Moonshine Ridge Mountain Men Volume 4

The Harts

Rocklyn Ryder

Magpie Press

Copyright © 2024 Rocklyn Ryder

All rights reserved worldwide

No part of this book may be reproduced, uploaded to the Internet, or copied without permission from the author. The author respectfully asks that you please support artistic expression and help promote anti-piracy efforts by purchasing a copy of this book at the authorized online outlets.

This is a work of fiction intended for mature audiences only. Names, characters, places, and incidents either are the product of the author's imagination or are used fictitiously. Any resemblance to events, locales, business establishments, or actual persons, living or dead, events, or locales is purely coincidental.

About
Raine Hart

I could give a rat's ass about fancy coffee, but what I do like about having the new cafe open on the mountain is the curvy little thing brewing it.

The first time I set eyes on April Holloway, she looks like she could use a month of good meals and a good night's sleep.

I tell myself I'm just trying to help her out-- make sure her business takes hold here in a small mountain town where bearded men in flannel can't tell the difference between light and dark espresso roasts and don't care.

Or maybe it's the haunted look about her that I know all too well that has me wasting six dollars on a cup of coffee every morning.

All I know is that she stirs up something inside me that I never thought I'd get for myself and now I'll do anything to keep it. No matter how hard April pushes me away, I'll keep pulling her back.

Because now I know what it feels like to want to be alive.

April's fighting demons even darker than my own and I'll slay every one of them to claim my girl.

Welcome to Moonshine Ridge and the rugged wilderness surrounding the remote mountain community where the history is long, the local lore is deep, and the men are as wild as the mountains they come from.

Protective, possessive, totally obsessed; the men of Moonshine Ridge will do anything necessary to claim the women they love and give her the happily ever after she deserves.

The Moonshine Ridge books contain a lot of insta-love, some swearing, some steamy scenes, zero cheating, and a lot of swoon-worthy happy endings. They're interconnected with recurring characters but can be read as stand-alones in any order.

Raine and April

<u>Promises on the Mountain</u>
The Hart Family of Moonshine Ridge
by
Rocklyn Ryder

Chapter One

April

Getting up at three thirty in the morning to start your day might sound crazy to most people, but I love it.

I love being showered and dressed and opening the cafe before the sun is even peaking over the mountain ridges to the east. I love the smell of fresh ground beans in the air while I watch the little mountain town wake up around me-- and I especially love that so many of them have begun to make me part of their morning routine.

Running my own coffee shop has been my dream since I was eight years old, the first time my aunt Jenny took me out for my first latte. Not that my mom was particularly thrilled with her sister for bringing me home spun up on espresso and sugar at that age, but I'll never forget watching the barista pull hand-packed shots from the ancient espresso machine with all the noise and steam of a Willie Wonka contraption.

It was magic.

I was hooked-- on coffee, and on the dream of owning my own cafe one day.

The mini blinds clatter as I pull the string to open them all the way up. I turn the hand-painted sign in the window around to show "open" to the outside world, and then I work my way through the small seating area, straightening chairs and the silk flower arrangement on each table while I wait for the people of Moonshine Ridge to start filing in.

It's only been a few weeks since I opened Mountain Mocha but things are going well. I've met a lot of good people, even made a couple of friends-- although, no one really close.

It's hard to get close to people these days. I tell myself it's the three-thirty a.m. alarm, or because I'm distracted with establishing the business, but the truth is that I turn down Terra and Zephyr's offers to hang out after work because I'm not ready yet.

The people here think I'm a normal girl, pursuing my dreams, filled with sunshine and optimism, and it's been so long since I was, I guess I just want to spend more time seeing myself through their eyes.

Real friendships mean letting people see who you really are. For now, I want to enjoy being the person they think I am. Someone a lot more like who I used to be.

Thinking about friendships has me wondering what things would be like now if Mia was still here.

We were going to do this together.

When we met, I'd been baristaing for two years already-- I'd begged Joy to hire me as soon as I was old enough to work for her.

Mia didn't drink coffee. She didn't even like the way it smelled. She hated working the opening shift, having to be up and faking perkiness at five a.m., but we hit it off and before I knew it, she was planning on opening the cafe with me.

The bells on the door jingle and the usual crew of guys head toward me, taking me out of my thoughts and giving me a reason to put a smile on my face.

"Tall oat milk cinnamon white mocha, right, Levi?" I confirm his order as he makes his way to the counter.

Levi smiles at me the way boys smile at girls as he nods in the affirmative.

"Oat milk? Really dude?" One of the guys teases his buddy.

"Shut the fuck up man, it's good that way."

These guys have become my regular morning crowd, a bunch of rough mountain men in their early twenties, sporting full beards, flannel, and boots. They're all handsome, tall, and jacked, jostling against each other and smiling at me while they do their best to flirt.

I'm guessing they don't see a lot of new faces up here, especially not single girls, but none of them do anything for me.

Honestly? I can't remember the last time I crushed on a guy. Probably back in high school, one of my dad's friends maybe, or that one hot history teacher I had my sophomore year. My crushes have always been older men and way off limits.

Probably why I got this far without doing much dating.

"What about you, Jake? Sticking with your usual or would you like to try something new today?"

Jake's cute. He's taller than his buddies but not as broad as Levi. He's asked me out a couple of times but I keep brushing him off.

"What do you recommend?" Jake braces his weight on the counter with one hand and leans over. He's definitely the fuck-boi of the three. He's smooth and confident and his smiles always start with his eyes. He probably knows a thing or two about showing a girl how things are done, but when I look at him, I can't see anything more than a customer.

"I've been experimenting with a maple sage thing," I tell him. He always takes whatever crazy thing I recommend, Jake's become my guinea pig for new drinks.

"Done." He slaps a bill on the counter and I know he doesn't want change. I say thanks as I slip it into the cash drawer and wonder what the fuck is wrong with me that I can look at those dimples and green eyes and feel nothing.

The guys continue to jostle each other and grumble behind me while I make Jake's drink, pulling shots for Adam's simple order while I'm at it.

The bells on the door ring again and I'm expecting Howard or maybe the guys that work up at the hydro plant on their morning run.

Instead, there's some grunts and protests. The guys go quiet, making the heavy foot falls on the tile floor sound loud in the small shop.

When I turn back to the counter, it's not Jake standing there. The boys have moved down to the far end of the counter, about as far as they can get from the man standing in front of me now.

"Thanks, April."

I hear Jake's voice somewhere off to my side as he takes the hot beverage from my hand, but I don't look at him. I can't. I can only look at the new guy in my coffee shop. All six foot four of him. With the beard and the flannel and the muscles bulging under the plaid cloth and the whiskey hazel eyes making me feel something I've never experienced before.

Raine

If I'd known Cane was going to order my ass down the mountain at the ass-crack of dawn this morning, I'd have made my own coffee before I left the house. Better yet, I'd have stayed home and let the lug do his own grunt-work.

Ever since Cane came back home, he's been bossing me around, giving me more work than I signed on for up at the camp.

But I can't deny that big bro has made a lot of improvements in the way camp operates and it's true that somebody has to be the one making the runs down to Slow River when we need lumber or hardware-- God knows Birch McAllister isn't about to give a Hart a fair price on local wood from the mill here on the Ridge.

The tavern doesn't open for breakfast till nine on the weekdays and the gas station coffee is barely better than boiled peat moss. Come to think of it, boiled peat might taste better.

The staff up at the camp have been raving about this new coffee place that opened in town and when I drive by, I see the place is open before it's even six a.m.

Pulling the truck into the parking lot that runs in the front of the building, I have to park way down in front of Eddy and Ginger's pizza place. Which is, of course, closed right now. There's already a line of trucks taking up the spaces in front of the cafe.

This is gran's building. Brick & Porter takes up suites eight and nine on one end of the long, ranch style building, with my grandmother's local history museum at the other end in the first suite.

The new coffee place is in between them, close to the pizza place with just one empty spot between them.

The windows are sporting curtains in a cutesy baby blue gingham check tied back with bows made of burlap and when I open the door, my ears are assaulted by what sounds like Santa's sleigh coming in for a damn landing.

It's cheerful as fuck in here. That gingham check and burlap is everywhere, with a few little tables with chairs that look like they'd collapse if I tried to sit in one. There are silk flowers in old Coke bottles on the tables and the whole place looks like one of those Pinterest boards my sister makes for her flower business.

There's no donuts or muffins in here, just a chalkboard mounted on the wall behind the counter with a drink menu that says everything but "coffee," and the cheapest drink I see is six bucks.

I sure as hell never need to step foot in here again, between the expensive, over-priced, citified drink menu and the country-chic decor like we're in Kansas or some shit and not the damn mountains. Not to mention the line of local assholes pressed up around the counter pretending they know the difference between a cappuccino and an Americano.

Fuck this. I'll wait till I get to the diner down in Keller's and grab a to-go order.

I'm about to turn on my heel when I hear it, a throaty, feminine laugh that goes straight to my dick in a way I haven't felt in years.

"What the fuck, man?" One of the guys says as I elbow my way to the front of the line. When he sees who I am, though, he shuts the fuck up and moves out of the way.

My brothers and I have a reputation on this mountain, everyone up here knows you don't fuck with the Hart boys unless you're ready to get punched-- hard. Looks like someone's already warned these kids about us and no one's willing to get in a fight before the sun's all the way up.

She has her back turned to me, working the big

espresso machine with an expertise that shows that this is her passion. She didn't come up here thinking a coffee shop would be a fun business to open after a few years of working at one the big coffee chains that uses automated machinery.

When she turns around so I get a good look at her I can't think right.

She's a fucking vision, with bright blonde hair piled up on top of her head and big blue eyes that stare back at me wide and screaming innocence. Like she's never set eyes on a man before.

A full apron that matches all the checkered shit in here is tied around her waist, accentuating curves that look like they could keep my hands busy for days.

A heart-shaped named tag pinned to the strap that wraps behind her neck says "April" in happy, girlish handwriting written in silver glitter.

I want to reach over and grab that name tag, scratch out her name and write "Property of Raine Hart" on it so every asshole that comes in here knows she's mine.

April holds the drink she just made out for the guy to take, but her eyes don't leave mine.

It's the guy that thought he was going to give me shit that steps forward from somewhere off to the side to take the cardboard cup from her.

"Thanks, April," he mutters as his buddy grabs his drink off the counter where she sets it.

The kids talk to her differently than when I first walked in. Polite but distant as they say thank yous and goodbyes, making sure to keep their distance from me.

If there's one thing men understand up here, it's the look on another man's face when he's looking at the woman he's meant to be with forever.

Chapter Two

April

"Did you save me anything today?"

Deputy Hawkins casually leans across the counter to eye the shelf where I usually hide a pastry for him.

Handing over his usual coffee and the croissant, he thanks me and heads toward Terra's table.

I notice my new friend is shooting a particularly menacing scowl in my direction and briefly wonder what I did wrong, but then she's yelling at her brother and Ozzie and storming out of the cafe, leaving the men laughing at the stunned deputy, and me feeling entirely confused. But I don't have time to catch up on their in-jokes because as soon as Terra walks out, *he* walks in.

Raine Hart looks better every time I see him. I swear he gets taller, more muscled, more handsome, with every day that he stops in. Which has been every day for over a week now, since that first morning.

A few people make a hasty exit, Terra's brother

among them. Other locals greet Raine warmly and ask about his mother.

"Hey sweetheart." His voice is molasses over gravel, it *does* things to my insides. "My asshole brother couldn't come up with enough busy work to keep me at the camp today, and I was thinking--"

Raine braces his weight on the counter between us and leans over. Irresistibly, I'm drawn toward him, stepping close enough that he could kiss me if he wanted to. I really want him to want to.

"I've got a cherry '79 that would look a hell of a lot better if you were in it. Are you up for a ride later?"

When he mentions his truck, his nods his head toward the window where the two-tone burgundy and cream truck is parked in front of the building.

When he asks if I'm up for a ride, his voice drops to a thick whisper that makes my thighs clench.

It's become our daily routine, usually he stops by much earlier in the morning, right after I open, but no matter who's in the cafe, the crowd always parts to let him through, regardless of who's next in line.

He always leans over the counter, dangerously close to hopping across entirely, and he always whispers something for my ears only.

Sometimes it's just a shopping list of whatever his brother is sending him down the mountain to pick up. Sometimes he asks how business is. Sometimes he asks if I dreamed about him-- but it's always a private conversation and it always sounds dirty, even when it's not.

"I can't go until I close up," I remind him, finding

myself leaning into him, magnetically drawn toward him till there's barely space between us at all.

"Good answer." His voice kicks back up to its usual volume, no longer telling secrets just for my ears. "I'll be back at three."

Before I can respond, he leans a little farther, jumping up to completely support his weight on his hands and dropping a quick peck on my lips.

So quick. Too quick. And then he's out the door just as quick, firing up the classic Ford and backing out into the road with a speed that says he expects traffic to stop and make way for him.

A few people in the cafe grumble about him as the truck tears back up the mountain highway, but I like the way he commands the space around him. What some people see as cockiness, I see as confidence. I like that way Raine makes me feel special. Safe-- like as long as I'm with him, no one will dare fuck with me.

I could use some of that these days.

Raine

No more distractions, and no more of Cane's stupid grunt work that he doles out on me just to keep me busy.

I know what he's doing, he's trying to keep me out of the tavern. Away from temptations, and out of trouble.

My older brother has developed some sort of fucking savior complex since he got back to the Ridge, and it seems pretty clear I'm the one he thinks needs saving.

But I'm not Hayle-- and I'm not Cane either.

I've done my share of waking up in places I don't remember getting into-- a couple of jail cells down in the valley, a few orchards in Keller's Ferry, once buck-nekked in a bull pasture that turned out to be on the Lazy P-- mostly in beds with women that were just as shocked to see me as I was to see them.

But I don't wrestle the same demons my brothers do. I can drink one beer and walk away. Even if I haven't always chosen to-- it's always been a choice. A choice I don't make anymore.

Can't remember the last time I lost myself in the bottom of a bottle.

Not true, I tell myself as I drive back up to the Gulch-- I remember exactly the last time I let booze drown out the pain, the night Hayle called to tell me he wasn't coming back.

He'd left the Ridge and he said it was for good. Cane was still playing at that time, and Hayle said that made me the man of the family. The youngest one of us, suddenly in charge of taking care of Mom and Gran and our baby sister when I wasn't even ready to take care of myself yet.

I couldn't step up like he'd asked me to. Not right away. First, I had to go on a bender in a Keller's Ferry roadhouse, drinking till I couldn't see and then smashing anything that got within reach.

Since then, I haven't done more than knock a few brews back while I kick Ozzie's ass at pool.

Of course, Cane came back as soon as he found out our oldest brother had skipped town. Gave up a future playing pro ball to move back up to the Gulch and take over running the Gold Camp for gran. Effectively demoting me to manual labor and reminding me that he's never going to see me as anything but his fuck-up little brother.

Joke's on him, because I don't want to run the damn camp anyway. Never did. And Cane's good at it, he's got a head for that kind of thing. I don't hate the hard work; it feels good to swing a hammer all day and I'll keep doing it voluntarily if Cane can get it in his head that I'm grown-ass man now and not the confused little kid that needed something to keep him busy so he didn't have to deal with the fact that his entire family had fallen apart.

In the house, I grab the blanket and the cooler I packed for our trip to Turtle Lake.

I told my brother to eat shit, the new cabins can wait another day. They don't have to be ready till May and we're ahead of schedule.

Today, I'm finally going to spend time with my girl.

I'm tired of stealing her time in fits and spurts between her customers. I'm done having to settle for learning about each other one double espresso at a time. I want to hear her whole life story. I want to know what crazy twist of fate finally delivered her to my mountain, and I want to claim those sweet curves of hers in the privacy of the old hunting cabin with the fire roaring beside us before I lose control and take her right there on that damn piece of blue Formica that's been cock blocking since I first laid eyes on her.

I throw the truck in neutral and kill the engine, letting her coast into position in front of gran's building, setting the e-brake to stop the truck before it can kiss the long porch. Gran would kill me if I take out one of the support pillars. Again.

The hand-painted sign in the window is turned to "closed" but the door to the cafe is unlocked when I pull the handle. Inside, chairs are stacked on tables, April's fancy espresso machine is torn down, the little tablet computer she uses in place of a cash register is powered off.

There's a heavy-duty, swinging door that separates the front of the coffee shop from the back room and it's propped open with the door-stop down. From somewhere beyond that, I hear April's voice and another female talking back to her.

"I can't wait to see it, I know Mia would have loved it...even though she wasn't really a big fan of the mountains, but I know the beach cities are so expensive and there's no way you could have opened up all by yourself out here."

"Actually, the plan was always to move to the mountains."

I don't mean to lurk, but when I hear the tiredness in April's voice, I need to know who she's talking to, what it's about. It's obviously not a conversation she's enjoying.

She's sweeping while she talks to the woman on speaker phone, her back to me while she works.

"Well, whatever, I'm sure you'd have been able to stay closer to home if Mia was...still with us."

April's shoulders slump, the broom in her hands coming to a stop.

"Hey, I can't wait to see the place!" the disembodied voice on the phone says, "I want to see my sister's dream brought to life-- you're coming home for summer, right? Mom really misses you."

"No, Kay, I have a business to run. I can't just close it down for months at a time."

My girl sounds tired. She sounds like someone who's been having the same conversation over and over and is staring to lose her conviction.

"It's a coffee shop, Ape. Who wants coffee in the summer time?"

"Actually, Kay, summers are really busy for most cafes and that's when Moonshine Ridge gets most of its tourist traffic, too. I'm expecting it to be a really good time for the shop."

"We'll see, I guess. I'm sure you're doing the best you can without your business partner. Hopefully moving to that mountain wasn't a total mistake. See ya soon!"

The call ends. April's body straightens with a deep inhale as she finishes her sweeping.

"What was that about?" Is all I want to know right now.

Chapter Three

April

Raine's voice is edged with irritation, its volume startling me as it bounces off the few stainless-steel shelves and prep tables scattered around the empty back half of the cafe.

"Just a friend checking up on me." I explain away Kay's call as nonchalantly as I can, doing my best to hide the pain from my voice.

This isn't how I want my first date with Raine to start off.

It is a date, right?

"Didn't sound like much of a friend to me."

He leans in the doorway, casually commanding the space just as easily as he does any space I've seen him in.

An image of him in my bedroom pops into my brain, totally unbidden. I feel the heat blossoming through my entire body and I rush to put the broom and dustpan back in the supply closet before he can see what he does to me.

"Kay's just--" how do I explain it without getting into the whole messy story? I'm sure this rugged mountain man isn't here for my drama, and to be honest? I'm happy to spare him. "She just has a different way of expressing her support."

"If by 'different' you mean, 'not at all,' you've pretty much nailed it. You about ready? I've got everything in the truck, ready to go. Let's get outta here and you can tell me who Mia is while we drive."

"Was," I correct. I say it absently, without even thinking about how I'm just opening a can of worms. So much for keeping my drama to myself.

"Sounds like there's a story there."

Raine's hands tighten slightly on my upper arms, his voice dropping down as if it's slunk off to someplace dark and distant.

It feels like a chasm just opened between us, even while so little space separates us physically.

"Let's git."

His hands fall away and he heads for the front door without waiting on me while I gather my things and lock up, but when I get outside, he's there with the truck already running, leaning against the side till I'm close enough to open the door for me and help me into the cab where the heater has already warmed the small space.

"Get over here." He slams his door as he climbs behind the wheel, then pats the space in the middle of the bench seat beside him, "I want my girl next to me when I drive."

His girl. The words make me giddy. I try not to read

into them as I slide across the leather until I'm sitting close enough that our thighs touch.

Raine's right arm stretches behind me, wrapping around my shoulders while the truck idles in front of the cafe.

Then he's turned toward me, his left hand cupping my chin and forcing my face up to his.

Warm, firm lips press against mine. The kiss catches me so completely off guard that I gasp, giving him easy access to slick his tongue into my mouth.

I've kissed boys before, but Raine is a *man*, and everything about the way he takes the lead reminds me of that fact.

My arms find their way around his neck, my fingers combing through the short hair at the back of his neck. My body instinctively twists, seeking his heat and the firmness of his muscled chest against my breasts.

Raine's hand leaves my chin and runs over my throat, across my shoulder and down to grip my hip and then my thigh so firmly that his fingers might leave marks.

Just when I'm about to throw my leg over his lap and straddle him with the steering wheel at my back, he breaks away with an agonized groan.

"Fuck." His hand releases its death grip on my thigh and pats it gently. "I need to get you up to the cabin or we'll be putting on a hell of a show right here."

He turns his body back toward the steering wheel,

pulling his arm off my shoulder and reaching between my knees to put the old truck in gear.

Raine drags his hand off the gear shift and up my thigh before he takes my hand out of my lap and places it squarely over his crotch, spreading his large hand over mine with enough pressure to cause me to curl my fingers around the hard length running under the zipper of his jeans.

"We've got a bit of ways to go, so you better keep me distracted on the way by tellin' me this story of yours. Otherwise, I'm likely to have you riding in my lap while I drive."

I'm so nervous about what he's implying that I'm almost relieved to start talking.

Raine

The educational camp that we run for the K through sixth grade students in the county is located on the lower river valley of the fourteen hundred acres that's still in the family from when my great something granddad struck gold in these mountains back in the eighteen hundreds.

Of course, most of our gold was pulled out of the original claim farther up in the mountains. Bill Hart used his fortune to buy up all the land he could get his hands on and then him and his buddies established the town of Hart's Gulch.

Unfortunately for the Hart's, this mountain was

already known far and wide for the whiskey running out of a still that was operated by a trio of sisters that had fled the war back east.

Mail addressed to "Hart's Gulch" got dead lettered in the valley post office until someone down there started re-labeling it as "Moonshine Ridge."

That's what got added to the census reports and that's what the town's called to this day.

Hart's Gulch lives on as the name of our family land. The forested acreage where my ancestor built his first home for his bride, where my family has been living and dying for over a century and a half. Where we've all built houses of our own, spread out among the hills and trees now.

"So, you all live on the same land?" April asks, when I point out the private road into the Gulch.

"A lot of the old families do," I tell her. "Just makes sense when there's so much land in one name up here. But we're all spread out, not like the Joneses. Guess we didn't really want to be that close together."

April looks over at me, her hand resting over mine where I've been keeping it on her knee whenever I'm not shifting gears, and I can tell she's about to ask questions I'd rather save for later.

"I want to show you the camp," I go on, changing the subject quickly, "but I don't want to get up to the cabin too late."

"Cabin?"

"Old hunting cabin on Turtle Lake." I squeeze her knee, "Nice and private, zero traffic up there this time of year. Thought it'd be a nice place to hang out and get to know one another."

And fuck yeah, when I say "get to know one another," I've got visions of April's curvy body spread out on the blankets in front of the fire while I *get to know* every peak and valley of her bare flesh and I don't plan on taking her back to town till I've figured out at least three ways to make her scream my name.

My dick thickens under my zipper again and I think about undoing my fly and having April jack me off while I drive. But something about the way she tenses under my hand tells me she's nervous-- interested, but nervous-- and I wonder how much experience she's had with men before me.

"Tell me about the camp?"

"I guess it got started by my grandparents in the eighties or so. They thought it'd be a good legacy project for the family. We host sixth graders in the warmer parts of the school year for one week sessions as part of the US history and science curriculum. Fourth and fifth graders get to come up for a day trip, and then we run a really popular summer program that's focused on the mining history of the area, but mostly it's just a typical summer camp experience for kids ages six to twelve. Older kids get to come up as counselors-- Gran makes sure no one's left out."

"Sounds wonderful. So that's where you and your brother work?"

A grunt comes out of me, being reminded of Cane. Working up at the camp used to be a lot of fun for me till he took over everything when he got back on the Ridge.

"Gran's getting up in years," I say, "she likes running her little museum down there by you. Cane's good with the business stuff...I'm good at banging things."

I shoot her a grin, liking the way she shivers under my fingers and taking it as a sign that it's okay to move my fingers higher on her thigh. She doesn't protest, so I let my hand linger, even though I'm aching to slip my fingers up between her legs and get her good and bothered while the old truck winds along the mountain road.

"There's enough money in the family to last us for the next several generations," I tell her. "Indefinitely, if we're smart with it. We grew up knowing we didn't need to go out into the world and find our own way.

"Probably didn't do us any good. Doing the construction shit at the camp is good for keeping me from getting too deep in my own head, I guess."

April nods silently, her head turned toward the window as she watches the forest and the meadows pass by outside.

The snow's been patchy this winter, nothing's really been sticking below eight thousand feet, leaving good views of the landscape.

"The cafe is kinda like that for me," she says low. "I like when it's busy, all the people coming and going keep me from thinking too much."

"Yeah, you're supposed to be telling me all about where you came from, what made you think a bunch of bearded assholes need fancy coffee-- and who that was you were talking to on the phone when I came in this afternoon."

April turns back and I see her looking up at me from the corner of my eye. I like the pretty smile on her soft, pink lips-- makes me feel important. Like maybe I could be worth something to somebody after all...worth something to her.

"I like hearing about your family, Raine. I like learning about the things that made you who you are today."

Her words hit me like a cold shower, causing me to tighten my jaw till my molars grind. I turn to stare out my side window, hoping she doesn't see how my mood shifts at the innocent words.

"Tell me who Mia is...*was*. And why is Kay giving her all the credit for your hard work?"

Chapter Four

April

I'm not sure what I said. Raine's laid-back demeanor goes stoic. His jaw tenses and he shifts in the driver's seat till he's sitting up straight, concentrating on the road even though it's clear he knows it well enough to drive it blind.

"Mia was a friend," I begin.

The thing is, I want to tell Raine about Mia. I want to him to know everything about me.

I can't explain it, he just feels like a kindred spirit, like someone who's going to understand and maybe that I can trust to keep me safe from the ghosts that haunt me.

Of course, it's not the ghosts that I'm having problems with.

"I always wanted to be a barista. I mean, I know it's not exactly a high-profile job and a lot of people don't really think it's a viable career path but..." My sigh is wistful, thinking back on that first latte, watching the barista pull the shots from the old espresso machine, the way I was awed by the way she expertly poured the foam into the ceramic mug to top it with a perfect heart.

"My aunt took me to a coffee shop when I was eight. Like-- an actual coffee shop-- where they hand tamped the grounds and steamed the milk themselves. Nothing automated. It smelled like heaven in there and the barista did latte art. I was hooked. I knew I was going to open my own cafe one day."

"Mia came to work at the same coffee shop I was working my senior year of high school. She was a year older than me and I thought she was the coolest person in the world...especially compared to me."

"I think you're cool."

I giggle at the mere thought. Raine's a good decade older than me, and everything about him screams *experienced*. It's crazy that he's interested in simple little ol' me who's never broken a rule or even toed the line.

"You would probably have liked Mia," I mutter. Thinking about the bad boy beside me, and the possessive way his hand lays across my thigh like it belongs there without question, so obviously used to driving girls up to this remote mountain cabin for "picnics by the fireplace--" if Mia was here, he'd have gone for her instead. I'm sure of it.

I shuffle my knees closer together, scooting on the leather seat to put enough space between us that I can't feel the heat of his hard, muscled body pressed against me anymore.

Suddenly, I'm feeling insecure. Unsure about the

man beside me. The same man that I've been swooning over obsessively for the last week, the one that I think about when I touch myself in bed at night, the one I was so eager to get in this truck with just half an hour ago when all I could think about was what he plans to do with me when we get to this cabin he's talking about.

He's used to a different kind of woman. Ones like Mia, that get high and go skinny dipping and are confident about what to do with boys.

"I like *you*, April." Raine's hand reaches to bring me back to his side and I can't help but melt into the silent command as his fingers wrap around my thigh. "You're the only girl I want to be with. Understand?"

He waits for me to nod and his hand creeps higher, strong fingers working deeper into the space between my thighs but not reaching high enough to relieve the ache that's growing inside me.

"Mia hated coffee," I laugh just remembering it, "she didn't even like the way it smelled. She worked at the coffee shop because she was into one of the guys that worked there.

"But we hit it off and then we started hanging out sometimes. Mostly, she got me into parties that I'd never have gotten invited to without her. For a while, I thought that was fun, but...it wasn't really for me, I guess. Mia always needed a sober driver and I wanted to make sure she was safe..."

My voice trails off, my thoughts going distant. Raine's hand tightens but it's not the sexy feeling like before, it's more for comfort. It feels like he's silently saying he understands something I haven't even said, bringing me into the present and out of my memories.

"She was going to come work for me when I opened my cafe." I laugh genuinely, thinking about how absurd it was. "I don't even know why she thought that was a good idea, but it just became our thing, you know? I guess I liked that she wanted to be my friend and it was fun to have someone to plan with."

"So, what happened to her?"

"She died."

I mean-- what else do you say, right?

"Sorry, baby." Raine's hand moves off my leg and wraps around my shoulders, pulling me close to him. It's nice. I get that he's trying to make me feel better, but it drags me into him so close that I pick out the individual scents of him-- the fresh, clean smell of laundry soap, combined with the warm, spicy scent of deodorant or cologne or whatever it is that makes my nerves light up with the hyper awareness of his masculinity.

I resist the urge to press my nose directly into him and squeeze my thighs together.

"Um yeah...she wanted to go out one weekend and I was kinda over it, you know? All those kids did was drink and smoke pot and-- *stuff*."

Raine grins without looking down at me.

"Was it the booze, the weed, or the *stuff*, that you didn't like?"

His arm tightens gently and I feel myself blushing.

"Uh well...I never really tried...*stuff*. So, I guess it

was the drugs and the alcohol," I confess, waiting for his reaction.

"Never?" This time he pivots his head to look down at me tucked under his arm. "Shit, girl, how old are you now?"

"Twenty-three."

He makes a noise that's either a groan or a growl, I can't really tell, but it vibrates through his entire body like a big cat purring beside me.

Silence hangs between us, heavy with unasked questions before he finally says, "So who's the Kay chick?"

Raine

I take the truck up to the gold camp, driving slow along the road that loops through the main areas where the offices and first aid station are, the big mess hall that doubles as meeting space and the outdoor amphitheater where we do stage shows and campfires after dark.

April seems more than happy to take a break from her story and I can't blame her.

The deeper she gets into her friend's death-- a single vehicle drunk driving incident on a night that April had insisted on staying home-- and the family that dealt with their loss by projecting their grief onto April, the more I'm understanding the dark circles that shadow April's pretty blue eyes have less to do with her early mornings and more to do with the guilt she feels about moving on with her life.

"It's hard, you know? Death changes people. Mia's sister just kind of re-wrote the whole story after she passed away. She got really attached to me even though we barely knew each other, and now she has this memory of her sister that's totally different from the way I remember Mia...for a long time, I started to believe Kay's version too."

"And now?"

"Now it's time to move on." April answers softly, snuggling into my side in a way that brings something protective to life inside me.

"It's been five years. I got a two-year degree at the local community college to help me with the business side of things, I went through a high-end barista training program. I won a national latte art competition. I researched locations for my cafe, wrote my own business plan, and got a small business loan-- I'm living my dream and Kay's acting like I owe it all to someone who didn't know the difference between Colombian and Ethiopian beans.

"I thought maybe if I wasn't so close anymore, she'd finally let go but, honestly, it's gotten worse."

Promising to bring her back up to the camp when it's warmer, I turn back onto the main road and head for the cabin.

Problem is, now I've got a lot more on my mind than just getting my face between April's legs.

"Oh wow, is that the lake?" April leans over me to

look at the lake below us out my window. "It's beautiful!"

"Not bad for a man-made reservoir, eh?"

Turtle Lake is part of the hydro-electric project that went in a few decades back. The power company leases the land from us for an outrageous amount of money, but it means allowing a wide easement around the perimeter that keeps the lake open to the public for recreational use.

"It looks like it belongs here."

"It does," I agree. I love seeing April wide-eyed with the beauty of the place.

The lower river valley is different than up at the top of the road where the hot springs are and where the Joneses run their river tours. There are still mountains all around us, but there's more open space for thick forests and meadows that fill up with wild flowers in the spring.

"We're going back there?" April's hand braces against the ceiling as the truck leaves the paved road and starts up the dirt track to the cabin.

Slipping the transmission into a lower gear, I notice she's holding her free arm across her chest. No doubt, she's trying to keep those pretty tits of hers from bouncing out of her bra on the bumpy back road.

Makes me think about picking up a Jeep that I could wheel fast and hard down the old lane instead of babying the old Ford.

"We have a hunting cabin back in there," I point toward the break between trees where I turn the truck in a few minutes later.

"Oh, it's so cute."

I try to look at the old place through April's eyes. It's just a shack. My dad put in a septic tank and hooked up a modern bathroom back when I was still too young to go hunting with him and my brothers. There used to be a generator, but I put in some solar a couple years ago that runs some LED lighting. That's really about all the power the place needs.

I think I'm the only one that still comes up here these days.

There's a couple feet of snow on the ground up here, but the driveway is still clear from when I came up yesterday to make sure the place was clean and the firewood was stocked for our date.

After helping April down from the truck, I grab the cooler out of the back and meet her on the porch.

"What's planted in here?"

Damn, she's cute. She's leaning over the porch railing, peering into the raised flower beds that Dad built for Mom a million years ago-- back when they were first married, before any of us kids came along.

Memories of summer, camping up here as a kid fill my head, with the planters overflowing with Mom's wildflowers in bloom.

I grab the hidden key off the top of the door frame and open the door.

"Nothing," I tell her. "No one's touched those planters since my dad died."

"Someone's been working in them. Recently, from the looks of it."

After I bring the cooler in and get it set up on the

counter inside, I go back out to see what she's talking about.

Sure enough, the soil has been worked recently, a thick top layer of mulch carefully applied over whatever's sleeping beneath it. A few small silver-green spikes shine up in places.

"My sister." I grunt. The stamped metal markers are a dead giveaway that Zephyr's been up here.

"Daffodils," April reads off a marker she pulls from one box. "Hyacinth," she reads off another after carefully replacing the first one.

"It's going to be beautiful when they're all in bloom in a few weeks."

The way she says it makes me wish I'd thought to raid Zephyr's greenhouse before I picked her up.

I'll make sure to bring her flowers next time. Right now, I want to get my girl inside so I can show her more things that'll put that dreamy look in her eyes.

Chapter Five

April

Raine's not joking when he says the place is small. Inside the little cabin is just one big room, with a door leading to a bathroom that looks like it was built on much later than the cabin's original construction.

A counter with a sink runs part-way along one wall, serving as the entirety of the kitchen, it seems. Next to the counter is a free-standing, wood-burning stove that stands on a brick hearth to give it some height. A small table and some chairs are the only furniture to be seen.

"I kinda expected just one bed." I laugh nervously, wondering what his plan is for the evening as he makes another trip out to truck.

"Even better," he says, kicked the door closed behind him as he drops the bundles he just carried in on the floor by the stove, "Just one floor. Lots of blankets."

Raine grins at me while I stare at the open space at

my feet and take note of the pile of sleeping bags and blankets he just tossed there. He crosses the short distance between us till he's standing close enough that his broad chest grazes my nipples.

His fingers reach to cup my chin and lift my head to his and those wicked lips meet mine again. This time the kiss is deeper, slower, more patient but still hungrier than the one he laid on me before we left the cafe parking lot.

The chill in the cabin is forgotten, Kay's guilt tripping and gaslighting fade into the distance.

There's only the silence of the small cabin, the stillness of the winter forest twilight outside, and the growing need waking up inside me as Raine claims my mouth with his.

"I'm going to start a fire." He doesn't even break the kiss completely, his lips are still touching mine when he whispers the words in a dark, throaty voice that makes me think that, surely, he already has.

But he means in the stove. It's not until he puts space between us again that I snap out of my daze.

"I can lay out the blankets." I volunteer, getting busy with unfurling several thick, flannel-lined sleeping bags and unfolding the softer, fleece blankets and layering them in a palette that turns the hardwood floor into a luxurious nest while Raine gets a fire roaring in the stove.

It's not long before the cabin is warmed up, but I'm way ahead of the air temperature.

"You really never tried...*stuff?*" Raine asks, a smirk on his lips beneath the beard as he blazes lingering kisses down my throat and along my collar bone.

Shifting my body in the nest of blankets, I move toward him, giving him better access to any part of me he might want to touch. Because I want Raine to touch me-- everywhere.

"A little stuff," I admit, feeling weirdly apologetic about my lack of experience.

I wish I knew how to take control right now. I want to impress this man, make him see me as more than just a nervous little girl who's hoping he'll show her what she's been missing. I want Raine to see me as a woman-- a woman that he could consider more than a fling with.

His lips twist into an inquisitive expression. Propping himself up on his elbow and bracing his head on his hand, he drags the other along my body slowly.

"A little," he repeats, "how much is *a little?*"

His fingers pull at my blouse where it tucks into the waist of my jeans till it comes free, allowing his fingers to skim along the sensitive skin of my belly where a kaleidoscope of butterflies has taken flight.

Raine dips his head down to mine for another kiss, this one soft and fleeting, and then he's looking down at me from that casual pose again while his hand casually skims up my ribs and over the padded cup of my bra.

"How 'bout this?"

His voice is a husky whisper, his eyes darkened in the firelit cabin as his thumb glides over my hardened nipple beneath the lace of my bra.

"Kinda?" I gasp out, fighting the urge to arch my back into his touch.

A smile stretches his lips, laughter teasing the lines at the corners of his eyes.

"How do you 'kinda' get to second base, baby girl?"

Raine's fingers tease along the edge of the lace before pushing beneath it to cup my entire breast firmly, pinching my nipple between his thumb and forefinger.

I lose my grip on whatever pretense of calm I was playing at, gasping sharply and pushing toward him, aching for more.

"Mmm, what about this?"

Raine lowers his face, pulling my blouse up high till it bunches around my neck, and takes my nipple in his mouth.

Oh fuck. My hands wrap around his head, pulling him tight, praying he doesn't stop.

Raine

April arches her back, feeding her breast to me, and I eagerly accept. Her fingers slide through my hair and her body twists to press itself against me in ways that have me fighting to keep my control.

She's nearly a decade younger than I am, it stands to reason she'd be less experienced but I hadn't been prepared for her to be so *inexperienced*. When she'd mentioned not having tried much when she was out partying with her friend, I thought she'd meant she hadn't gotten crazy-- hadn't gotten into some of the more experimental situations that some girls seek out at that age.

The woman writhing under my touch right now is one that's experiencing a man's touch for the first time. The truth of it slams into me as my fingers trail over the soft skin of her stomach on the way to a new destination.

April's innocent...she's mine, and she's going to be *all* mine.

My mouth moves to her other nipple, pulling it between my teeth and suckling till it's just as hard as I left the first one while I blindly work the buttons on her jeans and push my hand under the stretchy denim.

April gasps when my fingers slide over the soft cotton panties that have been hiding under her jeans.

She's got one hand trapped between us still, but the other slides down my neck and across my shoulder. Her fingers trace the muscles of my arm as I work my fingers between her legs.

"What about this?" I have to leave her delicious breasts to whisper in her ear, but the garbled sound of April confirming that this is new for her makes it worth it.

My dick is harder than I can remember it ever being, straining against the barrier of my belt, ready to answer the curvy woman under me that's begging to be claimed properly. But I'm not about to rush this. Even though it means torturing us both, I'm going to savor every one of April's firsts as we cross them off the list-- one. by. one.

"Was that a 'no,' baby girl?" I tease against her ear, sliding my fingers along the seam of her sex through the cotton that's thoroughly soaked through.

Aprils' eyelashes flutter, her lips are red and bruised from my kisses, her skin flushed with need and whisker-burn.

"Yes." She moans, bucking her hips to push her mound to meet my strokes. Her body is so needy already. It's killing me not to strip us both down and sink my shaft deep in her slick heat.

"Yes? You let some idiot boy touch your pussy before?"

I know the answer already, but my possessive asshole self wants to hear her say it out loud for me. Slipping my fingertip under the edge of her panties, I touch her bare sex and there's no holding back the groan that makes its way out of my throat when I feel the wet heat of her bare skin for the first time.

"Tell me, April," I rasp into the hollow of her throat, "who else has touched this pussy?"

"Just you," she whispers somewhere above me as my mouth makes its way down her body. "You're the first bo-- *man*-- who's ever touched me there, Raine."

"Good girl." It's more of something I'm thinking to myself, loving that she saved herself for me even if she didn't know it, but April gives up a sweet little moan when she hears the words whispered against her skin that has my dick twitching with need.

If my girl likes hearing me praise her, I'll make

sure to never stop telling her all the ways she's being good for me.

Right now, it's time to get rid of the layers of clothing that are keeping us apart. I need to feel April's skin on mine.

Patience is out the damn window, for both of us, it seems. April's working just as hard at yanking both layers of t-shirts off of me as I am at unbuttoning the pretty little flowered blouse she's wearing, doing my best not to rip the soft fabric that's catching on my calloused fingers.

I'm working blind for a few seconds as she tugs both shirts over my head as one but then she's shimmying out her blouse over her head with a giggle without waiting for me to finish with the buttons.

"Impatient?"

"Worried you're going to rip it off me," she says, tossing our discarded clothes aside while I make quick work of the hooks on her bra.

Those heavy tits swing free finally, landing in my eager hands and overflowing my palms while I knead them freely now.

"Baby, these are fucking perfect."

Knocking April back into the blankets, I crawl over her, caging her beneath me so I can get better access to her.

She bucks her hips under me and presses her mound against my hard shaft, tilting her hips so I can feel the hot center of her even though the jeans we're both still wearing.

"Missing my fingers, darling?" I smile between her

breasts that I've been enjoying having unobstructed access to but she's making it pretty fucking obvious that she needs my attention somewhere else.

"Yes," she mumbles shyly, then gives me another one of those delicious little moans when I rub a firm stroke along her center with the full length of the hard ridge beneath my zipper.

"Can't have that needy little pussy feelin' neglected, can we? Let's see if we can find something better than just my fingers to keep it satisfied."

There'll be lots of times when I'll get to slowly kiss my way down her entire body, right now, my girl needs some release and I'm determined to give it to her.

Chapter Six

April

Raine doesn't waste any more time teasing me and it's a good thing, or I might have rolled him over and attacked him.

I lift my hips to make it easier for him when he kneels between my legs and peels my pants off along with my panties in one easy motion.

The fire has the small cabin more than warm enough now, or maybe it's me. Cold is definitely not what I'm feeling, despite the shiver that runs through me when Raine sits back on his heels with his hands firmly holding my knees apart while he looks at my naked pussy.

"Damn, baby, that's the best thing I've ever seen."

His reverent tone has me believing him. Then he's pushing my knees up to my chest and settling his wide shoulder between my open thighs.

"Wrap those sweet thighs around my neck and don't let go," he tells me, right before his mouth makes contact with my clit.

Oh my God, he goes straight to the goal line, locking his lips over my swollen bud and sucking hard at the same time I feel the tip of his tongue flicker across me. Then I feel the thick, blunt tip of his finger sliding through my folds. The way his fingers glide along my seam makes me realize how fucking wet I really am for him and that does something to me.

It's like a confirmation of how bad I want this man. Like my body is screaming that he's the one I'm meant for and I need him to claim me now.

His thick fingers tease at my entrance, circling and pressing without entering me until I'm panting and mewling. My fists are clenched in his hair and my thighs are locked against his head. Who knows if he can even hear me begging him to give me more?

Then I feel a single digit breech my opening, pushing into me slowly, testing. All the fuzzy stars inside my head come into single focus as he slips a second finger inside me, his mouth still doing decadent things to my clit while he holds me firmly against him with one hand locked on my ass.

The whole world explodes. Sparks fly behind my eyelids as something breaks loose inside me. And then I'm coming, hard, flooding Raine's hand, his beard, his tongue while he rides out my orgasm, never stopping until I go limp in his grip.

Only then does he slip those wicked fingers free of me to begin kissing a trail up my sweating skin back to my lips.

"Fucking amazing, baby," he whispers, kissing me deeply so I can taste myself on his tongue. "Fucking amazing," he says again, flopping over on his back beside me and gathering me against his hard chest.

I love the hard thump of Raine's heart beating wildly under my ear and the rise and fall of his chest as he catches his breath, but I'm not done.

My hand trails down the column of hair that leads below a belt buckle that's been worked loose at some point. The tip of his cock pokes out above the waistband of burgundy boxer briefs below the loosened fly of his jeans, glistening with pre-cum oozing from the slit.

The sight has my mouth watering, and the places that Raine just worked to relax coil tightly again.

His hand covers mine when I reach for him though, holding me still against the rock-hard plane of his abdomen.

"April--" His voice is barely more than a growl, making my name sound like a warning, not the plea I hoped for.

"You don't have to, baby, we can stop here today...I'll make us something to eat."

Raine pushes to sit up, but I shove him back on the nest of blankets with my hand on his chest.

"I didn't come up here so we could eat sandwiches in front of a fire, Raine. I had certain-- *expectations*-- of why we were coming all the way up here."

He looks up at me with one of those infuriatingly wicked grins and cocks an eyebrow. "You did, did you? What kind of *expectations* did you have, baby girl?"

I can feel myself blushing, but I let my hand

wander back down over the thick ridge of his cock that's still hard as steel.

"Well, there are only two reasons a man brings a woman to a remote, mountain cabin in the snow, and if I thought you were going to murder me, I wouldn't have gotten in the truck."

Raine

F*uuuuuck*...Having April's hand on me has me losing my mind. It's taking all the self-control I can gather up to keep from ripping the rest of my clothes off and driving my cock into her innocent little pussy.

Which is exactly why my jeans are still on and I'm counting backwards from a hundred while I try to form coherent thoughts. Because April needs to understand something about me, about what's going on between us, what my intentions toward her really are.

"Baby, I can't think when you're doing that," I grit out between clenched jaws as April works my cock free of its confines and slides her fist down the throbbing shaft.

"Good," she leans forward to kiss me and when her lips begin to move away from mine, I follow. I'll follow this woman anywhere. "I don't want you to think, Raine, I want you to fuck me."

I'm on her in a heartbeat, pulling her hands above

her head and pinning them there as I drag my aching shaft along her naked pussy, inches away from giving in to what we both want.

"April, baby, you're right, when I threw these blankets in the truck, I had plans for how we'd be spending our time up here but I didn't know you were still a virgin then."

I hate the way she goes limp in my hands. Like all the air has left her lungs and now those pretty blue eyes are looking at me with so much sadness, I'm not sure what the right answer is anymore.

My brain wars with my dick, my better judgment battling against my instinct to claim my woman and make her mine without bothering with bullshit like civilized conversation.

"So that's it?" April's voice goes small as she looks up at me, her lower lip trembling, "You don't want me now?"

"Does it fucking *feel* like I don't want you?" I grind myself against her, making sure she feels how fucking hard I am for her. "I've never wanted anything more I want you, April."

My hand tightens around her wrists, pushing her harder into the layers of blankets under us, loving the way her eyes go wide with understanding.

"But before I wreck this virgin pussy, I want to make sure we're on the same page, here. I'm in this for keeps, April, and I don't want you thinking that's just a line of bullshit to be the one that punches that V-card."

"What do you mean by 'keeps?'" She's all raspy again, with those baby blue darkened by her blown-out pupils and when I slide against her again, there's a lot less friction where her pussy's leaking with need for my cock.

"I mean I want you to believe me when I tell you I'm in love with you. I need you to know I'm not just saying what I think you want to hear when I tell you I plan on marrying you and filling you up with babies.

"And I need to know you want the same thing, April, because I can promise you right now that I'm not about to let another man near you. Once you're mine, you're mine forever."

"I need you inside me, Raine." April's eyes are steady on mine, her voice is throaty as hell, and I can feel her pulse racing where I'm still clutching her wrists, but damn if she doesn't sound as serious as I've ever heard a woman be.

"Don't make me wait. I want to be yours, and I want to start now."

Never gotten my pants off so fast in my damn life, and that includes that time I found out the hard way I'd been standing on a nest of fire ants.

Notching my leaking tip against her entrance, I look down between us and damn near lose it just at the sight where our bodies are about to be joined together.

A thought hits me that has me reaching for my discarded jeans before I'm hit with the overwhelming urge to go in raw. I want to breed this woman, rut her deep and plant my seed in her fertile womb.

The need is so strong I can barely get the words out.

"Tell me you're sure about this, baby," I croak, pushing against her entrance, "I'm not putting anything between us. I'm clean but, if you're not on birth control, we could be fast forwarding those wedding plans."

April laughs, swatting my ass with a firm palm "I'm sure if you're sure," she says and I don't give her a chance to say anything else before I'm up to the fucking hilt in her tight heat.

"Shit, April, baby, you okay?"

Her nails are dug into my sides hard and the way her body tenses up reminds me too late that I should have been gentle. But dammit, a man can only hold out so long when he's claiming the woman who's going to have his children.

"I'm good," she says after a moment and then she opens her eyes and looks up at me with a grin that lets me know she really means it. "Really good," she adds with a wiggle of her hips that has me pulling back and thrusting into her till those pretty blue eyes of hers are rolled into the back of her head.

The sweet little gasps coming out of her have me on the edge and it's not the fire that's got sweat beading up on my skin as I drive back inside of April's tight little sheath.

As soon as her pussy starts to flutter, I know I won't be able to hold back if she starts coming on my cock but damned if I'm not going to make sure my girl comes for me.

Reaching between us, I press the pad of my thumb over her clit, and I don't have to do more before April's body convulses around me. Her legs clamped across the backs of my thighs to pin me in place while her perfect little tunnel clenches down and tries to drag me farther into her body.

My balls are on a hair trigger as I do my best to keep up with April's frantic movements as she milks my cock for my cum.

Then I hear my girl panting my name.

"Raine," April's voice is strained between soft cries, "I want you to come with me, come in my pussy. Fill me up and make me yours."

With that, my woman steals whatever control I was holding onto. Everything tightens and surges as I do what she asks.

Chapter Seven

April

Today is the best day of my life. Or maybe that was yesterday. Or maybe it started yesterday and every day from now on is going to be amazing.

That's definitely how I've felt all day. Even when the alarm clock went off far too early after Raine and I stayed up at the cabin later than either of us had planned.

We'd talked till he had to build the fire back up in the stove. I'd told him more about Kay and how she's made it hard for me to move on with my life-- even being hostile since I moved away. And Raine shared his own experiences with death, telling me how he saw his entire family torn apart when his father and grandfather were killed together in an auto accident on the old ferry road to the valley when Raine was only eleven.

I'd heard rumors about his oldest brother, who left town long before I came to Moonshine Ridge, and Zephyr had mentioned losing her father and grandfather in an accident when she was just a baby; but I had no idea how much their family suffered as a result of their loss.

I guess Zephyr was so young when it happened, she never really knew anything else-- but Raine explained how his grandmother blamed his mom for sending the men to Slow River to begin with, how his mother accepted the blame, and how his oldest brother channeled grief into anger and alcohol abuse while his other brother escaped the mountains in pursuit of a professional sports career.

Leaving Raine somewhere in the middle to make sense of everything that had happened, and find his own way through it.

Then he impressed me with his love-making skills again, before cooking me dinner on the stove, and then we made love one more time before we finally packed up and headed back to town.

I wasn't prepared to stay the night at his place, so he dropped me off at mine-- and didn't leave until my alarm went off at three thirty in the morning. Then made me late for opening the cafe.

Fortunately, Moonshine Ridge works on its own sense of time and it's not unusual for the small businesses here to keep *"ish"* hours. No one blinked an eye at me when I didn't turn the sign over to the side that reads "open" until five thirty-seven.

Deputy Hawkins came in at his usual time, this time smiling ear to ear.

Then Terra Diaz walked over from her daycare

center and shocked everyone by greeting the deputy with a kiss.

Like...a *kiss*. The *"this man is mine and no bitches better forget it"* kind that had the small-town gossip mill on fire less than fifteen minutes later.

That was great for business though. I think everyone in Moonshine Ridge has come through the cafe today to confirm the rumors.

Raine said he'd be by before closing today but he's running late. Cell service is spotty enough here in the heart of the town, but up at the camp where he spends most of his days, it's non-existent. So, of course, I haven't heard from him.

It works out well anyway, since I decided to stay open a little later to make up for the late start this morning and to accommodate any late afternoon gossip mongers looking for little town intel...and an afternoon caffeine boost.

I have a couple of bags packed, things Raine suggested I should bring with me up to his place so I'll have what I need to stay with him for several days at a time.

He's already making plans to move me in with him and I haven't even been to his house yet.

I giggle while I work, doing end of day cleaning with the front door propped open. It's a warm day despite the early February date and with the coffee makers running full blast all day, the cool air making its way inside feels good.

"Are you really still open?"

Maggie McAllister stands on the threshold, peering inside longingly.

"Yup, got a late start this morning so I figured I stay open a little later." I laugh at her visible sigh of relief as she steps inside, then turns around to motion at someone still waiting outside.

Her husband, Birch, fills the doorway, blocking the light as he moves inside.

"Can I interest you in a gossip-monger special? Or just your usual?"

Maggie and I share a laugh but Birch just stands behind his wife and glowers stoically.

I haven't seen much of Birch McAllister; he runs the local sawmill that's on the edge of town so he's not around much during my usual business hours. His brothers and their wives own the sporting goods store across the street from the cafe and the tavern just another block over. I've gotten to know Hyacinth and Chamomile pretty well but the men keep their distance-- something about their grandmother's feud with Raine's grandmother, who also happens to be my landlord.

Maggie only makes it in a couple times a week since she's up on their property doing the stay-at-home mom thing most of the time, but she comes in often enough that I have her tall, full-fat, double espresso maple pecan latte memorized.

"Do tell me what a gossip-monger special is first," Maggie asks, a hint of southern accent peeking through the words.

"It's just a standard vanilla latte." I hate to disappoint her, "It's been the default order of pretty much everyone who's stopped by to ask questions about the newest couple on the mountain."

"I'll stick with the usual," Maggie tells me, then looks up at her husband who leans down to place a soft kiss on her lips. "He'll have an Americano," she adds even though Birch hasn't muttered more than a grunt since coming inside with her.

I know he'd prefer a cup of hot, black, house brew, but the regular pots are already off and cleaned up for tomorrow.

"So, speaking of new couple gossip," Maggie hedges as she stands at the counter, off to one side so she can watch me pull the espresso shots, "Hyacinth says she saw you leaving the cafe yesterday in a certain classic Ford truck?"

The blush heats my face far more than the steam coming of the milk in the pitcher as I prepare her latte.

"You seeing Raine Hart?"

Birch's deep voice startles me. It's got a disapproving thing going on that makes it clear that he's questioning my taste in men.

"Um, actually, yeah I am."

I top Maggie's lattes with the thick, steamed milk and finish the pour with a tulip design before handing the drinks over.

"Be careful there," Maggie tells me, her teeth worrying her lower lip as she gives me a concerned look. She's not talking about handling the hot coffees.

"Why? What's wrong with Raine?"

I know all about the family drama between the Harts

and the McAllisters. You don't move to a town like Moonshine Ridge without getting the local tea spilled all over you before you've even had a chance to meet your neighbors. But no one's warned me off of dating any of the men on the Ridge and the way Maggie and Birch are looking at me now has me wondering if their concerns go beyond the bounds of the family feuds.

"I've never seen one of the Hart boys do right by a woman yet." Birch slides his arm around Maggie's shoulders as he grumbles. "I find it hard to believe one of 'em would start now."

"Just be careful there." Maggie finishes the transaction on the touch pad point of sale, tapping a button to leave a tip and signing the screen with her finger.

"Have fun with him." She gives me a wink and half a smile that has Birch scowling deeper. "Just remember it's just fun, okay?"

Ten minutes later, the door is still open and the open sign is still in the window but my mood is a lot darker. I still haven't heard from Raine, and Birch and Maggie's warning is ping-ponging between my head and my heart.

I have the La Pavoni torn down; the portafilters and the steam wand are soaking and I'm about to go turn the sign in the window to closed and lock the door when I hear the distinct idle of Raine's truck shut down and the sound of the e-brake being applied the way he always does.

This time there's no hesitancy. He jumps the steps to the boardwalk porch in two quick leaps and jogs across the empty shop space before jumping the counter in a lithe move, sliding over the surface like the Duke boys hood-sliding across the General Lee, and landing on my side with the heavy sound of both boots hitting the floor at the same time.

Before I have time to think, I'm pressed against the back counter, held tightly with one strong arm wrapped around my waist while he presses something into my hand, but I can't see what it is because I'm too busy swooning into the searing kiss that's busy wiping any doubts I was having from my brain.

Raine

"Sorry I'm late, baby. Did you get my text?"

Letting go of April's soft body shouldn't be so hard. Never thought I'd be jealous of a fucking espresso machine, but it was clear when I came through the door that she's busy taking the thing apart.

"No. I just thought you didn't have service up at the camp."

I fucking love that breathless quality to her voice and the dazed way she looks up at me. Letting her body lean into mine like she trusts me completely to keep her on her feet.

It's impossible to resist kissing her again. So I do.

"Couldn't call out of camp," I confirm when I let

her up for air again, "but I shot off a message when I was at the Gulch...do you like 'em?"

It's only then that she seems to become aware of the bouquet in her hand.

"Oh my gosh, Raine, these are gorgeous!"

My sister will skin me alive if she finds out I raided her precious greenhouse, but watching April bury her nose in the handful of mixed flowers I picked for her is worth it.

"How come you're just getting this place closed down?" I ask, looking around at the little coffee shop that's obviously been open an hour past her usual hours and feeling guilty about being late. "You weren't staying open just to wait for me, were you?"

Leaning back on the blue Formica counter, I kick my legs out in front of me and take her in my arms eagerly when she steps back between my knees for another long kiss.

I've been aching to get on this side of the counter ever since I first walked in here. Because this is where my girl is.

"No," she laughs lightly when I let her lips go. "It's been crazy today. Apparently, Terra and Hawkins are a thing now and everyone on the mountain had to come in to get the scoop."

"Everyone came in here? Damn, woman. If it's not bad enough that you got yourself hooked up with me, Alice McAllister is going to hate you for taking her gossip business away. She's used to her store being the tea capital of the Ridge."

A shadow crosses April's pretty face. She must

know she's easy to read because she pulls the flowers back up for another sniff.

"What's wrong? Alice wasn't over here giving you shit already, was she?"

The McAllister/Hart feud has never really affected me, outside of them and their friends not being keen on sharing space with me, but for an old lady, Alice can be a real bitch sometimes and if she's giving my girl trouble, I'll have to tell gran.

"Not Alice, no, she's only come in the one time when I first opened. But uh, Birch and Maggie were in."

Birch McAllister fucking hates my brother, Hayle, and while I can't say he doesn't have good reasons for it, Hayle's still my brother and kin is always where my allegiance is gonna lie.

I don't like the way April's shoulders sag or hearing her voice go small when she mentions Birch's visit. Like I said, I've never put much energy into the family bullshit, but messing with my girl is a quick way to change that.

"What'd he say to you?" It takes an effort to keep my voice even and I pull April back close to me, my fingers finding a firm grip in those wide hips that's almost enough to keep me calm.

"Ash and Hyacinth saw me leave with you yesterday," she tells me.

"Good." I like knowing they saw her in my truck. That means they saw the kiss I laid on her after she scrambled in. It means they saw her scoot across the bench seat till she was tucked right up against me. It means they know she's mine.

And if the McAllisters know April's taken-- then so does every other male on this mountain.

My shoulders straighten and I feel my chest swell with the pride of knowing this woman has been claimed and every asshole up here knows it now.

"So, what's wrong, baby girl?"

"They just wanted to warn me not to get too attached. Birch seems to think you're the kind of guy who makes promises he doesn't plan on keeping."

Fury burns through my veins and I've got a strong desire to go kick Birch's ass, but I swallow it down. Because the truth is, I've got no one to blame for that reputation but myself.

Somewhere under the pissed off feelings, there's a flicker of respect for the man that was just looking out for April.

That's the way it's supposed to work in the community. We look out for each other up here, family feuds or not.

Letting my breath leak out of my lungs in a slow, controlled, sigh, I wrap April up in my arms again. Pulling her so tight to my chest while I'm still leaning on her counter, that she has to push against my chest so she can look me in the eye.

"I understand why he might think that," I admit, "but I already told you I wasn't always a good man, didn't I?"

We had some hard conversations between us last

night. April knows all my secrets now, and she nods to answer me.

"I just want to know what to expect, Raine. Don't talk to me about weddings and babies just because you think that's what I want to hear. If this is just temporary, I'd rather know that up front."

"Hey, April," I cup the side of her face with my palm. Words aren't my super power and I'd rather make her believe me with kisses and orgasms but I know it's important to set the record straight in plain language. "You are it for me, baby girl. Knew I was about to start a whole new chapter of this life as soon as I saw you back here in your little blue checkered apron. You're my future now, and with any luck, that future's going to include a bunch of muddy kids running around. Hopefully, we got started on that yesterday."

My thumbs slide forward to caress the curve of her belly while I keep my hands wrapped around her hips. Thoughts of my seed already taking root deep in there have my dick thickening and a need to have her coming for me again surges through me so urgently, I really hope we've got this point settled.

Pushing us both away from the counter, I reach down and grab April up by the back of her thighs, giving her little choice but to wrap those shapely legs around my waist while I carry her behind the heavy, swinging door that leads to the nearly empty back room.

Setting her ass on top of one of the stainless-steel prep tables in the darkness back here, I've got my hands up her skirt and my fingers already easily slipping through her slick folds.

"Fuck, baby, you're already so wet." I slide a finger into her while I kiss her senseless.

April's hands are grappling with my jeans, pulling my belt from the buckle and unbuttoning my fly.

"Tell me you believe me, baby." I rasp it against her throat and then again, with my face buried between her tits. "Tell me you still want to be my wife, you're gonna let me fill you up with babies, and we're going to do the happy ever after thing together."

"I believe you." She pants the words, pulling my dick free and stroking it hungrily. "I believe you, Raine. I'll marry you and you can knock me up as many times as you want. Just. Start. Now."

Glad we got that settled.

Pulling her panties aside, I let April take the lead, pulling me close and lining up my dick with her opening.

"Hello? Ape, are you in here somewhere?"

Chapter Eight

April

The problem is that Kay didn't say anything until she'd already pushed the swinging door to the back room halfway open.

Raine sighs heavily and pulls back, quickly tucking himself back into his jeans while I hop off the prep table and do my best to put myself back together.

It's too late, Kay might not have gotten a good look at the details, but there's no way she doesn't realize what she just walked in on.

"You okay, baby?" Raine whispers low, his eyes seeking mine and looking far more concerned than frustrated at being interrupted.

I can't say the same for myself. I was really looking forward to feeling Raine's cock inside me again.

That's what I get for leaving the front door wide open, I guess.

"April, what's going on here?" Kay's eyes narrow as they move from me to take full stock of Raine's imposing figure standing beside me with his arm possessively wrapped over my shoulders.

"Maybe give us a minute?" I look up at him and offer my best *I can handle this* smile.

He doesn't look convinced, but he does bend to kiss me tenderly before reluctantly stepping away.

"I'm going to go visit gran," he tells me, but his voice is a stern warning to the woman standing in front of us. "I won't be out of hearing range."

His voice is icy as he glances at her on his way past, making it clear that he considers her a threat and that he intends to make sure she doesn't cause any trouble.

"Kay, what are you doing here?" I huff in exasperation, doing a second check of my skirt to make sure it's in place before leaving the back room and walking into the cafe.

"What am I doing here? What the fuck were you doing, Ape? I came all this way to visit you, and I find you fucking some stranger *in my sister's coffee shop!*"

Something snaps inside me.

"This isn't Mia's coffee shop, Kay! It was never going to be Mia's coffee shop. Mia fucking *hated* coffee, the only reason she didn't get fired a thousand times when we worked at Cuppa Joy was because she was fucking Joy's son."

Kay gasps.

It's not like she didn't know her sister, I'm sure that's not news to her. I think she's shocked that I'm done letting her get away with projecting her delusions onto me.

"I can't believe you would talk about Mia that way."

Her voice drops to a shocked whisper but it's laced with anger. "She was your best friend. You were going to open the cafe together; she shared her dream with you and you think that you can just cut her out of the picture now? Because you moved halfway across the country and opened up this little hole in the wall without her?"

In the five years since Mia died, I've let Kay latch on to me. I've let her project her grief and loss on me because I felt so fucking bad for her. Because I've felt guilty for not going to that party with Mia-- I would have been sober, I would have driven. Mia would have gotten home safe and spent our work shift the next day hung over and telling me about whatever guy she hooked up with the night before while I did all the work.

But dammit, I worked hard to open this coffee shop. I saved for years and bought second hand equipment from going out of business sales. I lived out of my car for almost a year while I explored possible locations for my new business and for my new home.

I thought Kay would snap out of it, that she'd eventually acknowledge the truth and stop giving Mia credit for my dreams and now-- for my accomplishments.

"Stop, Kay. Just stop," I flip the sign in the window to closed, but I leave the door open, knowing Raine's just a couple doors down, visiting Mable at her little museum.

"The coffee shop was always my dream and you know that. You always knew that. You knew that Mia didn't give a fuck about coffee. She liked the idea of being included in the business and when she started attaching herself to my dream, I let her do it.

"We were friends, but we weren't *best* friends and honestly, Kay, if Mia was still alive, we wouldn't still be friends. I think you know that just as well as I do."

"Yeah, well, that's pretty obvious, isn't it? If you'd been a better friend, my sister would still be here, wouldn't she?"

"What the hell does that mean, Kay? Are you seriously saying it's *my* fault that Mia's dead?"

"You were supposed to go with her that night, right? But you had better things to do, didn't you? You're the reason she was driving herself home after she'd been drinking. If you'd been a better friend, I'd still have my sister!"

My heart aches for her but I can't do this anymore. I can't be the scapegoat for her grief.

"Mia's dead because she decided to get behind the wheel when she knew she was too fucked up to drive. She knew better. She could have called me for a ride, she could have called someone else, she could have called a Taxi or an Uber or a fucking tow truck. She could have passed out in the back seat and driven home when she sobered up, or she could have stayed put and slept it off at the house where she was partying.

"She didn't do any of those things, Kay. She made a bad decision and I'm sorry for how it turned out but it's not my fault and I am done letting you steal my life away from me to give it to someone who never wanted it."

Unloading all that might make me feel better, but apparently, it's not the moment of catharsis for Kay that it proves to be for me.

While I feel lighter than I have since Mia's funeral-- the first time Kay mentioned the cafe being Mia's dream, not mine-- Kay's face goes dark with rage.

She grabs one of the vintage soda bottle vases off the nearest table and hurls it at the floor. It shatters into pieces, leaving the stem of silk flowers that was in it lying in the wreckage.

She lunges for the vase on the next nearest table. I'm so stunned that I just watch while she slams another bottle onto the ground, still calling me names and screaming about how I don't deserve any of this but my temporary paralysis lets go when she spins around and heads for the espresso machine.

"You are such a fucking bitch." She spits at me. "You were supposed to be Mia's friend and you're up here in the mountains, making lattes and fucking lumberjacks like nothing ever happened. Who was that guy you were humping in the back room, anyway? Is he the reason you picked this piece of shit little town in the middle of fucking nowhere? Is he your sugar daddy? Is the rent due?"

I manage to get between her and the Pavoni. I'm doing my best to force her back, yelling at her to calm the fuck down, when the sound of heavy footsteps running up the boardwalk have us both looking toward the open door instead.

Raine

"What the hell is going on down there?" Gran demands as the sounds of yelling and breaking glass interrupt us.

Another loud crash and the sound of breaking glass has me heading out the museum door.

"Go help her, Raine." My grandmother waves her hand at me, ushering me out the door without expecting me to wait for her.

There are only two empty suites between Gran's museum and April's cafe and at a dead run, it doesn't take but a few seconds to get to the door that's still standing open just in time to hear Kay questioning April's relationship with me.

"I'm her fiancé," I bark as I fly through the door. Assessing the situation inside in an instant, I jump the counter, putting myself between the girls and April's fancy coffee machine.

I know that thing cost her more than a lot of people pay for their cars and it's pretty clear this Kay chick has been busting the place up.

"Let go of April, now," I order.

Kay's clutching at April, one hand in her hair, and another twisted in her clothes while April tries to pry the younger woman's hands off of her.

"Fuck you," she screeches at me. "She's the reason my sister is dead."

April manages to get herself free and without hesitation, I pull her behind me.

"I think you know that's not true; from what I hear, your sister made a big mistake, but April had nothing to do with it. It's time to stop making April responsible for filling in the empty space where your sister should be."

Kay lets go of April and steps back, glaring at me like she hates me.

"What the fuck do you know about it?"

Pulling my girl into my arms, so that April's back is to my chest, I wrap her up and hold her tight. Making sure she's safe and taking some strength in the feel of her against me again.

"I know something about death," I answer the seething girl facing us. "I've seen the way grief can make people rewrite the facts so they're left with memories that they can live with. I've seen the way it can tear people apart when they should be coming together to support one another through hard times.

"I know you didn't come all this way to visit your sister's friend, or to support her success. You came up to my mountain to start a fight because you don't want to accept that your sister's the only one to blame for not being with you anymore and you're mad at April for moving on with her life when you haven't. But that's not fair to your sister, or to you, and I'll be damned if I'm going to allow you to keep making April feel like she has to be responsible for your grief as well as her own."

The girl stands there, working her mouth like a

guppy while she decides if it's worth continuing to fight with either of us.

"You don't know anything," she tells me, but her voice is sullen, lacking the rage she was venting when I came in.

"I know that April is part of this community now and there's not a damn person in town that's going to let a stranger come in and destroy the business she's worked so hard for."

"Not to mention that the closest thing we've had to coffee on this mountain before she got here was that swill coming out of McAllister's tavern there," Gran adds.

I hadn't noticed Gran standing in the doorway and now she jabs her thumb in the general direction of the tavern on the other side of the road, her voice sounding more emotional than I'm used to.

"It wouldn't be wise to get between mountain folk and good coffee." Gran levels a warning tone at the girl who's suddenly become aware of the crowd that's gathered outside the door.

Behind Gran, Current Jones stands beside his pregnant wife, Ginger, with more than a few others standing with them.

All the yelling must have brought them over from the pizza and brewpub next door.

At the bottom of the steps, I make out Ash and Hyacinth McAllister standing behind Ash's grandmother, Alice, who's alternating scowls between my grandmother and Kay.

"You should leave, Kay," April straightens up in my

arms. "Go home, find a good grief counselor, move on. But don't contact me again."

Kay sweeps the crowd that's gathered outside the little cafe.

"You heard my fiancée," I gently push April aside so I can take a step toward the unwanted guest, "it's time for you to leave."

"What are you going to do?" She scoffs as I move forward, "throw me out?"

My head swings toward the door, a grin stretching across my face before I turn back to Kay.

"I've never put my hands on a woman and I'm not going to start with you," I assure her, "but my grandmother doesn't have the same moral code I do."

With that said, Gran marches all four foot eleven of herself across the room and grabs hold of the younger woman's arm.

It's hard not to laugh at the look on the girl's face when she discovers that my grandmother is deceptively strong for her size and age.

"You heard that, didn'tcha, Hawk?" Gran crows at the local deputy who has joined the crowd and moved up front. "Get a good look at her, she's not welcome back here and if you catch her bothering my granddaughter again, I expect you to shoot her."

There's a combination of cheers and laughter from the audience and maybe Kay was expecting our local law man to step up in her defense. Instead, Hawkins tips his hat with a low dip of his head and a smile toward Gran as the whole town stands by and lets an eighty-year-old woman forcibly drag a girl in her early twenties to her car, telling her a few choice words along the way.

The crowd waits till the stranger's car has backed out of the lot and disappeared around the curve that leads out of town.

Drama over, the crowd from the Brick and Porter envelope the deputy and Terra Diaz, pulling the town's newest celebrity couple into the pizza place in a cacophony of congratulations and what-the-hells.

"You okay, baby?" I pull April into my arms, kissing the top of her head and then catching her lips with mine when she turns her face up to me.

"Thank you," she tells me, her pretty face shining at me like I'm a goddamn hero.

She looks down at the broken glass still littering the floor and sighs, "I need to sweep that up before I can go."

I'm about to jump on the task for her when I hear a labored sigh from the doorway.

"Oh Mable! Thank you so much, I'm so sorry you got dragged into all that," April gushes, side-stepping broken glass to go hug gran while I retrieve the broom and dustpan out of the back closet.

"It's no problem, sweetie," I hear Gran telling her while I sweep up the mess. "I'm sorry about your shop. Did she break anything important? I can have the deputy track down her information if you need to press charges."

"No, Mable, she just broke a few of the vases."

"Raine? Could you help me get back to the office,

sweetheart?" Gran calls at me as I finish dumping the broken glass.

"Just give me a minute with the boy and then I'll let you have him back." I hear Gran saying to April as I rejoin them at the door.

"Lock up, baby, I'll be right back. Gotta get you home so we can finish what we started." I whisper in April's ear and then let Gran take hold of my arm as she pretends to be too frail to walk back to the museum on her own.

"I take it April and that girl have some history between them." Gran makes the observation with a pat against my arm.

"Yeah, April had already told me about her. I don't think she expected her to show up here though."

"Well, that was a good speech you gave her."

Gran lets go of my arm as soon as we reach the door of the museum.

"Hopefully she's the type that's smart enough to know good advice when she gets it."

Bending low so I can kiss Gran's cheek, she pats mine with a soft smile.

"Better go get your girl, Raine." I get a soft kiss on the cheek in return for the one I gave her.

"I'm proud of you."

She whispers it so quietly, I wonder if I heard the words at all.

Chapter Nine

April

You'd think that after the day I just had, I'd be too worn out to jump Raine as soon as I climb out of my car when we get to his house-- his gorgeous, custom-built house set back off a private road in a thick patch of forest, out of view of the other homes he tells me are scattered around his family's property.

But I'm not. And I do.

"When it gets warmer outside, I'm going to set your pretty little ass on the deck railing and fuck you out here till you scream loud enough that Cane hears you on the other side of the hill," Raine purrs into my neck as he nibbles down my throat.

I'd have to be pretty loud if the closest house is on the other side of the hill. It's a pretty big hill.

"For now, I'll settle with fucking you in the living room in front of the fireplace."

Raine lets go of me long enough to unlock the over-sized wooden front door, making quick work of dropping my bags inside so he can shut the door behind us and get his hands on me again.

"Then I'll fuck you in the bedroom...and the shower...and the kitchen..."

"Sounds like a great way to tour your house." I giggle, pulling Raine against me and loving the solid feel of him.

"*Our* house, baby. Remember?"

Our house.

I like the sound of that-- and not because it's a gorgeous place to call home, but because I get to share it with Raine.

"How long will it take you get to get the fire started?"

My hands are working at the buttons on the flannel shirt that I've already untucked from his jeans and I pull my eyes off his chest just long enough to cast a glance at the stone fireplace taking up a corner of the big living room.

Raine takes a step farther into the room, careful not to move away from my busy hands that now have his flannel off and are enjoying the heat of his bare skin as I tug to free him of the burden of the black, long-sleeve tee that was under it.

He bends toward a small table at one end of a leather couch and grabs something off the surface.

"About that long," he answers, waiting for me to react to something other than the solid feel of his erection digging into my hip.

The fireplace jumps to life across the room with a

soft click from the remote that Raine drops back on the table.

"Cheater!" I accuse, with a playful slap to his arm.

"It burns wood, but it's plumbed with gas and an electric ignition for the remote. The logs will catch in a minute or two and it'll be warm enough that you won't even notice that you're naked."

"I'm not the one who's almost naked," I tease, waiting impatiently while Raine gets his work boots off so I can finish stripping his jeans off his impossibly muscled legs.

Seriously, all the construction work he does has paid off better than any gym.

My hands have a mind of their own, dragging up his thighs slowly, admiring the view of his lean body and the hard length begging for my touch under a pair of black boxer briefs.

"That's because I gave you a head start," he growls, pulling me back to my feet and then lifting me easily in his arms to carry me to a fluffy rug in front of the now-roaring fire. "I had to build a fire to keep my woman warm, remember?"

"Yes, I recall you worked very hard at that, thank you." I'm laughing as he quickly works to get caught up with getting me undressed.

"Show me how grateful you are to your man for taking care of you, baby."

He's still being playful as he kneels over me, putting that glorious cock at eye level-- or maybe slightly lower-- but when I slide his briefs down and take him in my mouth, his teasing is replaced by a groan.

Raine

Fuck. This woman of mine. I hit the fucking lottery with April.

Just yesterday she was coming on a cock for the first time in her life and even after the shit day she's had, she's sitting between my knees looking like a goddamn angel, stripped down to just her bra and panties with the firelight flickering over her skin and my cock halfway down her pretty little throat.

I thought tonight might go slow; I'd give her a tour of the house, maybe she'd want a hot shower or a long bath, while I made dinner. We'd talk about everything that went down today and then, if I was lucky, I'd get to make slow, tender love to my woman in the comfort of our bed.

April has made it clear that she had a very different idea of how our night is going to go. From the moment we had both our vehicles parked, her hands have been all over me and I plan on giving her whatever she needs.

Her fist works my shaft in strong strokes that follow her mouth as it slides up and down until I start to feel the tell-tale signs that we're approaching the point of no return. And damn do I want to shoot my thick cum down April's throat. I want to watch her gag on my cock when it swells in her mouth and see if she swallows it like a good girl.

But I need to come in her pussy again first.

I spent half the day hard as stone, remembering the feel of her and anticipating getting inside her again.

Then Cane and his bullshit last-minute meeting made me late, and when I got back to her, one of the asshole McAllisters had gotten inside her head and had her doubting I meant every word I'd said to her.

Then getting interrupted by an uninvited guest that just wanted to show up and cause drama.

"Lay down, baby girl, I need to taste that pussy before I come in it again."

Her mouth lets go of me with soft pop as I push her onto her back.

"Was I doing it wrong?" Her worried little voice asks as I do away with both our underwear.

All I can do is groan, thinking about her hot little tongue wrapped around the head of my dick and how close I was to letting her get me off with her mouth.

"Fuck no, baby, you were doing it way too good." I nestle between her legs, pushing her thighs wide and positioning them over my shoulders. "Don't worry, I'll let you mouth-fuck me later, but I've been waiting all day to get back in this sweet little pussy."

April's squirming on my tongue with the first lick, she's so wet already my beard's coated in her juices and I know it's not going to take any effort at all to have her coming all over my face.

"Raine, just fuck me, please." Insistent hands are

pulling at my hair and then tugging at the back of my neck.

"Am I doing it wrong?" I look up from between those heavenly thighs and give her a grin.

"You know you aren't." She practically scolds me, "I just can't wait anymore, I need you inside me now."

I think about teasing her, dragging it out and making her wait but that'll be for another night. Right now, I'm more than happy to give my girl what she needs-- because I need it just as bad.

Without hesitating any longer, I'm thrusting into April's heat, her tight sheath already pulsing around me and then she's clamped down on my cock, keeping me planted in her and I'm gritting my teeth to make it through her first orgasm because I'll be damned if she's only getting one.

"You're fucking incredible when you come, baby," I tell her as soon as she's coherent and I can speak again. "I want you to do that for me again, okay?"

"Okay, but roll over, I wanna be on top this time."

And that right there is my undoing. Once I'm on my back, I can only give her a minute before my thumb is pressed between us were we're joined, circling her little clit and building her up for her next release. Watching her ride me like that, with all her blonde hair loosened from the braid she wears it in during her work day, falling down over her shoulders and hanging off those perfect tits as they bounce and sway has me ready to explode.

One more time, I feel her squeezing tight around

me, the muscles deep inside her working to pull me deeper and milking me for my seed.

There's no holding back. I come deep and hard, spraying down her insides and hoping we'll be announcing the first wedding and the first baby in the family very soon.

Epilogue 1

1 1/2 years later
Raine

My brother is still an asshole, but at least we've finally found a way to work together that doesn't have me ready to put a hammer through his skull by the end of the day.

Or maybe Cane's control freak bullshit shit just doesn't get to me any more since I married April.

Knowing I get to spend every night of the rest of our lives wrapped up in her warm curves while my grumpy shit-head brother has nothing waiting for him at home but a chameleon and a couple of half-dead houseplants helps with putting up with him these days.

Walking into the house from the garage, I pull off my muddy boots and leave them on the mat. Then I drop my keys in the bowl by kitchen door and head for the shower.

April changed her hours after we got married, she wanted the extra time in the morning for the longer commute. Her old place was right in town, within walking distance to the cafe, but our house up in the Gulch is a solid twenty-minute drive in good weather.

That means she works a little later in the afternoons, especially when the weather gets warm like now and more people want to hang out on the porch later in the day.

I don't mind. It means I get a chance to shower before she gets home and gets me dirty again.

Eventually, my early hours will come in handy when we start filling the spare rooms up with kids.

We started off just hoping it'd happen, but it never did. For the last few months, we've been trying. Really trying. Which is a lot of fun...most of the time-- but we're about to the point where we're ready to start doing the testing in case there's more working against us than just impatience.

Stripping down as I go, I crank the knobs in the shower to right temp and jump in, grateful I put in the instant hot water so I don't have to wait.

I'm pawing through the bathroom cabinet a few minutes later, swapping out deodorant for cologne, then working a bit of product through my hair after getting it about as dry as I can with the towel, when I see something sitting on the edge of the sink on April's side of the vanity.

They've become a pretty common sight over the last few months. She takes one about twice a month. I figure she must have left it there while it processed.

When I pick it up, it doesn't look the same as the ones we've waited on before though.

There's a second line on this one. Two pink lines. I stare at the pregnancy test in my hand blankly for a minute, it doesn't look right to me. I know sometimes there's a line that shows up in the wrong place, meaning the test didn't work right, and I'm about to toss this one in the trash when I realize what I'm looking at.

Holy fuck. This is a positive test. I'm holding a positive pregnancy test in my hand. We did it, we're pregnant.

Maybe I should call her. Does she know? Did she leave it here for me to find? Fuck, I have to get to town. I have to get to April.

I'm dressed and in the truck in seconds, I couldn't be moving faster if the gulch was on fire. On my way to the main road, I pass the little lane that winds back to the open meadow where Zephyr's cottage is.

She's going to kill me.

After she found out I'd been raiding her greenhouse to pick flowers for April, my sister made it very clear that the only thing saving my balls was because she liked having a sister.

Fuck it. She'll get over it.

I gas it to the back of the property where Zeph's prize greenhouse sits with one side facing the south. She wanted her cottage built here because of the meadow that allows the sun to hit the greenhouse. And I guess it does the job because Zephyr's greenhouse is always full of flowers in bloom even when there's six feet of snow on the ground.

You'd think I'd have memorized some of the names of the things, but I haven't. I grab handful of the greenery that Zeph already has cut and make quick work of adding some of those tiny little white flowers that kind look like popcorn, and some of the purple ones that April always loves when they bloom in our yard, then I pull out my pocket knife and cut entirely too many of the two-toned daffodils for Zephyr not to notice. I'll buy my sister new plants, whatever she wants.

Before I leave, I see some pink flowers that are just starting to bloom and add them to the mix and then I'm back in the truck, gunning the engine into the town.

"You better not have been in the greenhouse!"

Something something in my sister's voice yelling at me as I run up the steps and into the cafe. Hopefully I set the parking brake when I shut the engine down. If not, I'll pay Gran back for the damage to the building.

No one's inside except my wife. My wife and our baby. Holy fuck, I've never seen her look so fucking gorgeous as right now.

I've jumped the counter a thousand times since that first day. April's a pro now at knowing exactly where to be standing so I don't have to take a single step to pull her lips to mine.

Her hand blindly accepts the bouquet, her other arm snaking over my shoulder and around my neck as

I push us behind the swinging door to the back room that's still empty.

"Wait, what's thi--" April feels the hard plastic wrapped in the flower stems with the rubber band I found on Zephyr's potting table in the greenhouse.

"Raine, what is this?"

To be fair, I'm not giving her much of a chance to see what it is, I'm still too busy kissing her. My hands are all over her, which she's used to by now, but not like this, with my palms spread out over her belly like I'm willing it to grow faster.

"Did you leave before you saw the results this morning?"

"Yeah, I figured it'd be just a negative when I got home as it was this morning, why?" She squints at the test in the dim light of the backroom.

"Ohmygod. Oh my God, Raine!"

"Tomorrow, you call the doc." I press my lips to hers and push her toward the little space we turned into her office. I need my wife now and I'm taking any chances on getting interrupted. "And switch to decaf."

Epilogue 2

Five Years Later
April

"Never thought I'd see the day." Maggie says what we're all thinking.

"It is possible that hell has frozen over," May-Ellen, my mother-in-law chuckles lightly, bouncing her grandbaby on her knee as she watches the sight unfolding before us.

"With the winter we just had, that's the only explanation." Howard says seriously, his hand over Grans as they sit together on the swing.

It's a mixed group of us, gathered around the duck pond on Hart's Gulch, sitting in folding camp chairs or on blankets spread out by the shore.

Gran and Howard have taken over the two-seater yard swing in the cleared area by the fire ring that Cane built near the edge of the pond a few years ago.

Robin Diaz is on a blanket with Ginger Jones, a couple of toddlers wracked out between them.

Kids are running everywhere, some of the older ones are racing kayaks from one end of the pond to the other, I think Jackson Jones is helping the men with their project.

It's crazy to see us all together like this, multiple members of four families that have been on opposite sides of a feud for three generations, but there's nothing like raising kids in a small town to cut through old bullshit, I guess.

We're out here with the kids, enjoying a summer afternoon on the pond with the kids while we wives keep an eye on our husbands to make sure they make actual progress on their project-- a tree house that Cane promised to the boys that's become a group effort among the dads of the Ridge.

With Terra Hawkins running the only daycare center and preschool on the mountain, our children have known each other since they were babies.

That's how Birch McAllister's son ended up making friends with Cane's oldest boy and our oldest is now bffs with a Diaz kid.

Of course, Terra and Zephyr had already broken the feud lines and it's no surprise that the Hawkins twins are inseparable from the Damiani girls and Basil Jones has already declared that she will be marrying Mesa Diaz's boy.

I guess it was inevitable that our kids would end up forging deep friendships-- even bonding over the old lore and gossip that once kept these families apart.

I watch with pride as my husband supervises the construction, explaining the plans to Mesa Diaz and Cane, who are manning the power tools as Birch McAllister and Hayle unload the lumber that Birch donated from the mill.

We have two of the McAllister families at the Gulch today, my husband and both his brothers, Mesa Diaz and his brother, Glen, and Ginger and Current Jones volunteered to fire up a set of well-seasoned Dutch ovens and are busy cooking a proper feast for the crew when the work day is finished.

Zephyr and Terra took a string of little ones out to the old greenhouse where Zephyr still tends a small garden that's open for the whole family to use now and with our two and half year old entertained in his grandma's lap, it's easy for me to lay back on my chair with my hand resting over my stomach where our daughter is growing, and think about all the promises that have been kept since I came to the mountain.

Next in Series

Whispers on the Mountain
Augustus Damiani

The lead engineering position at the remote hydro-electric plant is lonelier than a light-house keeper-- but the curvy beauty picking wildflowers is going to change that for me. Whether she wants to or not.

I've heard the whispers going around the mountain town of Moonshine Ridge-- rumors of who I am and what I'm hiding from...if they knew the truth, would they think any worse of me?

It's better if I keep my distance, so I let them gossip while I hide in my mountain fortress. I'm content to watch the seasons tick by in solitude-- until I see her. The curvy little beauty picking wildflowers on the land I'm paid to watch over has me wanting a life I don't deserve.

Zephyr Hart is young, and pure, with a light shining from inside her that I can't risk dimming. She deserves better things that I have to offer her. But when she calls my bluff, I'm a man unhinged and that's when we both discover the lengths I'll go to make her mine.

Thanks for Reading

It's been a long time in the series, building up to the Hart family and now that I'm finally here, I found it challenging to unwind their family history.

Ever since Cedar McAllister broke Hayle Hart's nose back in Surrender to the Mountain Man, I've been waiting to tell Hayle's story— I just hadn't realized at that point how interwoven it would be with his siblings' stories, or how it much it would reveal about Mable's character and even her battle with Alice.

Don't worry, my sources assure me that everything will work out, and I'm enjoying seeing how they get there.

~Rocklyn

About
Augustus Damiani

The lead engineering position at the remote hydro-electric plant is lonelier than a light-house keeper-- but one look at the curvy trespasser picking wildflowers and I know that's about to change.

I've heard the whispers going around the mountain town of Moonshine Ridge-- rumors of who I am and what I'm hiding from...if they knew the truth, would they think any worse of me?

It's better if I keep my distance, so I let them gossip while I hide in my mountain fortress. I'm content to watch the seasons tick by in solitude-- until I see her.

The curvy little beauty picking wildflowers on the land I'm paid to watch over has me wanting a life I don't deserve.

Zephyr Hart is young, and pure, with a light shining from inside her that I can't risk dimming. She deserves better things that I have to offer her. But when she calls my bluff, I'm a man unhinged and that's when we both discover the lengths I'll go to make her mine.

Welcome to Moonshine Ridge and the rugged wilderness surrounding the remote mountain community where the history is long, the local lore is deep, and the men are as wild as the mountains they come from.

Protective, possessive, totally obsessed; the men of Moonshine Ridge will do anything necessary to claim the women they love and give her the happily ever after she deserves.

The Moonshine Ridge books contain a lot of insta-love, some swearing, some steamy scenes, zero cheating, and a lot of swoon-worthy happy endings. They're interconnected with recurring characters but can be read as stand-alones in any order.

Augustus & Zephyr

Whispers on the Mountain
The Hart Family of Moonshine Ridge
by
Rocklyn Ryder

Chapter One

Zephyr

When I moved down to the valley last summer, I thought it was going to be permanent, but Slow River isn't home.

This is.

I stand up straight and roll my shoulders back, stretching my stiff muscles and enjoying the early summer sun on my face.

All around me, the mountains are waking up to the late spring. The snow has melted away this far up, although there's still plenty left on the highest peaks. Everything has turned green and the wildflowers are competing for best in show.

This is my favorite place to be any time of the year, but especially now. I have an impulse to spin around and sing, Sound of Music style.

I pick a song I actually know and throw myself a private dance party right here on the hillside, and when it turns out I don't actually know the whole song, I flop down in the grass and the flowers and laugh at myself for being such a dork.

No wonder I can't get a boyfriend.

Oh well, back to what I was doing.

Picking up my basket and the set of gardening tools I brought up with me, I walk up the hill to a patch of monkey flowers and dig the trowel into the moist soil so I can pull up enough to transplant. These are scarlet monkey flowers, *Mimulus cardinalis*, bright red flowers that will bring hummingbirds to the garden all summer.

There's just enough room in the basket for maybe one more plant. I'd love to add some elephants' heads to the garden, but it's too early for them up this high still so I just keep wandering around, keeping my eyes open for something that looks good.

Slow River is okay, I guess. It's a much bigger town than the little mountain community I grew up in. It has more restaurants to choose from, more bars to drink at, more traffic on the roads, and more options. As in, men.

I thought living there for a full year while I did a florist apprenticeship with Callie would get me out of my shell. I thought I'd meet a cowboy from one of the big cattle ranches in the valley and, well...I thought that even if I wasn't married by now, at least I wouldn't still be carrying my V-card.

Seriously? Doesn't this thing have an expiration date on it?

Obviously, neither my heart nor my virginity got claimed by a handsome rancher.

My apprenticeship is almost up and I'm already packing my apartment. Honestly, I can't wait to move back up to Moonshine Ridge. I miss Mom and Gran and-- yeah, I even miss my brothers.

Raine's mellowed out so much since he got married last year, and he and April just found out they're finally pregnant; Cane's still a brooding, control freak, but running the camp keeps him from getting too annoying; and even gran hasn't heard from Hayle in over a year now.

I miss my oldest brother the most, but he left the Ridge almost five years ago and hasn't done much to keep in touch with us.

After my dad and grandpa were killed in an accident when I was just a baby, my oldest brother, Hayle, always promised me he'd be the one to walk me down the aisle at my wedding and I can't imagine it any other way, so I guess it's just as well that I'm not in any danger of getting married anytime soon.

My fingers absently run along the worn fabric of the latest flannel shirt I stole from Hayle's closet. Mom and I have been taking care of his house while he's gone; making sure pipes don't burst in the winter, and that the mice and the bears stay outside, keeping the place ready for him in case he ever does come back.

But it's a beautiful day and the flowers are blooming everywhere I look; a perfect day for filling in the garden so I'll have flowers to keep in stock all summer.

Picking myself off the ground-- literally and metaphorically-- I grab my basket and tools and head farther uphill. Closer to the fence line that marks Turtle Dam Village. Population, one...smoking hot, brooding, mysterious as fuck, Italian electrical engineer that never seems to be around when I'm up snooping for another look at him.

A girl can dream, can't she?

Augustus

Even when the crews are here on their regular shifts, it's a lonely job, but it comes with a house, it pays well, and I know the company-- and its money-- are legit.

The hydro project went in in the seventies, the state leased the land from the Hart family-- who still owns most of the land I can see out my office window-- Turtle creek was dammed to create Turtle Lake, and the power plant went in and has been in operation ever since.

At some point, the company built an entire town up here at the plant-- houses, a school, a post office, even a general store-- whatever it took to get the employees they needed for the plant. It must have been hard to get people up here, it's an hour from the little town of Moonshine Ridge, and the Ridge isn't much of a town. It's another two hours down to Slow River where you finally start finding big box stores and fast food.

From my understanding, Turtle Dam was a

thriving company town through the seventies and well into the eighties but then, I guess the workers started choosing to make the commute up from the valley instead of living so far from the conveniences of civilization. The little village was a ghost town long before I came along.

I jumped at the chance to claim one of the company houses as part of my contract. Technically, my job description is Lead Engineer but as the only permanent resident of Turtle Dam Village, I'm tasked with more than just keeping the plant operating. I'm also the unofficial caretaker of the defunct little town...making sure the empty buildings stay clear of bears, raccoons, and unauthorized humans, and making sure the tourists who come up to make use of the reservoir's recreational status don't venture beyond the "no trespassing" signs designating the perimeter of the power plant's private lease.

Today's Sunday. The plant is operating a skeleton crew that spends the day deep in the belly of the machinery. Unless I get called in to handle an emergency, the closest thing I'll come to seeing another person today is watching the trucks passing by on the town road when the shift changes later tonight.

So, the sound of singing has me curious.

The area of the lake that's open to the public is too far away for me to hear all but the loudest of music when kids inevitably venture up from the valley to party over summer break.

No one should be close enough for me to hear, but there's a distinctively feminine voice accompanying the usual sounds of the early June river current coursing along the edge of the neighborhood and down to the reservoir and the constant chatter of birds and squirrels.

I have do have a few women on my crews, but no one who'd be on the grounds on a Sunday afternoon, let alone out there singing.

There's no way anyone can get this close without seeing the posted no trespassing signs the run the outer perimeter of the plant's private lease so whoever it is is either blind or blatantly ignoring the signs. Either way, it's my job to go out there and get them to turn back.

Heading out the door with my ID badge in hand, I follow the voice to the source.

Past the road that leads into the private neighborhood, I find her wandering the slope downhill from the plant's property.

From the road, I can already see enough of her to have me feeling unusually affected by the high elevation. My breathing has gotten labored and my heart is pounding, my brain says I'm standing still but my feet are carrying me toward her at an unusually fast pace.

Not standing still then, it's just that I can't take my eyes off of her, cataloging every detail as it comes into view.

Dark blonde hair with sun-kissed highlights gathered into a messy bun at the back of her neck. Curves that put the mountain roads to shame filling out a yellow sundress with all the best parts covered by a man's flannel shirt in a faded, blue plaid.

Something that feels suspiciously like jealousy rages through me, making me want to pull the oversize shirt off of her and toss it in the incinerator.

The ensemble is completed by a pair of short cowboy boots in a bright turquoise. She's got a basket in one hand filled with wildflowers in every color, and a small gardening trowel in the other hand.

Freckles are scattered over gently tanned skin like stars and suddenly, I'm thinking of the hours I could spend exploring their patterns and finding the constellations among them.

When she turns to look at me, I'm met with a wide gaze in stunning shades of amber and gold shining like tiger's eye as lips made for sin slowly stretch into a smile that looks like the best sort of invitation.

Everything in my selfish heart is screaming *mine*.

Chapter Two

Zephyr

Augustus Damiani. In the flesh and standing so close I could reach out and lay my hand on his impossibly perfect body.

Suddenly, I wish I'd worn a bra.

Or maybe I don't.

Gorgeous, dark eyes sweep down my body and linger where my hardened nipples are straining at the snug cotton material of the dress's bodice before dropping lower and making their way back up again.

He could just as well have used his hands to map my body for how completely I feel his gaze. In fact-- I wish he would.

Augustus Damiani has been starring in my filthiest dreams ever since the first time I saw him.

He's shaved since I saw him leaving Alice's general store last month, with a load of groceries and a beard to rival any of the local guys down in Moonshine Ridge.

I'm a mountain girl, born and raised; I like a beard

as much as the next girl, but the two-days-of-scruff thing that August has going on now is definitely working for me.

Now I can see the chiseled jaw that could cut glass, the high cheek bones, the lips that could... holy hell, those lips could do so much damage to me, I'd probably forget my own name.

"Huh?"

"What's your name?"

God help me. His voice matches his looks. It's a rich, velvety tone with a hint of accent that I assume goes with his Italian heritage. Now that I have a voice to go with the image, I retroactively fill in all the dirty things I've imagined him saying to me.

It's possible that I swoon a little.

"You're trespassing. This is all private land. You need to leave or I'll have to call the sheriff."

Wait. None of those things are what I imagined him saying to me.

"I'm not trespassing." I snap out of my stupor, getting yanked back into hard, cold reality. So much for my instalove fantasy.

Then he flashes me a grin that tightens my nipples and dampens my panties.

"You didn't notice the row of no trespassing signs posted every thirty feet apart?"

"But they're posted five hundred yards from the perimeter of the actual lease," I point out, "the power plant was granted the easement with the understanding that trespassing wouldn't be prosecutable until the fence-line was breached. The signs are warnings, not law."

"What makes you think that?"

He slides a hand into the front pocket of his pants, rocking back on the heels of his leather work boots, and giving me a grin that's annoyingly sexy considering how condescending it looks.

"It's my land."

Dark eyebrows shoot up his forehead.

"Your land? So that would make you Hart's Gulch Heritage and Holdings, I presume?"

"A major shareholder, yeah."

See? I can be cocky too.

Slipping the trowel into the basket with the plants, I cross my arms and stare back at him, careful to make sure that Hayle's old flannel is pushed off my boobs so that the motion puts them on better display.

Because I like the way he's looking at me. I want to give him reasons to keep looking, at least, until I can figure out how to give him reasons to start touching.

"So that makes you who, exactly, then?"

"Zephyr," I smile, hoping we're friends now, and hold out my hand to shake his. "Zephyr Hart."

Augustus

Hart. The surname bounces inside my brain like a bullet ricocheting through a China cabinet.

It's not bad enough that I'm head over heels for a

girl who's obviously too young and too perfect for me, she has to be a Hart?

Rumor has it, they're the richest family on the mountain. The family behind the trust that leases the land to the power plant.

This ray of sunshine with her basket of wildflowers was worth more money the day she was born than I'll ever see in my life time.

Taking in her ensemble, I let my eyes move over those dangerous curves one more time. The boots are well worn, quality material, but nothing fancy. The sunflower yellow sundress makes her look like a million dollars, but the dress itself probably came from one of the usual box stores in the valley or maybe an online catalogue.

It's the flannel shirt that has my attention as I take her hand and hold it a beat too long; fighting an urge to pull her to me, wrap her in my arms, and press my mouth to hers. But, if common sense isn't enough to keep my actions in check, that damn flannel sure is.

It's ridiculously big on her, the frayed hem hanging to her knees, skimming just above where her skirt ends, the sleeves must hang off her hands by at least six inches-- she has them rolled up several times and they still cover her arms to below her elbows.

That shirt belongs to a man, and the way she fondles it between her fingers when I remember to give her back her hand says it belongs to a man she loves.

Jealousy rears up and burns through my veins.

There's not a ring on her finger yet. Whoever the

asshole is, he's dragged his heels too long. He should have locked this little mountain sprite down the moment he saw her because now that I've found her, there's no way in hell I'm about to let her get away.

"Nice to meet you, Miss Hart." I find my voice, and my manners, while fighting my way out of those amber-flecked eyes, "Care to share what you're doing up here that couldn't be done three hundred yards farther downhill?"

Gesturing at the basket slung over her arm, I ask the question that's third on the list of things I want to know about her.

The first two being *who does that shirt belong to* and *why was he stupid enough to let you out of his sight,* but I like the way her pouty lips look every time she smiles up at me, so I'm not about to remind her of any reason she might have to stop doing it.

She laughs at me, the noise coming out as part squeak and part gasp that has my dick thickening against my thigh despite my best efforts not to imagine all other ways I could make her make that sound.

"Miss Hart--" she scoffs, rolls her eyes, and flutters her lashes at me, "please. Zephyr."

"August--"

"-- Damiani."

I swear to God she *sighs* on my last name and that's all it takes for my dick to grow uncomfortably hard.

"Have we met?" I genuinely wrack my brain.

I've only gone into Moonshine Ridge a handful of times to supplement my groceries from the little general store there between my monthly trips down to the big stores in Slow River.

How is it possible that I'd have crossed paths with this exquisite creature before and not remembered?

Her fingers fiddle with the sleeve of the over-size flannel where the handle of the basket loops over her arm.

That could be the reason. If I'd met her when she was out with her boyfriend, she might not have registered. Especially if he's big enough to actually fit in that shirt.

I'm not a small man, but I doubt I'd fill that thing out completely.

"Uh, no, not really," she answers on a shy note. I like the bright pink blush that colors her cheeks as well as her cleavage. "But you know, Moonshine Ridge is really small, so..."

Well, at least my dick isn't trying to strangle me anymore. Hearing that she knows me by reputation works faster than a bucket of ice water.

I've heard the whispers making the rounds of the small-town rumor mill down in Moonshine Ridge. I know what they're saying about me; the reason why I'm a recluse, hiding out in an abandoned village an hour from my nearest neighbor.

"And what about the flowers, Zephyr?" Steering the conversation off of me and whatever lies have already poisoned her mind against me, I ask about the basket on her arm again.

Up close, I can see that she's not merely picking wildflowers for a bouquet to brighten someone's kitchen table, she's been carefully digging them up as entire plants.

"I'm harvesting them for my garden," she explains. "Most of these will last into the fall if I transplant them into the greenhouse, but some of them will go in the big garden outside."

Tearing my gaze off her is hard, almost painful, she's like a wildflower herself, one that I'd like to harvest and transplant for myself. Watch her bloom in the privacy of my home and bury my nose in her petals to breathe her sweet fragrance every day.

This side of the hill is bare of trees, all open meadow down to the lake shore. Flowers just like the ones in her basket brighten the land in every direction right to the edge of the water.

"And the reason you needed to harvest plants from this side of the no trespassing signs?"

That blush colors her skin again and she gives me a sweet smile that's laced with naughtiness.

"I was hoping I might run into you," she admits with a quick shrug like it takes effort for her to come off as casual.

Insane thoughts take hold of me: I could steal her off this mountain right now, take her up to the house, burn that shirt, and spend the rest of my life making her forget whatever she left behind.

The way her nipples strain against that yellow fabric as she stares up at me through thick, dusty lashes tells me I have a very good chance at getting away with it too.

Chapter Three

Zephyr

Augustus Damiani glares at me and it's even better than I imagined it would be.

My insides turn to jelly and leak into my panties.

What are the odds that he'd be willing to help me out with the v-card problem? Because now that I've had a chance to meet him in real life like this? I'm even more convinced he's my number one pick.

I have to stop thinking about that. I have to stop thinking about *him* doing that. It's making me delirious and I'm likely to end up doing something so embarrassing-- like literally throwing myself at him.

I've been crushing on guys since I was eleven but this is the first time I've met a guy that made me understand what it means to feel your clit throb just by being close to him. I think I'm sweating; I feel hot. And kinda itchy.

It's probably just the warm afternoon sun. I'm being ridiculous. But I do have to get Hayle's shirt off of me, pronto.

"Do you mind?" I hand the basket over to August, and strip the old flannel off like it's a wool blanket. "Thanks, it was too hot for the shirt," I force an innocent smile, hoping he's not onto me as I reach to take my basket of plants back from him.

He doesn't hand it over. That discerning glare that has me in knots deepens and he watches me fold the old shirt over my arm with a frown like it insulted his mother.

"Nice flannel," he says in a tone that makes it clear he doesn't mean it.

"Huh? Oh...uh. It's my brother's," I stare at the blue and tan plaid laid over my arm in confusion, then up at August's dreamy dark eyes as I watch them soften as those sinful lips slide back into a smile.

"I can take the basket back," I offer again, holding my hand out for it and making the huge mistake of brushing against him.

"Whoa, you okay?"

Augustus Damiani is holding my hand.

I am both very much okay and not at all okay. I think I literally swooned when I felt those rock-hard abs against the back of my hand as he pulled my flower basket farther from me. Now he's got a firm grip on my hand and I'm sure he thinks he's holding me up but honestly, he's keeping me from floating away.

"Zephyr?"

This is a new tone for that silky, dark chocolate voice of his. A new look in those hauntingly deep brown eyes.

"Baby, you don't have any water in your basket. When was the last time you drank water?"

He sounds worried. Is he feeling protective? He called me *baby*.

"I have a bottle in my car for when I get back." I point in the general direction of where I left my car parked down by the lake.

"Come on, let's go take care of you."

August's arm wraps around me and I shamelessly take full advantage of the opportunity to lean into his body as he steers me up the private road that leads to into the Turtle Dam ghost town.

There are so many rumors going around the Ridge about this man, I can't keep track of them all, but one thing everyone agrees on it that he's hiding from something-- and that he's dangerous.

Gran told me he's a mafia hit man. That he's hiding out up here while he waits for heat to die down before he can go back to the city.

Then, when I was refilling the bouquets that Alice McAllister sells for me at her store, Alice said Gran has it all wrong and that August is hiding from the crime family he betrayed and that he's in the witness relocation program.

Terra said that Hawk ran a background check on August when he showed up in town and that he really is just an electrical engineer, working for the power plant. No exciting criminal ties but a couple of fancy degrees from a college back east.

Whatever the truth about Augustus Damiani is, I am one hundred percent into these daddy vibes he's putting off as he walks me into a big house at one end of the small village that's now nothing but abandoned houses and empty stores.

"Sit," he orders, pulling a chair away from a heavy, wooden table that sits between the kitchen and the living room.

"Drink."

A glass of cool water from a filtered pitcher in the fridge gets set in front of me.

I'm not even thirsty-- August stands across the kitchen from me and leans back against the counter, crossing his arms and then his ankles as he levels a stern gaze at me and waits for me to down the water-- well, not thirsty for water, that is.

Augustus

Her brother's flannel.
Relief has never felt more liberating, and that includes the day I made it back home in one piece.

I still don't know why she'd come up here hoping to find me. From the sound of it, she's already heard about me. Everyone else down in town steers clear of me, too scared of what they've heard to manage more than polite small talk. Except the deputy.

Hawkins seems like a decent guy. Under different circumstances we might have become friends-- but he's recently married, with twins on the way by the end of summer. And that's a stage of life I'm not likely to get to, myself.

The forest nymph at my kitchen table swallows down the last of the liquid in the glass and wipes her mouth with the back of her hand.

The gesture goes straight to my dick and the damn thing's hard as stone again as I imagine her wiping my cum from those lips and looking up at me with the same self-satisfied grin, like she's expecting a pat on the head for being such a good girl.

A growl escapes my chest.

"How are you feeling now?"

She still looks flushed. So many of those blonde highlights running through her hair have escaped the clip at the back of her head that they look like a halo shining in the sunlight filtering through the front windows.

Without *her brother's* flannel shirt covering so much of her up, it's easier to appreciate the fine curves filling out the top of that yellow dress, the peach-soft skin on display under the skinny straps that are doing double duty to hold up a set of truly magnificent tits, the full tops of which are tinged with a blotchy pink that contrasts with the light smattering of freckles.

I assume it's a bit of heat stroke, standing out in the harsh sunlight too long without drinking enough water.

Thinking of her out there, not taking care of herself, has me wanting to scold her or even take her over my knee-- thinking about the way her round ass would jiggle and redden with my hand-print has me tightening my jaw, silently acknowledging that my motivation has less to do with teaching her to take better care of herself and a lot more about getting my hands on her perfect flesh...and marking it as mine.

"Better, I guess." Zephyr's eyes don't quite make it all the way to mine when she answers. Her voice is breathier than when we were talking outside and I notice the way she chews her bottom lip as her gaze lays heavily in my direction.

"You sure?" She still looks a little out of it.

I'm about to force myself away from the counter where I'm reclining, desperately trying to find a casual position that relieves the ache of my dick. I'm planning to refill her glass, rummage through the fridge to see what I have on hand to get some sustenance in her, try to get her to tell me just what it was she was expecting when she came up here hoping to find me, when I see something that has me frozen in place.

A whispered oath moves past my lips in my second language. My fingers clenching the edge of the outdated laminate counter under me.

I cannot be seeing this. There must be a far more mundane explanation, flowers like Zephyr don't bloom in the garden of my life.

"You speak Italian?"

The finely controlled movements of her upper arm still momentarily, her hooded gaze widening when she hears the soft string of words under my breath.

"My nonna wanted to make sure we were able to communicate with family in the old country," I confirm with a nod, letting the knowing smirk that's been fighting the corner of my mouth have its way when I see her lips fall open on a quiet sigh.

"What did you say?"

"I cursed the devil for letting me hope for such a gift," I tell her truthfully.

The pink coloring her fair skin definitely has to do more with me than the high elevation sunlight. The blush deepens and spreads. Her eyes finally come all the way up to mine and a sly smile plays at the corners of her pretty lips while the small, measured movements return to the muscles of her left arm.

"*Fiore mio*, what are you hiding under my grandmother's tablecloth?"

Zephyr stills, her eyes wide and alert like a mouse that knows it's been spotted by a hawk.

"Nothing," she swears emphatically in a voice so quiet it isn't even a whisper.

A couple of quick steps is all it takes for me to cross the distance to her.

She squeals in shocked protest as I grab the chair by the seat beneath her tempting ass and pull it away from the table with a loud scrape across the tile flooring.

I might have embarrassed her, but she doesn't make any move to deny what I've caught her doing.

He left hand is tangled in the fabric of her skirt, tucked tightly between thick thighs exposed where she's lifted the dress and I know that if I brought her fingers to my mouth, I'd get a taste of the sweetest pussy that's ever tempted me.

"Come here, *fiore*."

Chapter Four

Zephyr

I swear. I am not sitting at this man's kitchen table, masturbating under the cover of the lacy table cloth.

Something about Augustus just has me feeling restless. My skin feels hot and prickly everywhere, but there's a pressure built up in my core that has me desperate for some relief.

When my fingers first pushed between my thighs, I didn't even realize what I was doing.

But the man is hotness incarnate and he's been leaning against the counter, all stretched out with his ankles crossed, those muscles on casual display like he's a model in a photo shoot. It's more than I can handle and I guess pressing my fingers against my clit to try to relieve the pressure there is probably a saner option than, say, climbing him like a tree.

I really did not think he could tell what I was doing and it is so not polite of him to call me out like this.

"Come here, *fiore.*"

When he calls me flower in Italian like that? Every time he says it, his voice goes to gravel and it comes out in a melodic accent that isn't as noticeable in his usual voice. It *does* things to me that have me acting purely on instinct.

Augustus pulls me off the chair and I'm hoping for hungry kissing.

Instead, he leads me around the table and lifts me surprisingly easily so that I'm sitting on top of the table cloth I was just hiding under.

Again, I'm hoping to feel his lips against mine. I want the short scruff of his beard scrubbing my skin. I want--

He doesn't move between my knees as my legs dangle off the edge of the table. Instead, he turns one of the chairs sideways so that I can rest my feet on it.

Warm hands grip my knees and I feel calluses as they slide up the outside of my thighs as he pushes the hem of my skirt up.

Thick fingers climb up my hips and hook into the elastic of my panties.

I'm all too eager to shimmy my hips helpfully as he works them off my ass and down my legs, his eyes never leaving mine.

Those heavy hands fold the fabric of my skirt up high on my thighs, till it's neatly gathered in my lap and I can feel the cool air of the room against my bare pussy.

But instead of moving close to touch me like I need him to, August rests those large hands on top of my thighs, only letting the rough pads of his thumbs barely brush me before he takes a step back.

His eyes sweep down my entire body, lingering on the place between my legs before taking my hand to his mouth, then they close tightly as he inhales the scent of me still on my fingertips before placing my own hand back to my center.

Augustus settles back in the same spot, leaning back against the counter a few feet in front of me. Only this time, the table isn't between us and I've been carefully arranged to be on full display for him.

My panties are a small wad of white satin in his hand as he raises them to his face and inhales deeply-- his eyes still on mine.

"Show me, *fiore.*"

His voice is soft, but there's no mistaking its command-- or his meaning-- as his eyes glance between my legs.

He...wants to watch me touch myself?

My knees fall together, my hand still wedged between them but far from where he put it.

"Why?"

I don't understand why he'd rather watch me than do it himself and I'm feeling silly and self-conscious.

"Because it's hot, and I want to watch," he answers with a sinful little grin as he lifts his water glass to his lips.

I'm shaking my head. It's never made sense to me why a guy would want to watch this. I don't think I can do this. Not even for Augustus Diamani's hungry eyes.

"I don't-- how's it hot?"

Oh fuck.

Augustus sets the water aside, his fingers sliding through the condensation that's built up on the outside of the glass as his hand moves off of it. It's surprisingly sensual and I feel my throat work in a hard swallow.

Then he pulls the hem of his shirt up and peels it over his head, letting it drop on the floor beside him.

Whoa. It's like a wall of eye candy. Inked up, olive skin stretched over defined muscles, and a perfect T of dark hair across flat pecs and trailing down between abs like a stack of bricks.

He stays casually reclined against the counter, his eyes never leaving my face, as his hands work his buckle and pull the leather belt free of the loops on his jeans before letting it drop on the floor by his shirt.

My eyes are glued to his hands as they undo the button on his waist band, lower the zipper, and reach beneath the black fabric of his boxer briefs to take his cock in hand.

Augustus

To be clear; fiore mio started this.

As soon as I realized what her hand was busy with under the table, I needed to see her. So this is her show and if she wants to know why it's one I want to watch, I'm happy to demonstrate for her.

It also provides sweet relief to my aching cock that's been hard for her since we met on the hillside.

Keeping my movements slow and intentional, I keep my eyes on the beautiful young woman sitting on my kitchen table as I take myself in hand for her to see.

Zephyr's lips part softly at the sight of me. The pink tip of her tongue slides across the edge of her upper lip appreciatively, making my cock surge thicker in my grip as I slide my fist up my length, finishing the first full stroke with a firm tug over the pulsing head.

It's obvious from the hooded gaze and the heavy rise and fall of her full breasts that she's learning the answer to her question; how it's hot to watch someone you find attractive taking their pleasure into their own hands-- especially while they leave no room to doubt that they are thinking of you while they do so.

My hand staggers on my second slow stroke. I have to hold my grip and squeeze my tip to hold myself in check as Zephyr's knees part before me. Thick, shapely thighs fall open, making room for her hand to slip between them and giving me a view even better than the mountains outside my windows.

Everything in front of me is perfection: the fine beads of perspiration that have formed along the crease of her cleavage, the goose-flesh covering her exposed upper arms, pebbled nipples straining under the dress, and the heavy-lidded, foggy gaze that's so focused on the movements of my hand as it works my cock, she might not even realize that she's lost her self-consciousness.

Those thighs fall wider, the yellow dress rucked up around her waist. Her delicate fingers slide between pussy lips that are swollen and dark with her desire, her honey glistening on her fingers as the wet sounds of her work fill my ears.

If you ask me, Nonna's hand-crocheted table cloth has never had a finer centerpiece set upon it.

When fiore comes on her own hand her body shakes violently with my name on her lips like an agonized plea as if I'm the only thing can ease her ache.

Even from six feet across the fucking room, her orgasm is more than I can last through. My free hand clutches at the counter under me as I fuck my own hand relentlessly, matching her rhythm while I watch her make herself come to the sight of me.

Cum shoots from me, arcing into the air like a fountain before splattering on the floor between us. I'll have a hard time mopping the floor later without adding to the mess at the memory of our afternoon.

For a long moment, both of us are still, our eyes locked on one another, both of us breathing heavily.

Zephyr's eyes slide down my chest and watch as I tuck my dick back into my briefs. The damn thing's still half hard and when Zephyr pulls her lower lip between her teeth and parts her knees so I can see her juices still glistening on her inner thighs, I know it won't be going soft soon.

"I need to taste you, *fiore.*"

The words are a prayer, falling from my lips as I slide onto the chair in front of her, swinging her leg over my shoulder and taking her by the back of the thighs to bring her to my mouth.

She's as sweet as I knew she would be.

My mouth collides with her center, my tongue seeking to savor every drop of her pleasure that still sweetens her skin.

"Ohmygod, that really does feel good."

Zephyr's hands tangle into my hair, her short nails scraping the back of my neck as she moves in my hands to give me more of her.

I'm so fucking lost in her that I miss any nuance there is to be found in her sweet cries. I only need her next climax and I need it on my tongue. This time, I need to be the reason her thighs are spread wide and when her body begins to shake and her cries become shouts, I have to be the only one bringing her such pleasure.

When her body has stilled, I continue kissing and lapping against every part of her that still carried the flavor of her orgasm.

My dick is hard again and begging for its turn with her.

Reminding myself-- and my cock-- that I am not an overeager school boy with no self-control, I reluctantly take my mouth off Zephyr's thigh. Leaning back, I take her hand and help her to sit up before carefully moving her skirt back down to cover the temptation in front of me.

I'm determine to let her rest but she's off the table and in my lap.

Her lips come to mine with a near violent force,

her hands at the sides of my head with her thumbs brushing the stubble on my cheeks.

I've never had a woman kiss me like this. Fiore leaves me breathless, with her hot little pussy finding my length and moving against it insistently.

In this moment, rational thought is a myth. I think I would grant this wildflower anything she asks of me.

"Augustus," she purrs, even as I continue to nibble at her sweet lips, "I want you to be my first."

Chapter Five

Zephyr

Augustus freezes, pulling away to give me a confused look. The way his brows draw together and his jaw clenches, makes him look like I hurt his feelings.

Then another soft string of foreign words gets muttered and suddenly I'm standing on the floor again while Augustus fixes himself back into his clothes. Including putting his shirt and his belt back on.

"What happened?" I wonder aloud, half in general and half actually asking.

"*Fiore mio.*" Augustus shakes his head, his eyes on the ceiling. "We've had fun today but it's getting late. You should go home and plant your flowers."

Five seconds ago, this man was touching me like he owned me and I was super into that, so what the hell just happened?

"Did I do something wrong?"

"No, *fiore*, you definitely did not do anything wrong." Augustus hands me the basket of plants as he herds me out the front door. "It's obvious that there are years between us, but if I'd known you lacked experience, I'd have behaved myself better."

My car is parked at the bottom of the hill, down by the lake shore. Augustus walks beside me the whole way, his hand resting lightly between my shoulder blades as if I'm his-- despite his obvious rejection that has me frustrated, confused, and increasingly pissed off.

"So, for the record," I whirl to eye him after setting the basket in the back of my Jeep, "is this a 'no?' or is this more like you want to wait till the third date sort of thing?"

This time he mouths the curses so quietly I don't even catch the words. I'm really going to have to study some Italian curse words if he's going to keep muttering like this.

"This is a *no, fiore,*" he finally tells me. "I am not the man you want in your memories that way."

Well, he's wrong about that. He's the man that was seared into my memory the moment I first saw him, and today has already guaranteed I won't be forgetting him pretty much ever. The memory I don't want of him is this one-- where he sends me home without satisfying the need that he only managed to make worse.

"What if I come back?"

Augustus inhales deeply, like he's gathering his courage, but he doesn't step away from me when I stand close to him,

"No means no, *fiore.*"

His lips curve in a smirk but his voice lacks conviction.

"Yeah, but you don't sound like you're not consenting so much as like you're telling me I can't have seconds on dessert."

"Hand me your phone, Zephyr."

See? That's what conviction sounds like.

When he gets very serious, his voice goes stern and loses the trace of accent. I haven't decided which way sounds sexier yet but I'm determined to hear more of both.

I unlock the screen and hand over my phone without hesitation. I don't care if he's going to put his number in it or if he's going to go through it looking for naked selfies or so he can delete any texts I might have from other guys. It's all good with me.

He has elegant fingers. Long and slender on hands that are at least twice the size of my own. Hands that were very recently wrapped around my thighs and my ass in ways that I'm kinda hoping left marks for me to admire later.

Those fingers tap against my screen for a minute and then he hands me back my phone.

"You let me know when you get home safely, *fiore*."

August waits till I'm settled into the driver's seat, watching to make sure I buckle my seat belt and then he nods at the insulated water bottle in the cup holder and reminds me to stay hydrated.

I don't even get a kiss goodbye.

It's like the whole kitchen scene never happened, but the whisker burn between my thighs says I absolutely did not hallucinate that-- that, and the fact that I'm driving home without my panties. Those are still in Augustus's pocket.

Augustus Damiani is the only thing I've been able to think about for weeks now. It's pretty obvious that he wants me too and I am determined to find a way into his bed.

Augustus

Fiore spends her days torturing me.

I should never have put my number in her phone.

I remind myself that I needed to know she had made it home safely; the road between the village and Moonshine Ridge is steep and winding and wildlife can catch drivers by surprise even in broad daylight.

The part of me that no longer lies to myself scoffs at my half-truth. I was desperate to maintain contact with the gentle breeze that's blown into my heart.

Since she called to tell me she arrived home safely-- called, mind you. I had expected a text. Hearing her sweet voice in my ear had only led to a night of misery as I soaked the sheets with my cum, painfully aware of the opportunity I'd turned down to have Zephyr in my bed and filled with my seed instead.

Now she sends me pictures daily. Of the flowers she transplanted in her garden and greenhouse; of the sunrise over the mountains from the back deck of her cottage in the family estate of Hart's Gulch; of her naked tits swinging free and beautiful with the blur of color from her greenhouse flowers in the background; of her fingers working between her legs, those dusky blonde curls wet with her arousal as she shows me what I should never have asked to see.

I'm too fucking weak to block her number; too fucking addicted to her light to leave her on read. So, like a fool, I reply. Every time.

I don't need my alarm anymore because I wake to Zephyr's morning texts. Another sunrise, the deer in the meadow, the steam rising from her coffee mug.

Her cheerful good mornings have become conversations: *how did you sleep? What will you do today? Did you dream about me-- I dreamed about you-- should I come visit?*

We chat through the afternoons, her cheerful photos of her gardens and the bouquets she makes to sell in the little store down there brightening days that I hadn't realized were so dull till now.

And my nights all end the same now, with me typing out a wish for sweet dreams for her in Italian because she says she sleeps best when I do, and then with me putting those dirty pictures she sends me to the shameful use she intends them for.

But I always evade her suggestions of coming back up to see me. I won't take her innocence. That's not a gift I deserve. It would haunt me forever if I became fiore's greatest regret.

Which is why I don't leave my desk on the day my front porch security camera alerts me to a visitor.

I watch her from my screen as she sits on the step far beyond the time she knows I'm usually home. I can't bring myself to open the messages she sends me; no doubt wondering if I've been delayed at the plant and when I'll get there.

If I answer her, if I see her, I won't be able to stop myself from claiming her.

So I sit at my desk in my office, behind the safety of a manned security gate that keeps her from coming up to the plant, and watch the live feed from the camera on my porch like a coward.

It's after dark when Zephyr has cried herself dry and gives up her vigil, leaving one of her bouquets resting against the bottom of my door.

Half an hour later, when I'm sure she's truly gone, I retrieve the flowers and read the note.

Sono venuto per farti cambiare idea.

"I came to change your mind." If she had caught me, she certainly would have been successful.

Inside, I find a vase and fill it with water and then her flowers, but I can't bring myself to set it on the table. My kitchen table has become a sacred place since Zephyr adorned it. I haven't even been able to eat a meal there.

The vase of flowers finds a place on the coffee table, but I can't stay in the room with them.

Hours later, when I haven't heard from her, I open the messages she sent from my porch and read through the progression from her usual bright demeanor asking if I'll be back soon, to worrying if everything is all right, to assuring me that she won't bother me anymore.

I should be relieved, but less than twenty-four hours later, after nearly no sleep and sending her several messages that she hasn't even opened, I'm a man possessed, pounding my fist on her front door.

"Who the fuck are you?"

The man who answers Zephyr's door does not look pleased to see me. The feeling is mutual.

"Who the fuck are *you*?"

Shouting at the man in front of me is proof that I've lost my mind. I don't care that he's bigger than me or that he's looking at me with murder in his eyes. I care that he's in my girl's house and I'm ready to put up a fight to get through him.

"I'm Hurricane." He growls at me like the name ought to mean something but all it means to me is that he's still in my way.

"Where's Zephyr? I need to talk to her."

Hurricane-- if that's his name-- crosses meaty arms across a barrel chest and glares at me. He's much stockier than I am, but we're similar in height, so at least I have that going for me.

"You're that mafia dude from the power plant, right?"

He's the first person to say it to my face, but it's not like I don't know what the locals are saying about me.

"Power plant, yes." I straighten to my full height, which actually gives me nearly an inch over the behemoth blocking my way. "Mafia, no."

"What do you want with my sister?"

Hurricane. Cane. Sister. Got it. He's her brother. Not the one she steals the flannel shirts from, that one doesn't live on the mountain anymore. This one's the one who used to play pro ball.

Standing face to face with Hurricane Hart, it's easy to see how he could easily have had a career in professional sports.

The last thing I want to do is explain my relationship with fiore to her huge, and obviously very protective, older brother.

"She said she has something she wants to give me."

But I can't bring myself to lie to him either.

Chapter Six

Zephyr

"The best way to get over one man is to get under another, right?"

My boss, Callie, winks at me as she watches me check my phone for the billionth time today.

"Go out, have fun, forget all about that idiot."

I'm still ignoring August's texts. Without opening them, I can only read the first few words of each one. They mostly start with "Please don't..." and "I can't...." and they all came in after I gave up waiting on him to come home last night.

Message received, loud and clear. I don't need to open his messages and give him the satisfaction of seeing that they've been read just so I can fill in the blanks that undoubtedly end each sentence: *"please don't*...come back to my house," and *"I can't*...be the man you want."

So I scroll past those and tap on the conversation with Brian.

"Sounds great, doll, I'll pick you up at seven. Can't wait!"

His enthusiasm makes me smile. I tap the heart reaction on his last text with a smile.

"He's picking me up at seven," I tell Callie. She been ready to leave for the last five minutes, but she's been waiting on an update about whether or not Brian and I are on for tonight.

"Good. You deserve a man who actually wants to be with you, sweetheart." She waddles back to me to give me a hug. "Lock this place up early so you have time to get dressed up. I want to hear all about it next week."

I watch my eight-months-pregnant boss make her way out the door, returning her wave as she drives past the flower shop windows on her way out of the parking lot.

Callie is much more enthusiastic about my date with Brian than I am, but she's right; there's no point in sitting around moping over Augustus.

He's been very clear from the beginning that he's not interested in going any farther than we've already been...and that maybe he even regrets that.

So I texted Brian when I got back to my cottage last night.

He's one of the locals here in Slow River. We met at O'Hare's last summer when I first moved down to Slow River for my apprenticeship with Callie. He seems like a nice enough guy, he's okay to look at, he's way closer to my own age, and, most importantly-- he's been trying to get me to go out with him for months.

Who knows? Maybe tonight will be the start of something good. If things with Brian look promising, I might even extend the lease on my apartment and stay on with Callie instead of moving back to Moonshine Ridge at the end of the month.

My phone chimes with another text from Augustus. Just seeing his name pop up on my screen has my fingers itching to cancel plans with Brian. Then I see the words, "Please understand that..." and my brain fills in the rest of that without opening the message.

I'm sure it finishes with something awful like, "please understand that..." what? Maybe that "...I'm not interested in seeing you again?" Or maybe he wants to reiterate his opinion about my age or my inexperience or tell me again about how he's "not the right man" for me.

While I'm preparing to close up the shop, my phone starts ringing. When I see Augustus' name on the screen, I cancel the call without answering.

The shop's landline rings while I'm sweeping and I don't even check the caller ID before answering.

"Slow River Florist, how can I help you?"

"Oh, thank God. Fiore, why aren't you answering your phone? Are you okay?"

Shit. I should have texted him back.

Augustus's rich voice pours into my ear over the line.

"Why are you calling my work?"

"You aren't reading your messages; you aren't answering your calls. You left my house in tears last

night and your brother said you went back to work early. I've been worried about you."

"How the fuck would you know I was crying last night, August?"

On the other end of the line is a weary sigh.

"I have security cameras on the porch, *fiore*, I saw you...I've been trying to get in touch with you so we could talk."

"You saw me sitting on your porch last night. You knew I was waiting for you. Did you get my messages? Were you ignoring me so you didn't have to see me?"

I'm pissed. There's no reason for him to be blowing me up just to confirm what I already knew; he was avoiding me on purpose.

"*Fiore*, when will you be done at the flower shop tonight? I think we should talk about things between us."

"We don't need to talk, Augustus. You've been perfectly clear about how you feel about me. I understand that you aren't interested in seeing me again. Don't worry, I won't come back up or bug you again. I have to go. I have a date."

Augustus

Zephyr says "date" and doesn't wait for a reaction before the line goes dead.

If she was only trying to get a rise out me, she'd have waited before hanging up so she could head my pained inhale. She would have heard my protests. She would have given me a chance to tell her how wrong she is about my reasons for turning her away... She wouldn't have me following her like a stalker as she leaves her apartment with a boy who doesn't even have the good manners to hold her door open for her as she climbs into the passenger side of his bright yellow muscle car.

It's easy to keep them in sight as I follow them to one of the steak houses in town.

Slow River is a ranching town, bigger than Moonshine Ridge but small enough that most of the businesses are still local independents.

The yellow car pulls into a space in front of the Branding Iron; a western-themed place with wagon wheels planted with the azaleas around the exterior of the building.

I'd been on my way down the mountain when I called the flower shop that Zephyr works at. Her brother had told me she'd come back down to her place in the valley early. That's why he'd been at her house today, taking care of plants that Zephyr had left instructions for.

By the time I reached the florist, she was pulling out of the parking lot-- despite there being another hour before the listed business hours said they closed. If I'd been any later, I'd have been left sitting there, desperately trying to convince her to answer her phone.

As it is, I was able to follow her to her apartment building, but couldn't see which unit she went to.

Leaving me waiting across the street, dialing her number repeatedly as my calls went straight to voicemail again and again, until the yellow car pulled up to the building and my fiore emerged from beyond the gate in a dress that would have had me rushing to toss her over my shoulder if I had been able to catch my breath before her date whisked her away.

Sitting in my own vehicle, several rows from where they might notice me, I know I'm fooling myself if I think there's any reason for me to still be here other than the jealousy raging through my veins.

The boy still doesn't open the door for his date. He stands near the tail lights and waits for her to join him.

He seems impatient for her to hurry, but the scene unfolds in my eyes in slow motion. First, one silver high heel meets the ground, then a second, as Zephyr turns sideways in the seat to pull herself from the interior.

Since this boy obviously learned his manners from the livestock in the pastures of the Slow River Valley ranches, he doesn't offer her a hand to help her as she stands.

Her hand grips the side of the car for balance and then she's in full sight of me. Those golden tresses falling in waves down her back, the emerald green dress hugging her body like paint, showing curves that have memories of her spread and panting on my table burning in my mind.

She closes the door herself and when she arrives beside him, he takes off walking ahead of her, making no effort to wait for her smaller steps in the sexy high heels that slow her pace, but make the view of shapely legs all the way up to the high hem clinging to her thighs well worth the wait.

This boy is an idiot. He hasn't taken notice of her yet. He's barely even glanced at the goddess accompanying him this evening.

I'm prepared to accept my punishment for being so stupid as to think I could resist the draw I feel toward Zephyr. I have the key in the ignition, ready to return to my lonely mountain refuge knowing I blew my last chance with fiore, when I see her date finally hold a door open for her-- I'm out of the car and sprinting toward the restaurant with murder on my mind.

Chapter Seven

Zephyr

Brian stands at the door of the steakhouse, waiting for me to move through the door he's holding open.

So far, the date's been pretty casual; he texted when he got to my place, he hasn't made much of a show of gallantry, but I guess that's not really a big deal. I'm a big girl, I can open a car door on my own.

"Ouch!" The pinch is unexpected as I walk past Brian through the door. So unexpected that I don't know how to react.

For one thing, it fucking hurt. My hand involuntarily covers the stinging spot on my backside where I'm sure a bruise is forming. Brian grins at me when I face him in shock.

"That hurt," I inform him coldly.

He just shrugs. "Ass like that's beggin' for it," he answers nonchalantly. "Let's go eat."

Inside, I hold back while Brian gives our name to the hostess.

"I'll meet you at the table," I tell him, pointing in the direction of the ladies' room to let him know where I'm headed.

"'K, see ya in a few." Brian shrugs and follows the hostess into the dining area.

In the restroom, I check the spot that still smarts from Brian's pinch. It's not showing any marks yet, but I have a feeling it'll be purple by the morning.

Washing my hands, I give the girl in the mirror a serious look. It's not like I wasn't expecting him to touch me. Or even like I didn't go into tonight with the full intention of letting him.

It's just that-- I'm not really having fun. Brian does nothing for me and the ass grab didn't feel sexy, it felt gross. Tonight is obviously not going to be the beginning of anything.

The woman in the mirror tries to assure me that has nothing to do with a certain, brooding, Italian engineer and tells me to at least enjoy dinner.

Determined to take her advice, I open the bathroom door and walk straight into a wall of warm muscle and spiced cologne.

"Let's go, *fiore*, your date is over."

Augustus's hand splays across the small of my back, steering me out the door with a commanding touch.

When we get on to the sidewalk, I expect him to stop, thinking we'll talk and then I can go back to my evening.

Instead, August continues to navigate me into the parking lot.

"What the fuck are you doing, August? I'm on a *date*."

"Not anymore. You're not going anywhere near that boy again, Zephyr."

August's SUV is parked a few rows away and it dawns on me that he expects me to leave with him. Despite the forceful hand at my back, I come to a dead halt between the parked cars.

"You can't just steal someone's date, Augustus," I huff up at the dark eyes glowering down at me.

Even with the heels, August towers over me. His black hair hangs around his eyes as if he hasn't combed it with anything but his fingers; his eyes are narrowed, dark brows knitted together in consternation; and those wicked lips pressed in a hard line, his jaw ticking near one ear.

He lets me vent but it's pretty clear I'm not getting through to him.

"What the fuck is right, Zephyr, that asshole is lucky all I'm taking is his date. I'd have also relieved him of half his teeth and his dick if he'd touched you again. Let's go."

No, no, no. Nothing about that made my belly clench or my clit throb with need. Lies, I tell myself, but I'm still not going anywhere with him.

"For your information, I was into it." More lies.

"Sure as fuck didn't look like you were into it." August leans close to level his gaze to mine, fire blazes in the dark irises, his nostrils flaring as he challenges me to disagree when I realize what this means.

"'*Looked like?*' You were watching? Have you been following me?"

Augustus straightens back to his full height and when the firm tug he gives my hand doesn't get me moving again, he moves so quickly that I don't have time to do more than let out a surprised squeal as I'm tossed over his shoulder and carried the rest of the way to his vehicle.

For the record, I do consider beating my fists against his back as I'm carried. I also enjoy the view of his ass. The way the muscles flex and bunch with his purposeful strides-- and I think about reaching down to cup my hands around those strong glutes to feel them move. August's shoulder digs into my stomach, which is less than comfortable, but his arm is wrapped around the back of my thighs like a steel band and I feel his free hand tugging at the hem of my dress to keep me from flashing anyone before he yanks open the passenger door of his SUV and carefully, but roughly, places me on the seat, fastening my seat belt before closing me in and sliding behind the steering wheel on his side.

I'm furious, but I'm also turned on, which makes me more furious.

"Where are you taking me?" I demand. As he starts the engine and pulls out of the parking lot, I hear the door locks automatically engage.

"Home." His tone is resolute as he very noticeably heads in the opposite direction of my apartment.

"My place is in the other direction."

"Not your home, *fiore*."

Augustus

"You don't seriously expect me to ride all the way back to the Ridge with you?"

My flower's voice is cold and I don't have to glance beside me to know the angry glare she's leveling at me.

"No. I expect you to ride all the way back to Turtle Village with me." I grit between my clenched jaw.

The cabin of the car is filled with the sound of fiore's frustration.

"That's a three-hour drive, August. What do you expect me to do when you get me there? Play checkers with you?"

I roll to a stop at the flashing red light that marks Keller's Ferry's only major intersection. I hear the click just as the bell on the dashboard chimes and suddenly Zephyr's fist pounds on the door beside her.

There are no other vehicles at the intersection, so I press my foot to the pedal and start the journey up the two lane, mountain highway that leads to our destiny.

"Do you have the child locks on?" Her voice is filled with awe and laced with real fear. It sets my jaw on edge and has my heart pounding with uncertainty.

"Augustus? Are you *kidnapping* me?"

"Shh, *Fiore mio*, please put your seat belt back on." I don't recognize my own voice; it sounds flat and far away; dim under the white noise of my blood rushing through my veins.

Flipping the switch to turn on the high beams, I keep both hands on the wheel as I take the car around the sweeping curves that follow the contours of the mountains as we climb in elevation.

This section of the highway is far from any settlement, clinging to the side of a cliff that was blasted into the mountains over a hundred years ago. The only light on the road comes from the headlights and the moon overhead.

Zephyr has gone deathly quiet beside me. The light on the dashboard that said her seat belt was unfastened has gone out.

Beside me, I can sense her apprehension, her hand tightened on the door handle beside her, the other periodically reaching to tighten the seat belt across her chest, her inhalations rough between held breaths.

We round a bend and a deer bolts from the side of the road into the forest. Zephyr startles beside me.

Reaching for hand in the darkness between us, I'm relieved when she takes it and squeezes my fingers tightly.

This is the stretch of road where her father and grandfather hit a deer nearly twenty years ago. It caused them to lose control of the vehicle and run off the road-- killing both of the men somewhere in the process.

She told me she doesn't travel this road at night.

I am the worst of selfish men.

I'm proving the whispers about me true; I am not a

good man. Not someone who should be trusted or welcome in their community. I've literally kidnapped a woman and now I'm taking her to my home in a remote, abandoned, mountain village-- and, God help me, but I do not want to play checkers when we get there.

It's not until we level out on the stretch of road that enters Moonshine Ridge that I feel fiore's grip soften, allowing the blood to flow back into the fingers she's been strangling in our silent ascent of the mountain.

"Why are we going to your house, August? Why would you bother kidnapping me just to drive me up there so you can tell me one more time how you aren't interested in me *'that way'*."

She drops my hand to make the air quotes as I make the turn onto the road that will take us past her family estate, the educational camp they run for school children, and up to Turtle Village.

"You still haven't read any of the messages I've sent you today, have you?" I grumble at the obvious.

She scoffs beside me, more relaxed now that we're on level ground with wide clearances on both sides of the road that's more familiar to her.

"I got the gist of it from the previews-- 'I can't be the man you're looking for,' 'I don't want you to regret meeting me.' Same shit you've told me already, August. I get it. I don't need to hear you say it in person. Why do you think I stopped trying to talk to you and agreed to go out with Brian?"

My hands clench on the steering wheel at the mention of the boy's name. I'm still not committed to letting him get away with putting his hands on my *fiore*.

"I want you, *fiore*. I've never wanted anyone or anything more in my entire life."

"Bu-- wait. I thought you said we were going to your house?"

Zephyr's first thought is lost in her confusion when I make the turn into Hart's Gulch.

"I'm taking you home. You can call me and I'll give you a ride back to Slow River tomorrow."

I pull in front of the storybook cottage she lives in and release the safety locks, fully expecting her to jump out without hesitation.

"What happened to 'I want you more than anything in my life, *fiore*?'"

Her seat belt is unbuckled, but instead of moving to exit the vehicle, she turns toward me. I go ahead and kill the engine, turning the headlights off manually so as not to draw attention from her neighbor.

Who I've already encountered today and would prefer not have bashing my skull in for kidnapping his sister.

My own seat belt unbuckles and I twist toward her.

"I do want you, Zephyr. Since the moment I saw you, I knew you were the only woman who will ever own my heart. But you are young and you have no idea what lies ahead for you between the age you are now and mine. I cannot have you. Once I do, I will want you forever."

"Are you going to kidnap me from every date I go on? Because I'm not going to play the 'I won't touch her but neither will anyone else' game. I'm not going to die a virgin because the man I want is too chickenshit to take me, August."

Her challenge is not lost on me and it proves to be my undoing.

Chapter Eight

Zephyr

I'm still mad at him. Even as I'm caught in his arms and pulled across the center console. Even when my lips are crushed to his, and his tongue slips against mine. Even when his hand arranges my thigh over his lap and the hem of my dress is pushed up above my hips.

When August's hands slide forward from my back until his thumbs flicker over my nipples, I'm still pretty pissed off at him.

Bra unhooked? Still mad.

Breasts kneaded in his strong hands while his mouth devours each nipple?

Pretty sure I'm still mad, I just don't exactly remember why anymore.

It's not until one of August's hands slips between my thighs, moving my panties to the side so he can slip one of those sinfully long fingers inside me that I forgive him.

Second finger? I was never mad.

My hands scramble over his shoulders, my fingers clutching in the soft fabric of the button-down shirt he's wearing. My head brushes the ceiling of the car, reminding me where we are.

"*Fiore mio*, come for me, baby."

Insistent fingers stroke me from inside, finding a spot that has my feet threatening to cramp as my toes try to curl in my heels.

"Yes." August purrs between my breasts as he keeps a steady pace, adding pressure to my clit with his thumb as I ride his hand, my cheek pressed hard to the back of his head as we curl against each other in the cramped space. "That's it, Zephyr...baby...let me feel your tight little pussy coming for me...begging for my cock to be inside you next..."

Honestly, I'm not sure if August can still breathe. I have my hands wrapped so tightly around his head that I'm probably smothering him in my cleavage.

I'm pretty sure he's still alive because he hasn't stopped the delicious way he's moving his hand, even when I come so hard that I must nearly break his wrist where it's trapped between us.

Soft swears in Italian are mumbled against my breasts between kisses and light nips before August withdraws his fingers and licks them clean.

"Fuck." His eyes roll back and then onto mine in the moonlight coming through the sunroof above us.

His hand paws blindly at the door to our side and then the latch releases and the door swings open.

"Time to get out, *fiore*," he whispers hoarsely as he fixes my dress back to cover my breasts and moves to help me onto the ground without tripping in the heels.

Oh, right. I remember how to be mad at him again.

"If you think you're--"

"Shh--" his hand reaches to get my clutch from the seat beside him and he already has one long leg on the ground as he moves toward me, "--I'm coming with you."

Augustus unfolds his lean form from behind the steering wheel, wrapping one arm around my shoulders with a possessive grip as if he's suddenly afraid I might actually make a run for the house and leave him hard and wanting in my driveway.

Not. A. Chance.

We move as one, making space for him to shut the car door softly before climbing the steps to my front door where he stands without loosening his grip while I fish the key from my purse and open the door.

Then, my feet are suddenly no longer in contact with the ground as I'm swung into Augustus's arms and carried inside bridal style. August kicks the door closed with a foot and heads for the short hallway.

"Which one?"

His question is breathless and impatient as we near the two doors opposite one another.

"Left."

No one reaches for the light-switch as we crash through my bedroom door and onto the bed. Moonlight spills through the windows with the open blinds that look out onto the garden in the back and it's plenty enough light for me to admire the dips and planes of Augustus's body as we work together to unburden him of his clothes.

He's down to pants and whatever is under them as he stands on the floor to kick off his shoes after he's peeled my dress off and cast both my bra and panties into some dark corner of the room as if they offended him.

I reach down to unbuckle the straps on my shoes but August *tsks* as he brushes my hand away.

"Leave them on, I promise not you won't need to walk anywhere soon."

The black jeans he had on fall to the floor and then the boxer briefs that were beneath them.

I scramble backward into the middle of the bed to make space for him as he easily steps out of the pile of clothes and crawls between my legs.

August

We'll have our conversations later. Right now, fiore has been clear that she's tired of waiting to feel my cock splitting her virgin pussy apart and if I manage to breed her this quickly and we find ourselves bound together for it, I vow I'll spend every moment of this life and the next making sure she never regrets it.

Thoughts of Zephyr's curves enhanced with the swell of our child growing inside her cause my already painfully engorged cock to twitch in anticipation.

In the pale light of the moon shining through her windows, the glittery high heels sparkle, but not nearly as beautifully as her glistening pussy.

"I promise to wake you up with my mouth on your clit, *fiore*." I gasp out the words between the hungry kisses I steal from her lips. "Forgive me if I lose my manners, baby, but I--"

My words are stolen by a rough nip to my lip and the feel of Zephyr's hand wrapped around my shaft. The only sound left in my throat is a harsh and pleading growl.

"Just fuck me already, Augustus."

Her teeth catch my earlobe to punctuate her demand, leaving me with no choice but to obey.

"I don't want to hurt you." I slide two fingers back inside her impossibly tight channel, working to ready her for my intrusion. "You're so tight, *fiore*, have you never had anything inside your little cunt?"

"My vibrator's almost as big as you, August."

Her crass confession has me choking on my swears as I allow her to take the lead and line my weeping tip against her opening.

"Did you just ask the Holy Mother Mary for the strength not to come too soon?"

Fiore mio giggles beneath me, tilting her hips to bring me closer.

"You've been studying Italian in the wrong schools, *fiore*." I nip at her nose with a grin. "You should not be able to decipher such filth."

"I'm going to make you say filthier things than that, Augustus."

It might be a threat, or it might be a promise; either way, Zephyr brings her hands to my waist and guides me past that point that no other man has ever been...or ever will be.

She's hot and slick, lined in velvet perfection and so tight that I can feel how her tunnel has to stretch to accommodate my size.

Now that I know she's been learning to decode my curses, I let the words dry in my throat as I mouth them silently against her throat.

If this woman is this tight even after taking care of herself with a toy that's nearly my own size, there's no hope that I'll ever stretch her well enough that I'm not on the edge of spilling my seed as soon as I've entered her.

Despite her claims, Zephyr's eyes go wide at the feel of being filled so completely by the real thing. The kiss-swollen lips that no longer bear a trace of the lipstick she had applied earlier, pop open in a perfect *O* that has me slipping my thumb between them.

They seal around my digit, her tongue slipping around the tip as she sucks gently, her hooded gaze back at me causing me to lose all hope I had of staying in control.

Pulling back, I gasp at the feel of her sheath suctioning in my retreat, pulling to bring me back.

It's a call I answer quickly, thrusting forward with force and immediately retreating again in response to the sharp gasps and mounting cries Zephyr makes as I fill her to completion over and over again.

Through the rising fog inside my brain, I feel the

sharp bite of fingernails in my back and the scrape of the high heels behind my thighs. Zephyrs cries are getting louder and I can feel the muscles in the sweet walls wrapped around my dick beginning to pulse.

I know I won't last through her climax. Not this time and possibly not any time after this.

Reaching between us, I press my thumb to her clit and circle, eager to feel her clench down on me, knowing she's about to rip my cock from my body when it happens.

My name rings off the walls around us as Zephyr comes as hard as I'd hoped. Just as expected, the feel of her milking me for my cum is something I can't deny.

I let loose inside her, spilling my seed in pulsing jets that have me blacking out momentarily.

"Never doubt that I belong to only you, Zephyr," I whisper into her hair when I've regained enough strength to speak. "I love you, *fiore mio*. Forever forward."

Chapter Nine

Zephyr

"...If you knew then, why did you fight it so hard?"

Cuddled together under the blankets, I'm enjoying feeling August's hot skin against mine while we talk quietly-- and seriously-- into the early hours of the morning.

He says he knew his heart was no longer his the moment he saw me on the hillside picking wildflowers.

Literally how he said it too, *"I knew my heart was no longer my own."* Swoon.

"It hurts my feelings that you don't remember that day well, *fiore*. I did nothing at all to fight it." He chuckles softly and kisses the top of my head.

I'm wrapped around him, with my head on his chest, his arms banded around me possessively while one hand strokes the small of my back.

"Uh, you threw me in my car and barricaded yourself in your mountain fortress as soon as you found out I was a virgin. That's what I remember."

"And young, Zephyr. There is a lifetime between us. The years you see in your future are already in my past. I know how easy it is to look back with regrets and I don't want to be one of yours."

"You keep talking about regrets and past mistakes, August. What happened in your past that makes you so sure I'm going to regret whatever I do in my twenties?"

Uncurling from his chest, I wiggle so I'm eye to eye with him with my head beside him on the pillows.

"Were you really in the mafia? What did you do? Are you hiding out, is that why you live up at the plant?"

August fixes his eyes on me in the dim light. The corners of his eyes crinkle with the smile on his lips.

"No, *fiore*. No mafia. I've never even seen the Godfather. My mother is a school teacher, my dad's a plumber. I grew up in a small town in upstate New York."

I swear I'm not disappointed. I mean, the whole dangerous past fantasy is hot as hell but this man is going to be the father of my children-- it's probably better if he doesn't have a violent, criminal past.

The twinkle leaves his eyes and his face goes sad. August picks up my hand that's been drawing lazy designs over his inked chest and laces his fingers through mine.

"I was young, impatient, and filled with greed. When I graduated with my four-year degree, I was offered a job as a private contractor for a company that operated in Iraq. They offered me more money than I could make in the states with only my bachelor's degree and the extent of my vetting of them didn't extend beyond assuring that their offer was legitimate.

"I took the job. I made a lot of money. I was able to pay off student loans that many of my classmates still struggle with today.

"It was only a few months before I started to suspect that the company was involved with the wrong sort of people-- but I stayed anyway."

His voice goes remorseful at the confession.

"I worked for them for two years before problems started and my colleagues began to disappear only to return in pieces."

I can't help the gasp. This was not a story I'd expected, even in the darkest of my scenarios.

Before I can say anything, August presses his lips to mine with a kiss designed to shush me.

"The company had made enemies that weren't the sort of people to confine their battles to the courtroom. We were taken over and my contract was due for renewal. The new leadership very much wanted me to stay on. I very much wanted to leave with my head attached."

"What happened? I mean-- you got out, obviously."

"But it took the US military's help and many weeks of investigation while it was determined whether or not I was a threat to national security. I spent a year with family in Italy before I it was safe to come home."

"At least you picked up the accent," I tease, drawing a finger along the side of his mouth.

"And I did learn the fine art of Italian swearing

from my cousins while I was there." August kisses my fingertip and laughs gently.

"I was the age you are now when I took that job. That's how I know what foolish decisions we can make in our youth. I'm afraid that you will wake up one day and realize that I am nothing but a fantasy that is best left in your past.

"You will break my heart that day, *fiore*. You will leave me a broken man."

"I want to marry you and have a family with you, Augustus," I point out plainly, "that's a big difference from 'escaping terrorist overlords.' I think your odds are on this bet are way better."

He only gives me enough time to watch the smile spread across his lips-- the smile that takes his eyes with it, creasing those sexy crinkles at the corners, the smile that says he's not fighting me any more-- before he's on top of me, pinning me under his weight with his cock hardening against my thigh.

"I will give one year, *fiore*." Kiss. "One year to change your mind. If you haven't broken my heart by then, you will marry me." Another kiss. "You'll marry me on the hillside where I found you." Kiss. Slower, savoring. "When the wildflowers are in bloom again, on a day when the sun is shining as brightly as the faith you have in me."

Then he slides into me, this time asking a saint I've never heard of for strength to last till I stop screaming.

Augustus

Zephyr left the shower minutes ago, with my cum leaking out of her, saying something about breakfast.

Seeing as the only thing I ate last night was fiore's sweet pussy, breakfast is a promise that has me rinsing quickly and searching her bedroom floor for my clothes.

Underwear, pants, socks, and shoes are found but my shirt is nowhere among them.

Leaving the shoes and socks behind, I emerge from the bedroom to the sound of Zephyr arguing with a deep, male, voice that I recognize as her brother's.

"...because the only button-down shirts Hayle ever owned are all flannel, that's how."

"I'm twenty-three, Cane. Legal adult. Grown woman. In my own house. You're lucky I'm wearing anything at all. Maybe knock before you just let yourself in next time."

"You said you weren't coming back till we move you out of your place in Slow River next week. I thought I was supposed to water your damn plants."

"You saw August's car outside and thought you'd barge in here on one of your typical control-freak tirades. What are you going to do, Cane? Tell me I can't have sex in my own house?"

That-- does not bode well for my safety, and I strongly consider retreating back to Zephyr's room before I'm spotted by her brother. But this is a confrontation that has to be faced, even if I'd have preferred to do it under different circumstances.

Clearing my throat to announce my presence-- please don't let fiore taunt her brother with any more images of me defiling his baby sister, I would like to live-- I step into the big room that is both kitchen and living room to discover what has Cane so outraged.

Zephyr is wearing my shirt. Possibly, *only* my shirt. It hangs to her knees, she could easily add a belt and call it a dress, but perhaps she could consider doing one or two more of the buttons to cover the view of her generous breasts as they bounce with her movements.

Now is not the time for me to be focused on that, not with Hurricane Hart, former professional football player glaring at me.

"August says you've already met," Zephyr tells her brother. "Be nice to him, don't make your niece or nephew grow up without a father, Cane. It sucks, I know first-hand, remember?"

The man's eyes widen on his sister with a look of horror at her implication.

"You are not helping my cause, *fiore*." Skirting Cane's reach, I join Zephyr in the kitchen, paying for the mug of coffee she hands me with a kiss.

"Go put more clothes on," I tell her, doing my best to behave and not reach my hand beneath of the hem of my shirt to see what might not be under it. "I'll be fine."

Zephyr gives me a withering glance, then shoots her brother a warning one.

"He'd better be," she tells him with a wagging finger as she heads back for her bedroom.

I watch Cane watch his sister, knowing all too well what's going through his head right now.

"Fuck her over and you'll be the next body they never find up here, got it?"

"I have sisters too." Is the best assurance I can offer him.

I remember the first time I caught Bella with a man in her house. She was twenty-six and he only made it out alive because she already had a ring on her finger.

My brother-in-law is a good man, but he knows he'll go through the turbines up at the plant if my sister so much as asks.

Cane's response is a grunt.

I reach for another coffee mug, lifting it in an invitation to the man I intend to also call my brother.

"Nah," his eyes dart back toward the hall where Zephyr still hasn't reappeared, "she'll fucking kill me if I stick around."

I set the mug back on the shelf and try to breath my sigh of relief invisibly.

"Take care of her, man. She deserves at least one man she can count on not to leave her."

I've heard her stories about the loss of her father and grandfather at an age too young to remember them, and Cane's words remind me of what she's said about the way her brothers handled their grief.

His own guilt for leaving the ridge for his career rings heavily in his words, as well as the anger he carries at the missing brother for having abandoned the family he'd left in his care.

"If Zephyr and I ever part, it will be her choice, not mine."

Another grunt, this one more resigned.

Zephyr returns, wearing leggings with my shirt buttoned high this time.

"Are you staying for breakfast so you can hover over us all day?" She asks her brother as she pulls a carton of eggs from the refrigerator.

"No. Got shit to do at the camp." He answers as he heads for the front door. "Maybe you guys come get pizza with us after we move you back up here, yeah?"

"Sounds good, Cane." Zephyr and I watch the door close behind him on his way out.

"Are you okay, *fiore*?"

She melts against my chest with a deep sigh of relief.

"That wasn't how I wanted to spend our morning."

I'm already working the leggings back down her legs.

Fiore proves to be excellent at multi-tasking, coming sweetly on my fingers while she cooks for us and riding my cock at the kitchen table while I feed her from my plate.

A nap, another shower, and a few hours later, I stand in the outdoor garden that stretches to the open meadow on the south side of her property behind the big greenhouse looking over the transplanted flowers from the day I first saw her only a couple of weeks ago.

We've been discussing plans for the future, her

visions for our wedding, naming our children, and making me the happiest man alive.

"So that's the plan," she hands me the bouquet she's gathered while she tells me my future, "now we live happily ever after."

"*Si, fiore mio,*" I laugh as I bend to her kisses, "as long as your brother doesn't kill me, we live happily ever after."

Epilogue 1

5 months later
Zephyr

"COULD YOU PLEASE REMIND YOUR GRANDMOTHER THAT I HAVE TEN-WEEK-OLD TWINS?"

I can hear Terra's terse voice through her texts.

"I WOULD LIKE MY HUSBAND TO BE HOME WHEN HE'S OFF DUTY, NOT DOWN AT THE GENERAL STORE WAITING FOR A LOCKSMITH FROM THE VALLEY BECAUSE 'SOMEONE' CHANGED ALL ALICE'S LOCKS WITHOUT MENTIONING IT."

Whatever truce our grandmother's agreed to ended when Raine and April got married a couple of years ago.

This morning, Alice found she couldn't open the store because the locks had been changed and now my bestie's husband, our local sheriff's deputy, is sitting in a snowed-in parking lot waiting on a locksmith instead of being home with his wife and new babies.

"I'll remind her." I type out.

"ARE YOU ALL MOVED?"

I look around at the company house that I officially share with August now. We decided to make this our full-time place; it has four bedrooms that August is eager to fill with cradles and cribs and it's much closer to his job which makes me feel better in winters like we're having this year when we already have a few feet of snow up here.

We'll keep the cottage as our love nest, or rather, my business headquarters. Since I still have the gardens and the bee hives in the Gulch, I'll use the spare room for my office while I build my floral empire.

"YEP. ALL MOVED NOW."

"ANY NEWS?"

August put a ring on my finger officially a month ago so that's when I sent Hayle the email asking if he's still going to give me away at my wedding.

"YEAH, ACTUALLY..."

I wasn't sure if I should expect any kind of reply at all. God knows, my oldest brother hasn't bothered to stay in touch with any of us since he disappeared five years ago.

"WELL? WHAT HAPPENED?"

"DID HE FINALLY ANSWER?"

"IS HE COMING BACK?"

Three more of Terra's texts bombard me while I'm trying to answer her.

Sifting through the messages, I find the one in question and copy/paste it into my conversation with Tee.

"'OMW'" is all it says.

"SO, WTF DOES THAT MEAN?" Terra asks.

I shoot off a shrug emoji.

"I GUESS THAT MEANS HE'S ON HIS WAY."

She responds with an eyeroll and goes silent. Twins must have woken up.

"Ready to go?" August's hand splays between my shoulder blades as he bends to kiss the top of my head, "I'd like to be back before late."

"We can stay at the cottage," I remind him.

"Good point. Why don't we just plan on that? That way no one has to drive."

His intonation isn't lost on me. Augustus says I'm a kinky drunk but it's so much more fun when he can drink with me.

We're going down to Mom's for dinner, so we'll be able to walk back to the cottage afterward.

We went so many years all of us living in our own little bubbles, I'm not about to miss out on the family bonding that we're just beginning to work on.

This family dinner routine is new for us since Gran and Mom mended old fences and, since June and Donner showed up, Cane's even mellowed out some.

Looking down at the message on my phone before I close the app, I wonder how that's going to change if Hayle is really coming home.

Epilogue 2

Five Years Later
Augustus

"*Lasciala con Celia.*"

I let my lips brush the shell of fiore's ear when I whisper to her.

The shiver that moves over her golden skin is the response I hoped for.

My cousin waves us off without need for an excuse to take our daughter off our hands for however long we trust her not to teach her Italian.

Celia's language tutoring is how I learned to swear, after all.

"Where are we going?"

"I want to show you the old house," I answer, leading my wife by the hand across the Italian landscape.

"August, we saw the old house when we got here."

Zephyr giggles, onto me for sure.

"Si, but you didn't get to see it in the good light."

My family's estate in Italy is a collection of more modern villas nestled among ancient olive trees. The old house is a crumbling square of four stone walls on a hilltop with a view of the sunset.

When we arrived a week ago, we walked up to see it in the morning. I showed her the view and gave her what history I know of it.

This evening, I have very different plans.

It's a short hike up the low hill and when we get there, the sun is already kissing the horizon.

"Ooh, that is pretty." Zephyr stands beside the outside of the stone walls and gapes into the distance, her hand still entwined with mine.

"It is, indeed."

When she turns, she sees that my eyes are only on her.

I watch the blush spread up her body, fanning from her deep cleavage and into her cheeks. We stand and watch as the fire of pink and golden hues lighting the sky fades to blues and pastel hues of lilac.

"Oh." Zephyr's eyes are drawn to the interior of the structure beside us as the string lights begin to go on.

"Romantic," she coos as she moves beyond the arch that no longer holds a door on the rusted hinges.

Inside, she finds the blankets I laid out over the packed, dirt floor, the candles gathered on the crumbling stone heart, strings of tiny fairy lights crossing the open ceiling, and the basket of local wine and tapas waiting for us.

My hands are already sliding up her full thighs,

taking the gauzy sundress with them on their way until she's freed of it completely.

Her bra joins the dress in a corner to give my mouth access to her breasts, savoring each nipple in turn till they're hardened points against my tongue. Then I move to my knees, filling my palms with the soft feel of her ass and lowing the tiny scrap of cotton she calls panties to the ground.

As she steps free of the last remnants of her clothes, fiore mio pushes me back into the soft palette of blankets, returning the favor of relieving me of my own clothing, then straddling my hips to torture my hardened cock as she slides her wet folds along my length.

"Did you bring me up here to get laid, Mr. Damiani?"

"I had planned to eat first, Mrs. Damiani." I have to grit the answer through clenched jaws because Zephyr is doing everything in her power to destroy the slow seduction I'd had planned for her.

"Celia will watch Brezza all night, won't she?"

My wife smiles down at me with mischief in her eyes as she takes me inside her in a tortuously slow stroke that gives me time to appreciate every inch of her tight, slick, smooth, interior.

"Celia will keep our daughter for as long as it takes us to make another niece or nephew for her to dote on."

"Is that what we're doing, tonight?"

Zephyr falls over me, catching herself on hands planted above my shoulders as she takes my mouth with hers-- as if the kiss will distract me from the way she's begun to move up and down on my cock.

In the years we've had together so far, my wife has learned many ways to drag my seed into her womb, this is one of her favorites; riding me slowly while she watches me unravel under her spell with an uncanny talent for timing her release to mine.

It's only due to the miracle of modern birth control that Brezza is our only child so far.

"Si, fiore...."

My fingers grasp her thighs, my hips pistoning upward to meet her strokes, as she takes me to the brink of control.

"...we are not going home till you are ripe with my child again."

"Good thing I got off the pill then."

And then there is no sky above us, no walls around us, there's only Zephyr, with her nails in my arms, and her tight channel convulsing around my cock as she begs me for our second child, which I am eager to give her.

Next in Series

<u>Secrets on the Mountain</u>
Hurricane Hart

Five years ago, I gave up a career in pro ball after it cost me everything.

My family thinks I returned to Moonshine Ridge because they needed me here, but they don't know the secrets I keep from them.

Turns out, neither do I.

When the past I thought I'd lost forever comes looking for me, she does it with a four-year-old boy by the hand. One that looks too much like the man in the mirror for me to question anything other than why the hell did it take her this long?

I thought Junie was gone, another casualty of my downfall, but it turns out we've both been lied to.

The question is; do we take this second chance, now that we know that our first one was stolen or am I about to lose everything important to me one more time?

Thanks for Reading

Try as I might, I could not get Augustus Damiani to growl. Despite multiple author/character conversations between us, the man refused to be reduced to a monosyllabic, grunting, mountain man. He just kept insisting on speaking eloquently, in complete sentences.

I am so sorry.

I tried.

I really tried.

Sometimes, characters refuse to follow the script and go full improv.

Nevertheless, I fully understand why the man makes Zephyr swoon and I hope you do too.

I'm not sure Alice and Mable are convinced he's not ex-mafia though. But they do agree he's very easy to look at...and they've been very insistent on learning to swear like an Italian.

~*Rocklyn*

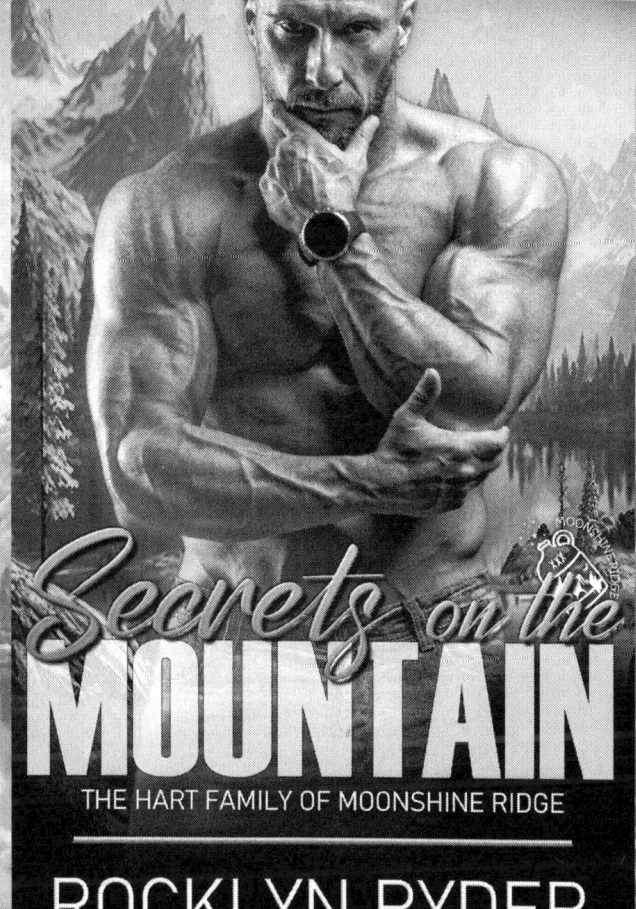

Preface

This book has a companion scene that's been included at the end of the story.

It takes place immediately before the story begins and is told from the point of view of Mable Hart. If you would prefer to read it as a prologue, skip ahead to "Love at First Sight" before beginning Cane and Junie's story here.

The book will make just as much sense if you wait to read the bonus scene at the end-- or even if you don't read it at all.

About
Hurricane Hart

Five years ago, I gave up a career in pro ball after it cost me everything.

My family thinks I returned to Moonshine Ridge because they needed me here, but they don't know the secrets I keep from them.

Turns out, neither do I.

When the past I thought I'd lost forever comes looking for me, she does it with a four-year-old boy by the hand. One that looks too much like the man in the mirror for me to question anything other than why the hell did it take her this long?

I thought Junie was gone, another casualty of my downfall, but it turns out we've both been lied to.

The question is; do we take this second chance, now that we know that our first one was stolen, or am I about to lose everything important to me one more time?

Hurricane & June

Secrets on the Mountain
The Hart Family of Moonshine Ridge
by
Rocklyn Ryder

Chapter One

June

Hart's Gulch Gold Camp.

The sign points to a dirt road veering off to the right.

I follow the well-maintained dirt and gravel road as it leads me into the mountains. Past the fence, through a wide gate with a high sign overhead. There's signage on the side of the road with a rudimentary map etched in wood that shows the location of an office, visitors centers, mess hall, and amphitheater.

A quick glance in the rear-view mirror shows Don in his booster seat behind me, still engrossed in the pack of stickers that the ladies at the museum in town gave him where we stopped for directions.

He slept most of the way up here, and before we stopped in Moonshine Ridge to ask around, he'd started asking questions again. Ones I don't know how to answer. So I'm grateful for the old ladies that gave him the activity packet that's kept him busy for this last leg of our journey.

Please-- I pray silently-- please let Cane be here and let us get this over with quickly.

I wish I hadn't had to bring Donner with me but there was no one I could leave him with for over a week while I made this trip. If Cane doesn't like it, he should have responded to my attorney's attempts to do this without having to track him down in person.

A few buildings come into view and I pull into the lot in front of a wooden sign that says "administration."

"Are we here?" Donner's voice is all excitement at the prospect of exploring something new as he climbs out of the booster seat. Immediately, he's a whirlwind of four-year-old energy, spinning circles in the gravel lot and making what I assume are airplane noises.

Out on the dirt road, a two-tone, classic pick-up barrels past, leaving a cloud of dust billowing behind it before coming to a stop that has it locking up the brakes and skidding several feet along the gravel before making a sharp U-turn back to us.

"Ma'am? You looking for Hayle maybe?"

The man that climbs out of the cab looks so much like Hurricane; my breath catches in my throat before I'm able to answer with a shake of my head.

"Cane," I clarify, "I'm looking for Hurricane."

This man's eyes flicker over me, then onto Donner where they stay even as he arches an eyebrow and shakes his head as if he didn't hear me right.

"Raine." He extends his arm and gives me a cautious smile, eyes still following Don.

"June," I answer, taking his hand for a brief shake.

"The ladies at the museum in town said I'd find Cane up here. Do you know where he is?"

My memory scrambles to connect dots. Raine Hart is far from the scrawny kid his brother always spoke about. The man in front of me now isn't built like Cane, but he's far from scrawny and not a kid at all.

There's a gold band on his left hand and when he pulls his phone out of his back pocket, I catch a photo of him with his arms around a blonde woman before he opens an app and starts typing.

"And who are you, big man?" Raine asks as Donner studies the stranger with a look that leaves me unsettled.

"Donner, like thunder." Don does his famous hand gesture for thunder. I don't know where he got that, but I've rarely seen him introduce himself without including it. I guess I'm glad he's proud of his name, I've often wondered if I made a mistake by keeping a family tradition for a family he'd never know.

"Ooh, German. Very cool. Well, my name is Raine, so we kinda go together, I guess."

Raine squats on his haunches to get on eye level with my son. This time, it's me that Raine's eyes keep moving to.

"Cane's in the office," he tells me, his voice switching back to the talking-to-another-adult tone as he gets back to his feet. "You, uh--" his eyes drop down to Don, "want some privacy?"

"Thank you."

I'm so grateful for the implied offer, I can't stop shaking my head. Or maybe I'm just shaking.

"Hey, buddy, you like horses?"

"Yeah! Are there horses here?"

Raine smiles down at Don. "Yup, we got about twelve of them right now, wanna go see 'em?"

Donner's already two steps ahead of his new friend, waiting impatiently for a clue which direction he should be headed in.

"Through there," Raine turns to me and points at an open space between two buildings, "there's a door on your left marked *'private'* but it's not locked, the top of the stairs. Says 'office' on the door."

He gives me a nod and then points ahead to give Donner a direction to head. A few steps and then Raine stops and looks back at me.

"The stables are just over there," he hooks a thumb toward a roof in the distance. "We'll be in hollering distance."

Hurricane

The paperwork here in the office doesn't usually get to me. Since I got back to Moonshine Ridge and took over running the gold camp for Gran, it's been the one thing that's kept me sane. Normally, I find it easy to get lost in the spreadsheets, keeps the noise in my head down to a dull roar.

Lately it's been a lot harder for me to stay in the present, and that dull roar isn't the distant white noise that my past should be.

Maybe it's Raine. My kid brother; married and expecting a kid of his own next spring has me feeling some ways for sure.

He grew up while I was off the mountain. He'd been a lanky teenager: ditching school, fixing up that old truck, and chasing girls.

He was on the right path to end up just like our older brother when I left to go off to college.

Of course, at the time, Hayle was holding his shit together, stepping up to the plate after we lost dad and grandpa both at the same time. That's the only reason I took the scholarship, knowing I could count on my big brother to be back here, taking care of our family.

It's been five years now since I got back home.

They all think I left the league because Hayle went MIA. What they don't know is that I left because playing ball meant selling my soul. And, since it had already cost me the only thing worth making that trade for, I didn't see the point.

It wasn't until I got back to the Ridge that I even found out Hayle had walked away. Left Gran to run the camp on her own, left Mom to raise our baby sister on her own, left our kid brother to fill shoes he was still too damn young to wear, left everything and everyone in pieces for me to have to pick up as soon as I got back when all I'd wanted to do was crawl back into my cave and lick my own wounds.

Instead, our big brother started a bar fight he deserved to lose, tucked his tail between his legs, and disappeared. Left his house in the Gulch exactly the way it had been the night Cedar McAllister broke his nose.

Now my baby sister is worrying about whether or not her big brother is going to show up in time to keep his promise and walk her down the aisle at her wedding next year, and all I can think is that if that fucker ever does show up, I'm going to break his nose again.

The restlessness finally gets to me. Trips down memory lane never end up in a good neighborhood, and if I don't get some fresh air, I'm likely to smash something that'll take more time to replace than I have patience for.

Leaving the office unlocked, I stomp down the stairs and throw the door down there open with more force than it was built to handle.

By the time I make the turn to follow the narrow space between the buildings, I'm about to break into a run, feeling the anxiety building, I know old demons are catching up to me again.

Something stops me cold in my tracks. I might as well have run face first into a brick wall for the way the air gets pushed out of my lungs.

Because standing right in front of me is the last person I ever thought I'd see again.

She looks different. Different than she does in my memories or the dreams I like to pretend I don't still see her in. Different than I thought she would if I ever found her.

Her curves have filled out, plush and ripe and not hidden at all under the loose-fitting tunic blouse that hangs long over a pair of leggings. Her hair's pulled back tight. No-nonsense, in a clip that hides the rich chocolate color that doesn't show the blonde highlights I recall, and gives no hint to the length it is now. A few strands of gray highlight the fine hairs near her ears.

There's not a trace of make up on her face.

She doesn't look much like the woman I last saw, sitting beside a hospital bed in a post-op surgery center. But those sea-glass green eyes are unmistakable.

There's only one reason I can think of why Junie would be here and the fool I am doesn't question it.

Sweeping her into my arms, I pull her in for the kiss I've waited five and a half years for.

The woman in my arms stands stiff, her lips cold and sealed against mine. Such a contrast to the eager warmth that I remember that it jars me back to the present and I remember that's not us anymore. But not before Junie melts against me, opening for me and letting me in. Returning the kiss with a hunger that has me forgiving her everything.

"Cane."

Small hands push against my chest, my name throaty and breathless on her voice.

"Cane," she says my name again but all I hear is God granting me absolution.

"Stop. Cane, I--"

"Mom!"

A child's voice cuts her off and it only takes Junie half a second to put enough distance between us that no one would guess we were more than casual acquaintances.

"Mom, you gotta come see the horses with me!"

There's a photo on mom's mantle of me as a kid: I'm holding Raine when he was just a baby. I must have been about four when that photo was taken. I see it every time I visit my mom.

Right now, I'm staring at a boy who's talking a mile a minute at a silent June as he runs toward us.

It's like looking at myself if I'd stepped right out of that photo from Mom's mantle.

The way Raine eyes me as he and the kid get closer tells me my brother sees it too.

Chapter Two

June

My lips still tingle from the kiss and my brain is filled with a low humming noise that's making it difficult for me to focus on what's going on.

"Mom, come see the horses, Raine said I can ride one if you say yes. Can I?"

Donner's words are incoherent jabber as his little hand grabs mine and tugs me in the opposite direction of the man we came to see.

The man that just kissed me like it hasn't been five years since he had me kicked out of his house without an explanation or even the decency to do it himself.

Kissed me like I'd expected he'd do for the rest of our lives.

To say I'm confused is an understatement, but when I turn my eyes from Donner back to Cane, it's clear that if this is a contest to confuse each other-- I win.

"Hey, Donner," Raine flattens a hand over my son's head, halting his insistent tugging on my arm and forcing his attention toward the giant man glowering down at him with his arms crossed over his broad chest. "This is my big brother, Hurricane. Most of us just call him Cane though. Don't let him fool you, he's more afraid of you than you are of him."

Raine's joke is enough to break the spell, causing Cane to take his eyes off Donner momentarily to deepen his scowl on his brother while Raine just laughs and shakes his head.

Donner keeps a loose hold on my hand and watches the two older men with fascination.

"Go home." Cane's voice is deeper than I remember it, and I remember it being deep. Maybe it's just the way he barks the order at his brother without even a hint of the humor reflected in Raine's smile. "Don't you have a pregnant wife waiting for you--"

Cane's words fade as both men glance toward me and away so quickly it's easy to think I imagined it.

"You know where to find me." The smile drops off Raine's face.

"You ok?" Raine asks me so quietly, I have to read his lips.

I never got to meet any of Cane's family. There just hadn't been time to make the introductions before he was injured, and afterward well, by then he'd changed his mind.

The man hovering protectively between me and Cane right now, asking me if I feel safe for him to leave us alone together doesn't fit with the way Cane used to describe his younger brother. It's obvious that Raine's grown up to be a good man.

My heart aches deeper, knowing that this is the only time Donner will ever get to spend with his uncle. That Raine has a wife that will never be my sister-in-law, that he has a baby on the way that will never get to know his older cousin.

With a forced smile, I give the worried man a falsely confident nod. Letting him get home to the life he's so obviously excited about, while the man that once had me convinced he felt that way about me glares in silence the entire time it takes for Raine's truck to disappear down the dirt road.

"What do you want?"

Whatever he was thinking when he kissed me earlier has long since left his mind, reminding me not to get any ridiculous ideas in my own head about second chances and happy endings.

Which was easy before I felt his lips on mine again, before he went and reminded me what it feels like to have those massive arms wrapped so tenderly around me, and feel his chest so warm and solid against me.

"I need some paperwork signed," I answer cautiously, not wanting to have the full conversation in front of Donner.

Cane's eyes drop down with a hard scowl, but as soon as Donner looks back at him, those dark eyes soften. But just for a moment before he's wearing his scowl just for me again.

"Is that it?"

"That's it," I promise, relief flooding my stiffened muscles.

"Do you have this paperwork with you?" He eyes

the messenger bag style tote under my arm expectantly.

Slipping the strap off my shoulder, I open the bag and pull out the over-sized envelope with his name on it.

He takes it from me, careful not to make contact as the envelope passes from my hand to his.

"Just a minute," I assure Donner when I get a tug on my hand, "we're almost done."

An impatient huff sounds to my right.

"What the fuck is this, June?"

"Cane!" I pick Donner up and position him over my hip. Like that'll protect him from the profanity-- or whatever else is about to spew out of Cane's mouth that I can't control. At least it does the job of reminding Cane that there's a curious pair of four-year-old ears present.

Cane gives Donner an apologetic look. Don sinks his little head onto my shoulder.

He's a good kid. He likes to observe things quietly, but he'll be all questions on the drive back down the mountain. I haven't told him much of why we're here today or who these people are, and with luck, Cane will put his name on every one of the lines where there's a little blue flag sticking out of the stack of papers and I won't have to explain anything to Donner until he's much older.

Of course, that's not what happens.

Hurricane

"You're out of your goddamn mind. There's not a chance in hell I'm signing this."

Running the camp means I'm around kids plenty enough to have learned how to hold my damn tongue but the swears won't stop coming out of me.

The boy-- *Donner*...

Shit. My son's name is Donner.

As if it wasn't plain as day from looking at the kid, the papers Junie handed me spell it out in printed legalese across sixteen sheets of paper that are marked with no less than six places where she expects me to sign away my parental rights to a son I didn't know I had.

"Fucking hell, June!"

She lets the boy scramble into the back seat of the little rental car and I stand rooted to the fucking ground while I watch her hand him a bag of snacks from the front seat and give him smiles and nods and then a kiss before she heads back to me.

"Could you keep your voice down? I don't want to have to explain why you're so upset."

It's like there are too many words trying to get out of my mouth at the same time. All I can do is spit and huff and curse some more.

"You don't want to explain why his father was mad about not knowing he existed?" I pull at my hair and pace the breezeway between the administration building and the first aid station.

"I don't want to explain why the *perfect stranger*

that mommy had to come visit was mad at knowing he existed."

June hisses between her teeth, low enough that she won't be overheard and lethal enough to mistake her for a diamondback.

"This isn't going to happen." I hold up the papers she expected me to sign without question. "When you said you needed papers signed, this is the last thing I was expecting."

"What were you expecting, Cane?"

Sounds like the fight's gone out of both of us.

Junie leans against the wall like she needs it to hold her up and my pacing slows to a stop not far from her, both of us careful to keep the car within sight and our voices low now.

"I thought you'd be handing me a bunch of shit about child support," I admit. "I was looking for the request for a lump sum for back support, what you expect me to pay you going forward. Figured your attorney would be smart enough to go after a portion of the family trust, make sure my boy gets the inheritance he's entitled to.

"I thought I'd find a custody proposal in there, for fucks sake. Not a bunch of places to sign away my rights like he's not even mine."

Junie's staring at me with wide eyes that tell me my reaction is a far cry from what she'd been prepared for.

"We don't need your money, Cane." She sounds insulted.

"Don't tell me you came all the way up here with him in tow thinking I'd sign your papers and let you walk out of my life-- *again*. Shit, Junie, you know me better than that.

"At least...you used to."

"You're right, Cane; I *used* to know you better than that. The man I knew would never have let us get to this point in the first place. But that man disappeared a long time ago. So, yeah, I kind of figured you'd be more than happy to sign off and let us get on with our lives."

The feel of the legal envelope in my hand is dry and suddenly a lot heavier than a few sheets of paper ought to be.

A few years back, Rapid Jones adopted Doc's boy. I remember the Joneses threw a big father's day party for him and Jackson up at their River Bend property, with half the town coming out to celebrate the fact that the kid's deadbeat dad was so happy to sign away his parental rights and let another man be a real dad for his kid.

"You married now?"

My eyes slide to Junie's left hand. I shouldn't feel so relieved to see the bare ring finger, but the feeling still barrels through me like a train.

Junie clenches her hand up and rolls the bare fingers into the dip of her waist like the mere suggestion caused her physical pain.

Her movement stretches her loose-fitting top tight across her breasts and presses the fabric so that it shows the curvy figure that's matured since I last saw it.

My cock twitches behind my zipper and I curse the damn thing for noticing her.

She's not mine anymore. The claim I had to that sweet body has been a long time over now. Broken the day I find out she'd been gone long before I came home to an empty house.

"No. I'm not married," she answers quietly after a long pause.

The taste of her still lingers on my tongue. That one, reckless, kiss I stole from her when I foolishly gave in to the fantasy that she'd come back here after all these years for me. For us.

The way she'd softened in my grasp, melded against me, opened up and let me in like nothing had changed between us after all this time-- I don't know if there's another man in her life now, but it's clear she still belongs to me.

"You got a new man? Is he thinking he's going to adopt my boy? Is that why you never told me about him before now?"

Junie must have gotten her second wind. Rage darkens her face and, God help me, but even seeing the fury of hell itself etched on the woman's features isn't enough to keep me from wanting her still.

"Fuck you, Hurricane," she spits as she pushes away from the wall she's been leaning on. "You're the only reason you didn't know you had a son, so don't try to play the victim in this one.

"Now that I know where the fuck you are, you can talk to my lawyer instead of putting me through your gas-lighting bullshit."

Before she can take more than one step toward her car, I have my hands planted against the wall on either side of her.

"You two aren't leaving my sight." It comes out on a snarl. I've seen men near my own size cower in fear from me, but the woman caged between my arms doesn't look the least bit scared of me.

The pulse in her neck is beating visibly, her breaths are quick and shallow, and her pupils are so blown-out that the darkness makes the clear green irises take on a stormy gray hue.

Her lips part, maybe she was planning on telling me to get fucked-- being this close to her, with the fruity smell of her shampoo invading my nostrils and the heat that's rolling off of her body making my dick respond like it's answering a call neither of us made-- if she wants me to get fucked, I'm willing to comply.

"You're not going to take my boy away from me, June."

Chapter Three

June

It wasn't supposed to go this way.

That's all I can think as I double-check on Donner, who's thoroughly crashed out in the spare room he'll share with me for as long as we're stuck here in Cane's house.

Cane made sure we followed him back to his place and, after a few phone calls, his brother dropped by with a couple of pizzas from a place in town and I got to meet Raine's wife, April.

In the few hours I've been here, I've also met Cane's little sister, Zephyr and their mother, May-Ellen, and overhead more than one conversation between Cane and his grandmother, Mable, who turns out to be one of the women we met earlier at the museum where I stopped to ask how to find Cane.

"Six hours." Cane mutters, as he sets his phone on a charging pad. "You managed to keep Donner a secret for five years and within six hours of walking into gran's museum, the whole damn mountain knows about the both of you."

"I didn't keep him a secret," I mutter back.

A dark, amber glare shoots toward me from behind a large piece of polished granite that serves as both kitchen island and breakfast bar.

"You keep sayin' that, but I don't remember taking any birthing classes or handing out any cigars."

I stand on the other side of the counter, making sure to keep space between us at all times.

You might think that's because I'm worried about what he might do to me if he gets his hands on me, but honestly? It has a lot more to do with being afraid of what I'll let him do to me.

Cane pours tea from a pitcher, filling two glasses while he continues muttering.

"...don't remember--" he counts off with the fingers on his spare hand-- "four? Four or Five? birthday parties...Christmases, Halloween costumes, fathers' days..."

He pauses to look at me, gesturing to the second glass of iced tea.

"...mothers' days..." he adds the words to his rant in a softer tone.

"How sweet is it?" I ask, meaning the tea. I'm ignoring his running commentary.

"Ain't changed that much, Junie-bee," he tells me in the same soft voice as he slides a sugar bowl across the island to go with my tea.

Cane never sweetened his tea. The stuff he makes is downright undrinkable, if you ask me.

He goes silent as he watches me measure several teaspoons of sugar into my glass before I deem it acceptable.

When I replace the lid on the sugar, I look up to see him staring at me, shaking his head with a vague smile ghosting his lips beneath the beard that's grown out thick and full since I last saw him. For a second, I see a shadow of the man I loved.

Looking around, I catch a fleeting glimpse of the life I was supposed to have.

Reality crashes into me hard, bringing me back to the here and now that's so far from what I'd expected.

"If we're going to stay with you, we need to discuss what we're going to tell Donner." I finally speak, working hard to keep my voice steady and my mind focused on what's best for my son.

Our son.

Cane keeps saying there's no way he'll sign the papers I brought with me. He's already put in a call to his family's attorney and emailed the documents I brought so that they can be addressed.

He wants to be part of Donner's life and he's refusing to let us leave until we have an agreement in writing-- but I don't know how I'm going to explain this to Don.

In a million years, I never thought I was going to have to introduce Donner to his biological father.

Cane motions to the deck through a set of French doors and I let him guide me into the cool night air.

"Here." His deep voice is gruff as he wraps a wool blanket over my shoulders, like he's mad at himself for being nice to me. "I can light the fire too," he motions dismissively at a stonework fire-ring filled with colored glass. "It's propane."

He doesn't wait for me to answer, just turns a key on the side of the structure and a moment later, flames lick through the colorful glass pieces.

We sit in Adirondack chairs, my feet propped on the wide edge of the fire ring and Cane pulling his chair close beside mine.

Just so we can talk without worrying about being overheard, but something inside me is all too aware of the cozy scene we make: a couple enjoying adult time after the kid's asleep. Anyone who saw us from a distance would think we were a scene from someone's honeymoon Pinterest board.

"You've really never told him I exist?" Cane speaks directly to the fire in a voice laced with pain. "He's never asked who I am?"

"He asked." I answer the fire. "I wasn't ready yet. I didn't think he'd start asking till later. Maybe when he got into school."

"What did you tell him?"

"The truth. Or, at least, the closest thing to the truth that I thought a four-year-old would understand."

"Which was what, exactly?" This time he's not talking to the fire, in the shadows of moonlight and dancing flames, Cane's head is turned toward me.

"Um..." Okay, June, if you could explain it to a four-year-old, you can explain it to the brick wall of muscle and scowl that still manages to turn you into a mess of hard nipples and wet panties despite making it all too clear that done is something he's been with you for half a decade.

So what was up with that kiss when he first saw me today?

I shake my head like I'm trying to clear an Etch-a-Sketch, sip my sweet tea, and try to pick up my train of thought before it derailed.

"He asked if he had a dad and I said that of course he does. Then he asked if he'd ever get to meet his dad and I--"

"Please tell me you didn't say I was dead."

I shake my head. "No. I just said I didn't think he would."

Hurricane

"He didn't ask any more questions?"

I'm trying to remember how we explained things to Zeph when she got old enough to start asking questions.

My brothers and I were old enough to remember our dad, but he and pops passed when our sister was still a baby. She doesn't remember them and I guess she was about four or five when she started asking why she didn't have a daddy.

Of course, up here on the Ridge, families tend to stay together unless something outside their control rips them apart. Zeph didn't have other kids at school growing up in single parent households to compare her own situation to.

Maybe that's why she asked so many questions.

Maybe kids are just different.

"Not really. He's in a preschool with some other kids that don't have dads around. He didn't seem to think it was unusual."

"We'll figure it out, June-bug," I promise, not even noticing the way my hand reaches for hers to give her a reassuring squeeze when I hear the concern in her voice. "But I'm going to be part of his life from now on."

Our hands stay connected. It feels so natural to have Junie's small hand wrapped around two of my fingers as our hands rest on the arm of her chair. Like old times; Junie always said it hurt her hand when I'd try to lace our fingers together-- my hands are so much bigger than hers, it made her fingers spread apart too far-- so she'd change our grip till she had her delicate little fingers wrapped around just two of mine.

Just like they are now.

But it doesn't take long before darker thoughts ruin the feel of having her beside me again.

"What did you mean earlier, when you said I'm the reason I didn't know?" My voice is low and I don't like the way it comes out sounding hurt when all I want is to be mad.

Something tugs inside me at that thought, letting me know that's not exactly the truth. I don't want to be mad at June-bug. I want her back. I want her to have never left me. I want to wave a magic wand and make the last five years look completely different.

That's not gonna happen though. She didn't come all the way up the Ridge to start over with me and our son, she came up here to sever the only claim I could still have on her.

Pulling my hand back, I hold on to that thought and grasp at the anger it gives me so I don't make a damn fool of myself thinking the way she kissed me back earlier means there's still a chance for us.

"I meant you're the one who wouldn't return my calls, Cane." The irritation in her voice tells me she's grasping at the same anger. "You're the one who blocked my number, you're the one who instructed his people not to transfer my calls. You're the one who returned all my mail unopened--" Junie's voice is rising, she's moved so she's on the edge of her seat, twisted to stare at me in the low flames of the gas fire.

"You're the one who had his lawyers threaten to charge me with stalking me if I continued to 'harass' you.

"The only reason you didn't know about Donner as soon as I did is because you kicked me out of your house and cut me out of your life like a fucking tumor before I even realized I was pregnant...you made it crystal clear that you didn't want to know what happened to me and you didn't care."

June's not the only one balanced on the edge of her chair and the nonsense she just shouted makes it a lot easier to stay mad at her.

"What the hell are you talking about? You're the one who walked out on *me*, June."

"Fuck you, Hurricane! Don't tell me what happened, I was there!"

"No, fuck you, June! Because I was there too. I know what happened too. You realized I wasn't making shit up when I said addiction was a problem in my family. You found out I was quitting the game and you didn't want to marry a junkie has-been, so you left."

"Excuse me, I *what?*"

The house is built solid. I used eight-inch studs in the exterior walls to beef up the insulation to save on heating costs through the mountain winters. June and Donner's room is on the front side of the house, with plenty of space between our sleeping boy and our rising voices out here on the back deck, but we both shoot glances toward the French doors now, aware that we're shouting.

"What the fuck are you talking about, Cane?" Junie's voice lowers in volume, but it doesn't lose its bite. "Rick came up to the house after you went on to rehab, gave me an envelope of cash and an apology for having to be your messenger boy."

Chapter Four

June

I can't read the look on Cane's face. Maybe being confronted with his actions after all this time has him realizing just how fucked up they were.

If he's processing just how his behavior led to him not knowing I was pregnant-- good. I hope it fucking stings. I hope the look I'm seeing on his face right now is just over five years of agony hitting him between the fucking eyes. I hope that look means he's feeling every day of hell I went through when his manager showed up at our door to tell me that Hurricane wanted me gone before he got home from physical therapy.

"Rick. Said. What?"

But when Cane grinds the words out slowly in one syllable sentences, I realize that what I'm seeing raging across his face is something far more intense than regret.

Most people would be afraid of the giant man staring at me with murder in his eyes right now. Most people would be smart to be afraid of Cane right now.

I'm not most people. I never was and, apparently, I never will be.

Despite the fact that he broke my heart, and the crappy way he did it, there's not a cell in my body that believes for a second that Hurricane would hurt me.

Right now though, I can't say the same for his former manager.

"Rick said you went into a rehab program that included intense training to get you back on the field after the surgery. You weren't allowed to have visitors or phone calls."

I take a moment to breathe, to give Cane time to breathe. He's clutching the edge of his chair so tightly, I'm worried he's going to split the thick wood slats into splinters.

"You'd been gone for about two weeks." I hear myself speaking slow and calm, like I'm trying to talk a grizzly bear down from a rampage. "Rick stopped by the house one afternoon. He was apologetic, he felt really bad, but he handed me some cash and said that you'd told him to move me out."

Cane's head drops, so I can't see his face anymore. He nods though, silently bidding me to keep going.

"He said that you were committed to getting back in top condition and you'd come to the conclusion that I was a distraction. You sent him to move me out of the house. You wanted me gone before you got home."

"You believed that?" The lethal look has left his eyes and when he looks at me now, all I see is misery. "You really thought I'd do that to you? To us? Shit,

Junie, you really think I'd have chosen the fucking game over you?"

"What was I supposed to think, Cane? I didn't know where you went. Your phone was off, your voicemail was full. Rick seemed really upset, he said he'd tried to convince you to wait, see if you still felt the same way when the program was done.

"He said he told you to at least have the decency to tell me yourself, but you insisted that I had to be gone before you got back. He had a moving company come in and pack all my stuff up, he gave me money so I could relocate. He said he was sorry but that you never wanted to hear from me again."

Cane's body goes slack. The sturdy wooden chair making a protesting groan as the big man slumps back into the seat.

"He told me you left."

He pinches the bridge of his nose and squeezes his eyes shut tightly.

"He told me he went to the house to give you an update on how I was doing and you were gone. Packed up and disappeared. Changed your phone number. Didn't even leave a note."

Now it's my turn to fall back in my seat. For a long time, we both stare silently into the flames.

"Why would I do that, Cane?" I finally speak, feeling seriously wounded that he thought I'd have abandoned him.

"Because you knew I was in rehab, because you knew I'd told Rick I was breaking my contract. You didn't want me if I wasn't a pro-ball player. You didn't want me if you knew I was hooked on the painkillers. Because you didn't really want *me,* you wanted the lifestyle. That's what I thought. That's what that bastard let me think."

Something in his words catches my attention and I can't help but zero in on it.

"Hooked on painkillers? What do you mean?"

Cane swivels his head to look over at me, one eyebrow quirked above a squinted eye.

"Rehab, Junie. They gave me morphine in the hospital. I couldn't kick it. That's why I went to rehab right after."

"I don't understand, why would they give you morphine if you told them you were prone to addiction?"

"It wasn't an allergy. My manager ok'd it. Nobody asked me."

"I thought it was physical therapy. I couldn't understand why I couldn't talk to you."

Hurricane

Part of the story she got was true, at least. Those first two weeks sucked ass. I didn't want anyone to see me like that. I had my manager take over my calls and my emails, but I expected Junie to start visiting me when I got past the worst of it.

I was nobody in the big picture of pro sports, so there wasn't any press to worry about.

Of course, Rick was planning on changing all that as soon as I got back to the game.

It had just been a stupid knee thing, nothing that should have even slowed me down for more than a couple of weeks after the surgery. I'd been laid up in the hospital for a couple of days for no good reason, while Junie crawled up in the bed beside me and watched TV with me and we talked about our plans for the future.

I kept asking her what kind of ring she wanted.

We'd only been together a couple of months, but I knew the moment I saw her that she was going to be my bride one day.

All this time, I thought she'd found out that I'd checked into the program to clean that shit out of my system and left when she found out I'd told my manager to eat shit and tear up my contract.

I didn't care how much money it cost to get out of it. I wasn't going back to a business that didn't give a fuck about me.

Mom lost a brother to drugs when she was still a kid, her dad had been down the wrong road more than once before he finally got clean for good.

I'd watched my older brother dance with the bottle since long before he was old enough to know he had a problem.

The idea that I might have that gene terrified me. I've always hated the idea that anything could take hold of me like that and I'd been careful to avoid finding out.

It was in the pre-op paperwork not to give me anything stronger than aspirin, and by the time I knew what had happened, it was too late.

I told Rick I wasn't going home till I got clean. He found me a program and I went straight there from the hospital.

Yeah, I did entrust him to deliver a message to Junie for me. Just not the one she got.

"I was a week in and still crawling up the damn walls when I told Rick I was breaking my contract."

I'm looking into the firepit, but I'm seeing my manager's face when I told him I was buying myself out of the contract I'd signed. I didn't care how far I could go in the game, I cared that he'd been unapologetic about giving the order to go ahead and give me painkillers that I'd been clear I didn't want.

The way he'd shrugged and told me it was no big deal, and that "next time" they'd plan for the rehab program in advance. As many times as I got injured, that's how many times they were willing to get me hooked on something and put me through hell to get off it again.

It wasn't about me; it was about how much money I was worth to them.

Football was never my passion. It hadn't been my plan. I was good at it and it gave me an escape from the chaos back here at home after we lost my dad and my grandfather at the same time.

My mom and my grandmother were at each other's

throats over it, Zephyr was just a baby with no clue that her whole family was coming apart at the seams. Raine was a kid-- hell, I was just a kid! Fourteen years old, full of confusion and anger tailor made for knocking guys down to keep them from getting to a dumb ball.

Hayle was a senior in high school. He was already a wild kid. Our family's money meant we'd be set from birth and my older brother was never headed in any direction but self-destruction. Suddenly he was seventeen years old and the man of the family.

Football gave me something to focus on and it let me avoid the family drama.

Hayle was holding his shit together when I took the scholarship. He was working at the camp and helping Mom with Raine and Zeph. I thought the responsibility had finally given him some meaning in his life. Thought he'd grown up.

If I'd known how that was going to turn out, I'd have never left the Ridge.

"Cane?" Junie's hand waving in front of my face breaks the vacant stare I have aimed at the fire. "Hey, there you are."

When I come back to the present, she's right there; standing in front of me looking just a beautiful as she ever did.

She let her hair down at some point and now I can see it flowing in long, chocolate waves that fall over her shoulders, the ends skimming the barest outline of nipples poking through her bra.

For a second, I forget that's probably due to the

chilly night air. Hell, I forget everything. Everything that's happened in the last five years, everything that we've learned today, everything but the woman standing in front of me looking too fucking much like mine.

Chapter Five

June

When the far-away glaze leaves his eyes, the man looking up at me is the one I thought I'd never see again.

The one I thought I'd never *want* to see again.

My lips buzz with the memory of the kiss we shared too briefly earlier.

When Cane's hands grip my hips and tug me onto his lap, my traitorous body eagerly complies.

The chairs are wide enough for Cane's bulk and still leave room for my knees to settle on either side of his hips as he positions me to straddle him, but the hard wood and deep angle of the chair's design isn't the most comfortable place I've ever made out.

Cane's lips move against mine, our tongues sliding in time with one another in a slow, sensual dance. When his hands move under the hem of my blouse, I lean into the warm, callused feel of them as they slide up my skin. And when he pushes the cups of my bra aside and his thumbs graze over my hard nipples, I don't remember that the chair isn't comfortable. Or that the night air is cold. Or that we need to be cautious of getting caught by a curious child.

I only remember the way Cane's hands have always felt so right on my body. Just like they still do now.

"Junie." Cane's hands push the hem of my shirt up high, and he mumbles against the exposed flesh of my breasts. "I need you, baby girl. So bad."

He takes a nipple between his teeth, his hands pulling my hips down so that there's no mistaking the hard length straining against his zipper.

Feeling his desire pressed to my core is almost enough to make me come right then.

The only answer I have for him is a needy whimper as I rock into that hard ridge.

Cane responds with a groan that blows hot against my breast. Suddenly, I feel myself being hoisted out of the chair along with his strong body.

It's only under protest that he loosens his grip and allows my body to slide down his till my feet are secure on the ground while Cane flips a switch to kill the fire. Before the flames have died, he has my mouth captive again, as we slowly make our way back indoors.

The master suite is at the other end of the house from the guest bedrooms. Smart planning for a couple who hopes to raise a family while maintaining some privacy, but in our current, awkward predicament, it presents a slight challenge-- it gives us a moment to come to our senses.

"I just need to check," I whisper as soon as we've come inside.

It means losing contact with Cane's solid build.

Apparently, I'm not the only one who's afraid of breaking the spell.

My hands linger against Cane's chest, my palms flattened over the hard planes of his pecs but refusing to leave his warmth just yet.

One large hand moves beside us to latch the doors now that we're in for the night, but his other hand remains possessively draped around my shoulder.

Cane's eyes glance over my head, toward the hallway that leads to the guest bedroom where Donner is, no doubt, still fast asleep, then back to me.

Giving me no more than a firm nod that he understands what I'm saying, we move together toward the guest bedroom door.

Cane stands just behind me, his hand on my hip holding me just firmly enough that I can still feel the length of his cock pressing against the small of my back. Not letting me forget that we're in the middle of something and he expects to pick up where we left off.

This is part of my nightly routine, checking on Don before I head to bed for the night, but the feel of Cane's fingers pressing into my side as he also tilts his head to peer around the edge of the door to view the slight form of our sleeping son, reminds me this is new for him.

Is this what it would be like? If things had worked out differently for us? If we were a real family, raising our son together? Would we put him to bed every night, spend a few hours of adult time, and check in together before we head to bed ourselves?

A thrill runs through me but I can't be sure if it's hope that we might still be able to have get there, or if it's fear that it's too late to go back.

Closing the door softly, I turn to look up at Cane.

There's a silent question brooding in his intense gaze and I wonder if he's thinking the same thing.

He holds out his hand and I stare at it dumbly for several seconds.

This is my chance to shake my head and slip through the door to the safety of the guest room. This is my chance to save myself from whatever heartbreak is coming next. When the attorneys have mashed together a temporary agreement and Don and I are on our way back to our lives. When this moment is over and Cane realizes I'm not the woman he was in love with so many years ago, and he sends me back to reality.

When we pick up where we left off-- yesterday, not five years ago.

Taking his hand, I let him lead me back to his bedroom.

I'll deal with whatever come next later. Tonight, I want to remember what it feels like to make love to the only man who's ever owned my heart.

Hurricane

M y boy is asleep, stretched out in the middle of the queen size guest bed, oblivious to the world.

If he's anything like me and my brothers at that age, a jet could land on the roof and he'd sleep through it.

Something squeezes around my heart so tight; I have to take a step back while Junie closes the bedroom door.

This should be us. This should have been our lives every night right up till now.

Knowing everything we lost out on has me desperate to get it back.

As I hold my hand out, waiting to lead Junie to bed, I don't miss the flicker of doubt that clouds her features.

For a moment, I think she's changed her mind. My gut clenches and I steel myself for the apologetic shake of her head that I sense is coming.

I've never been terrified in my entire life.

I've been scared, I've been disappointed, I've been angry as fucking hell; but until this moment, waiting for Junie to put her little hand in mine and let me take her to my bed where I can start to put us back together, I can honestly say that I've never known the kind of terror that has my blood going to ice when she hesitates.

We make it out of the hallway and past the kitchen before I spin around and catch June up in my arms. Pulling her off her feet is so easy, even with the new fullness to the curves that always made me crazy, she weighs about nothing. It feels natural to have her in my arms, carrying her, bridal style, through the door to my master bedroom with her arms wrapped around my neck, kissing the breath out of me while I kick the door shut behind us.

"Fuck baby, I thought you were going to blow me off."

I throw her on my bed and don't give her a chance to move before I'm climbing over her. My hands can't get her clothes off fast enough, and even the words I'm saying are in the way of getting my mouth on my woman.

"I remembered how much I liked blowing you." Junie giggles, pushing against my shoulder like she actually expects to roll me onto my back.

For a second I'm a kid in his twenties again, rolling around in a hotel suite bed with a hot little college coed that has me thinking about buying a diamond ring and getting down on one knee-- before the game that would be my last, where the knee I was planning on getting down on ended my career and my relationship.

It's just me and June-bug and our whole future ahead of us still.

Our bedroom was always full of her sweet laughter while we tussled for control until one of had the other panting and moaning.

"You put that hot little mouth on my cock right now and I'll be out of the game way too soon."

I hook my thumbs into the waist of her stretchy leggings and peel them and her panties off together.

The lamp on one of the bedside tables is on, casting the dips and rises of June's body in warm light and shadows that have me letting my breath out in a low groan at the sheer fucking beauty of her.

"Baby, what's wrong?"

June's arms cross over her middle as if my heated stare makes her self-conscious.

"It's been a long time, Cane," she whispers, as I take my hands and gently move hers so she's not hiding herself from me anymore. "I'm not twenty-five anymore...things change. I had a baby."

"You had *my* baby," I growl, running my eyes over every perfect inch of the skin she's so shy about before crawling down so I can kiss every place my eyes have already been.

"You're just as fucking perfect as you've always been, baby girl." And I'm not saying that to make her feel better. Junie's body really is everything I remember plus a little better.

"I love these curves," I mumble, dragging my finger, and then my tongue along her ribs and then over the soft swell of her belly. "Love the way you're all soft and rounded out now. Like a woman should be."

Junie giggles softly, her fingers tangling in my hair as I nip and lick my way over her body.

"I was always curvy," she says, as if I need reminding.

I groan again and get to my knees, with her legs spread open on either side of mine while I make quick work of undoing my jeans and pulling out my cock.

"And your curves have always done this to me,

Junie-bee," I wrap her hand around my hardness and let the sensation take me to heaven.

Chapter Six

June

You'd think nothing had changed from the way Cane looks at me. Like I haven't put on weight, like my boobs are still perky, like I don't have stretch marks like tiger stripes all along my abdomen.

Meanwhile, Cane's still in great shape. His body is still made of hard slabs of solid muscle that haven't gotten hidden under padding from age or a sedentary lifestyle.

As much as I enjoy the view as he peels his shirt off and tosses it aside, I can't help but feel self-conscious about not being able to offer him the same in return.

When he wraps my hand around his shaft, however, I can feel it throbbing in my grip. If there's any room left to doubt that Cane's still as attracted to me as he ever was, it's erased when I see the way his face pinches tightly as he thrusts against my hand as if he's on the verge of losing control.

"Fuck baby, I can't let you touch me like that yet."

Cane grits the words out at the same time he steals his thickness from my hand. "I'll be making a mess of you way too soon for either of us to be happy about it," he whispers hoarsely as he moves south, kissing his way quickly down my body till he reaches his destination.

With his head between my thighs, I don't have anything to do with my hands except thread them through his hair.

It's been so long since I touched him and now that I have, it's like I can't stop. I need to feel him, to have my hands on him just to remind myself he's really there.

Then I feel Cane's warm breath against my drenched core, the pads of his thumbs rough against my most delicate skin as he spreads me open and dips his tongue into my center.

"You're so fucking wet, Junie." His voice is a rasp between exploratory strokes of his tongue. "You still taste as delicious as I remember."

Those are the last words I hear from him for a while. Two thick fingers slide in and out while his mouth goes to work on my clit.

It's a good thing I have a grip on him--the feel of his hair caught between my fingers, the rough grip his free hand has on my ass as he uses it to pull my body closer and keep it sealed to his mouth, the solid resistance of his neck between my thighs when I involuntarily squeeze them together so ·tight that I'd be worried about suffocating him if I could think at all-- or I'd be convinced this was just another dream.

I come much faster than either of us expected and

harder than I have in any of the last five years that I've been taking care of myself.

"That was fast, baby girl," Cane coos reverently as he peppers soft kisses along the insides of my quivering thighs. "I thought you'd make me work harder."

"I'm thirty now," I point out with a little laugh at myself.

"Thirty is a magic number?" Cane's kisses are beginning to linger, as if he can sense my body waking up to his touches all over again.

"Apparently women hit their sexual prime in our thirties."

The conversation is still light-hearted, with Cane working his way back up my body between slow kisses and tender caresses, but there's tension behind his tone as he jokes with me.

"So you come that hard with everyone now, then?"

"I wouldn't know, Cane," I take his hand, looping my fingers around his and letting him easily pin my arm to the pillow beside my head.

My voice loses the playful tone I've been trying to keep up this whole time, and maybe it's too soon to show my cards and I'll just end up heartbroken and angry about it tomorrow, but if we're doing this tonight it's only fair to be honest.

"You're still the only man I've ever been with."

With that confession, Cane's fingers tighten on mine, his warm caramel gaze going dark as he stares back at me while he puts together what I mean.

In seconds, he's finished peeling his jeans and boxers off. They land on the floor somewhere outside the circle of dim light and then he's between my legs again.

This time, with his hips holding my thighs apart, one hand gripping his own length firmly as he slides the slick tip of his dick through my own wetness before pausing just shy of pressing inside me.

"There's not a condom in this whole damn house, Junie-bee," he tells me, his voice ragged and coarse, "because I haven't been with anyone since you either."

He pushes in by millimeters, like he's trying to finish this conversation but can't quite hold himself back.

I don't want him to. I widen my thighs, lifting my knees, and tilting up to beg him further inside me.

"...and I hope you're not on birth control, because I plan to fuck another baby into you tonight and this time, I'm not going to miss a minute of it."

Hurricane

It takes every ounce of control I have to give her time to stop me.

There's still some part of my brain that's working right, screaming something about good ideas and too soon and taking time, but that voice is small and far away and not making a whole lot of sense right at this moment.

At this moment, the only thing that makes any sense at all is the primal part of me that's screaming to take this woman, mark her, claim her, make her mine in every possible way.

Thank God, Junie doesn't try to talk any sense into the caveman that's taken over me, I'm not sure he'd listen.

Instead, she writhes underneath me, clutching at my sides and whimpering as I enter her slowly, savoring every inch of her as her interior walls are forced to make room for my intrusion.

"Hurricane." Junie's whimpers become insistent little mewls under me. "Don't tease."

"Baby, you're still so tight--" I push in farther, savoring the feel of her sealing around my hard cock with every inch I get deeper, "--I have to take this slow or I'm going to explode."

But she's not paying attention to my words anymore. June's eyes have closed, her bottom lip drawn between her teeth, and her fingernails dug deep in my back as she rises up to meet me and takes me all the way in.

Feeling June's sweet little pussy hugging my cock is more than I can handle.

It's been too long since I've been inside her, too long since I heard the needy little sounds she makes when she's desperate for me to fuck her hard and thorough, too damn long since I felt her greedy little channel clenching around me when she's coming undone with my name on her lips.

"Junie," I warn her, catching her lips in a kiss to steal her next moan, "I won't last if you keep making those noises, sweetie."

"Fuck me and make me come, Cane." She slips her tongue out to draw over my upper lip but doesn't kiss me. "Fill me up and make me yours all over again. I need it, baby, I need you."

She does it on purpose, just like she always did, and I fucking love her for it.

Drawing back, I slip my hand between us and tease her clit.

Another time, we'll make love slow and easy; I'll roll her over and watch her ride me with those pretty tits of hers bouncing up and down on her chest for me; I'll bend her over the edge of the bed and take her from behind while she says all those filthy words while she watches me over her shoulder just because she knows I could never hold out when she did that.

We're going to have a lot of chances to make up for lost time, but right now I need to make sure Junie gives me another one of her delicious orgasms before I lose control altogether.

It doesn't take long. Just the lightest brush over her swollen little bud and she's arching her back and crying out for me while her tight little pussy squeezes my dick so hard I can't move.

I'm lost to her climax. Helpless to resist when I feel her muscles milking me for my cum.

Holding on to Junie so tight I'm sure to find bruises on her in the morning, I slam home one more time and release everything I've got deep inside her womb. Filling her to overflowing, branding her with my DNA, and praying we'll be starting a new life tonight that we'll get to bring into the world together this time.

"I love you, June-bug."

They're the only words I can think of and the first thing out of my mouth as soon as I can speak again.

It doesn't even occur to me that we're moving fast, in my mind, we're just picking up where we left off. Five years got taken from us and I want them back, but the best I can do is make sure we don't waste another second that we're given.

Pulling my woman into my arms, I cradle her close and tell her again.

"I love you, Junie. Don't leave. Never leave again, no matter what, and I promise we'll figure it out."

"I love you too," Junie says, snuggling against my chest and letting me hold her. "I know we'll figure it out, Cane."

But she doesn't relax and drift off to sleep like I want her to.

"Where are you going?"

When she wriggles out of my grasp and crawls out of bed, I realize she's not just heading for the master bath. She's picking her clothes up off the floor and getting dressed.

It has my heart clenching, my hands itching to pull her back into bed with me. Didn't she just tell me she loved me too? After everything today dumped on us, that we'd figure it out together?

"Donner expects me to sleep in the guest room. I need to be there when he wakes up."

Junie crawls onto the bed and leans in to kiss me. Slow. Tender. Like she's telling me not to worry, she'll be here in the morning.

"How do you think we should--"

"Shh. We'll figure it out," she tells me again. Giving me a small smile and adding a soft kiss to my furrowed brow before slipping out of my bedroom and leaving my bed empty and my thoughts jumbled.

Chapter Seven

June

"Mom, I'm hungry."

"Give me five more minutes." I beg, trying to keep a straight face as Donner's tiny fingers pry my eyes open.

It's a game we've played for a long time. He's always been a morning person, like his father.

"I already gave you five minutes before I woke you up."

I can't think of an argument to his logic, and also, I'm eager to join Cane in the kitchen and see how our first day as a family is going to go.

"Can I take a shower at least?" Asking the four-year-old for permission isn't part of our usual routine, but things are off for us and I want Donner to spend his first full day here feeling safe and confident.

My simple request is met with a pointed frown that tells me he's probably been awake for an hour already, patiently waiting till he saw the big seven on my phone's clock before waking me up.

"Let's go explore Cane's kitchen and see what we can find for breakfast. I'll take a shower later, sound like a plan?"

"Hurricane, Mommy," Donner corrects me, pulling my hand to drag me out of bed. "His name is Hurricane, remember?"

Despite the awkward introductions yesterday, Donner took to both Raine and Hurricane, immediately deciding that men with equally stormy names were meant to be his people. Raine taking him to see the horses didn't hurt either.

"I remember, baby. Mommy's known Hurricane since before you were born, so she can call him Cane."

I'm met with a skeptical eye as I let Don lead me out of the guest bedroom and into the kitchen.

I'm surprised to find the house still quiet. Cane was always up with the sun and usually had coffee brewed and waiting for me by the time I crawled out of bed.

The early morning sunlight seeps through highlights along the high ceiling, giving the kitchen and living room a warm glow that makes it hard to stay groggy for long as I bumble through the process of discovering where the coffee is kept and how to work the automatic machine.

"Do you think Cane has cereal?"

Donner climbs up on one of the chairs that flanks the wide, granite island, and stares hopefully up at a cabinet.

"I do *not* have cereal," Cane's voice reverberates off the walls, loud in the sleepy house and entirely too chipper for such a tender hour of the morning. "But I can make pancakes shaped like dinosaurs, how's that sound?"

Cane looks different than he did yesterday, as he closes the door of the room he just emerged from behind him. He's showered this morning, his dirty blonde hair still damp and uncombed, looking like it did after I'd had my fingers in it. He's dressed in worn jeans that fit loose at the waist and snug across his massive thighs and a navy-blue t-shirt that clings to his sculpted torso in a way that has me remembering exactly what those muscles feel like.

This morning there's a smile playing at the corners of his mouth as soon as he sees Donner and I in the kitchen. The furrowed brow has relaxed, and the stiff set of his shoulders has eased.

Heat blooms in my core and I try not to give away the way his molten stare flusters me as he joins us in the kitchen.

"Coffee for you-- in forty seconds." He flips a switch on the machine I was just trying to figure out, and it instantly begins to fill the house with the rich aroma of God's apology for making mornings come so early.

From the cupboard overhead, he hands me a heavy, ceramic mug with Moonshine Ridge's town logo stamped into a clay medallion on the front.

A minute later, there's enough coffee brewed to fill my mug and Cane has Donner helping him by adding a worrisome number of miniature chocolate chips to a bowl of pancake batter.

"I think I heard you saying you wanted to ride the horses yesterday, is that right?" Cane hands Don the whisk to mix the chocolate pieces into the batter while he heats the griddle on the stove top and searches a utensil drawer for a small soup ladle.

"Yeah, Raine said I had to ask Mom but she wasn't in a very good mood yesterday."

I find creamer in the refrigerator and let the caffeine work its magic, doing my best not to think about the bad mood my son is referring to.

Cane laughs and shoots me a knowing side eye and a grin that's about as far as where we started yesterday as the moon is from Neverland.

"Maybe you should ask her now," Cane says with a chuckle as he ladles pancake batter onto the griddle in an oblong shape.

Donner peers around Cane's bulky frame and watches me wearily as I sip from my coffee. Then he straightens back up and looks up at Cane.

"She not done with her coffee yet," my son whisper-shouts, schooling Hurricane on the best practices for how to deal with me before noon.

Hurricane

Junie pretends to hide her smile behind the rim of the mug when Donner warns me that asking her for anything during the first cup of coffee is a sure way to start the day off wrong.

I make a show of leaning over to look into Junie's mug, checking to see how much longer we have to wait. When I give her a wink, she blushes so pretty, it's hard to remember that we're nowhere near the point of early morning breakfast kisses yet.

"I think you can ask her as soon as the stegosaurus is done," I report back to Donner as I flip the pancake in question.

"That's supposed to be a stegosaurus?"

The kid seems skeptical.

"You gotta use your imagination," I explain, "the chocolate chips throw the effect off, makes 'em look like they have chicken pox."

Don bursts into giggles and only laughs louder when I point out general outline of the dinosaur to be found in the pancake's vague shape.

Junie reaches for the coffee pot and refills her coffee mug.

"Okay, ask her about horseback riding now," I fake-whisper out of the side of my mouth to Donner.

"Mom, can we--"

"Yes, if Cane is okay with it, then we can go horseback riding today."

I hold up my fist and wait for his tiny fist to meet mine knuckle to knuckle. Donner's wide grin has my chest feeling tight.

This is harder than I want it to be.

I hate pretending like I'm just a friend of Junie's. A nice guy who wants to be cool, make pancakes and take him horseback riding. I want to be Donner's dad and I have no idea how long that's going to take.

I slide a golden-brown pterodactyl onto the stack

of pancake blobs and ladle out batter in the shape of a velociraptor.

Maybe she sees the tic in my jaw, or maybe she still knows me all too well, but Junie slides her fingers down my arm, stopping shy of taking my hand and giving us something we'll have to explain to Donner.

"Do you want the T-Rex, or the Loch Ness Monster?" June asks Donner as she moves him back to the bar counter where I've set out plates, and silverware beside the butter and syrup.

"I don't think it's supposed to the be Lock Ness Monster," I hear Donner correct her.

Junie's obviously never seen a brontosaurus before.

June-bug has been smiling almost as much as Donner all day. Well-- once we got a second cup of coffee in her. Some things will never change.

"Did he wake up at all?" She asks, as I return from the guest bedroom.

"Didn't even move when I put him down," I answer, settling into the space beside her and pulling her into my lap.

We did get up to the camp and take a couple of the horses out after breakfast. Donner rode with me and I showed him how to maneuver the reins to tell the horse which way to go. Junie rode one of the mares and needed almost as much guidance on how to ride but the horses are used to inexperienced riders so it was an easy afternoon on the trails.

When we got home, I grilled burgers on the deck while family blew my phone up.

I gotta hand it to my kid brother, he's been pulling double duty for the last forty-eight hours, keeping Gran and Mom at bay; reminding them that they aren't the only ones who just found out Donner exists.

Don crashed right at the table. Set his burger down, half-eaten, took a big gulp of milk, laid his head down and he was out just like that.

I carried him back to the guest room once we figured he wasn't going to catch a second wind.

Now it's just Junie and me, cuddled on the sofa in the big living room, enjoying our first real chance all day to enjoy each other without having to explain ourselves.

"I was surprised I didn't find you in the kitchen already making breakfast this morning," June leans into me, letting me wrap my arms around her while she snuggles against my chest.

"I was making phone calls, waiting for you guys to get up." I move her hair aside so I can kiss the back of her neck.

"At seven in the morning?"

"Started at six. Talked to the east coast office for my attorneys to see what we can do about Rick and shit his agency pulled on us."

June twists, looking at me over her shoulder.

"They stole five years of my family from me, June. Five years that you should have had a husband and four years that my boy should have had a father in his life. I can't let them get away with that."

Chapter Eight

June

The pain is evident in his words, and Cane's usually commanding voice breaks on his final sentence.

I'm not surprised that Hurricane is planning on going after his former manager and anyone that was in on breaking us up. If it wasn't bad enough to discover that Cane's manager had lied to us about how and why I moved out, thinking it was our relationship that had Cane ripping up his contract with the agency and leaving the league; add in Donner and the fact that Cane lost his own father at a young age and I'm glad I'm not Rick.

"You haven't even questioned that he's really yours." I kiss Cane's nose and let him catch my lips with his. "Most men would have demanded a paternity test."

Cane scoffs loudly enough to make me jump, but he holds me firmly around my waist so I know he wants me close, even for the serious conversations.

"There hasn't been a doubt in my in mind who Don's father is since I first laid eyes on him," he tells me, softly.

"I'm sure the lawyers will want us all tested before we're through, but that'll just be formalities."

"So what did your lawyers say this morning?"

"They'll need you to write out your side of the story and we'll need to do a deep dive into your expenses for the last five years, but what they're really interested in is pursuing criminal charges."

"For what?"

I mean, sure, everything we've found out is pretty fucked up but it's pretty hard to prosecute people just for being assholes.

"For over-riding my medical directives, for starters," Cane says it calmly, like it's not that big a deal to him.

"Didn't you sue when it happened?"

"Didn't even think about it," he admits. "I was young, already had all the money I'd ever need from the family trust-- I just wanted to get the drugs out of me and go home to you. Breaking my contract and telling Rick to fuck himself felt like enough at the time."

"Do the lawyers think they can go after him for the way they broke us up?"

Cane shrugs slightly, pulling me close and holding on to me like speaking about it might make it happen all over again.

I'm all too happy to snuggle into his broad chest and lay my head on his shoulder.

"They said they'll have to find the exact charges

that might apply, but they think they can get him for extortion or blackmail or something similar because he gave you cash to get out. And they're looking into what they can do about the intent to deceive."

"Cane...why didn't you try to find me? That's the thing I still don't understand? You knew where my parents lived, you had my full name-- why didn't you come after me?"

It's the question that hasn't left my mind since we started talking things through. The last thing I need to understand if I'm going to uproot my and Donner's lives and give us a chance at being a family like we should have been.

Lifting my head off his shoulder, I stare into a whiskey-tinted gaze that's looking back at me with a troubled expression.

"I tried, Junie-bee." He rasps out, sounding anguished, "I fucking tried. I was out of my goddamn mind when I found out you were gone.

"Rick acted like he was just as upset about it as I was. He swore he'd find you for me, told me all I had to was concentrate on finishing the program."

Cane's arms tighten on me, like he's making sure I'm really here.

"That fucking asshole lied to me," he growls. "In fact, his whole damn agency lied to me. He wasn't the only one telling me they were looking for you."

New questions line his handsome face, his lips set back into the same scowl I saw when I arrived yesterday, then he tilts his head as if he's just thought of something else.

"Did your parents ever mention being contacted by a private eye?"

I shake my head vigorously. "No, they would have mentioned that. Even if they thought you were a jerk that I didn't need in my life--"

Cane stiffens and I don't blame him; explaining all this to my family back home will be something we'll need to tackle together and sooner rather than later.

"-- they still would have let me know. They knew I was trying to contact you to tell you I was pregnant, and they sure as hell would have liked to have seen me getting some child support."

"They told me your parents wouldn't talk to the investigator except to make it clear you didn't want to hear from me."

"Your phone was off, you moved out of the house," I offer my own response. "I was trying to get a hold of you through the agency and they told me if I kept trying to contact you that they'd file harassment and stalking charges. By the time I hired the attorney, you weren't their client anymore and we got all our papers returned unopened with a statement from their own legal team that they weren't responsible for forwarding anything to you."

Cane's hand runs down the back of my head, sliding down my hair and twirling the ends around his finger as he studies me.

"You stopped highlighting your hair," he says, finally. I don't know if he's changing the subject on purpose or if we've both just hit our limit for the night.

"I don't think I ever saw you go out without makeup, Junie-bee."

His fingers brush my cheek, indicating my skin's natural state.

"It was too much trouble to keep up with," I admit. Not wanting to go into the details of all the ways I died inside when I left our house that afternoon five years ago, thinking that Cane didn't love me anymore.

Hurricane

The way her voice goes small tells me more than her words mean to.

New rage bubbles in me, making me want to track down that sleaze bag that represented me and the agency he worked for back when I was playing. I want to pound the fucker's head into the concrete and put some blood stains into one of those thousand dollar suits he used to wear that no cleaner will be able to get out.

I hate that so much time has been stolen from us, but mostly, I hate seeing the traces of worry and heartache etching my girl's sweet face.

June's a beautiful woman. She was beautiful the day I first saw her, when she was a college grad student out with her friends, spending all her money on a rigged arcade game on a carnival midway to win a stuffed panda bear with hideous tie-dyed fur where the black should have been.

Thank God for growing up target shooting using Hayle's old .22 with the sites all out of alignment. Made it a cinch for me to fill that tiny star on the target with holes so I could meet the girl with the blonde highlights running through her chestnut hair and the glass green eyes that had been carefully accented with the winged eyeliner back then.

If she never visits another salon, she'll always be just as pretty, but it kills me that somewhere along the way she stopped taking pride in those little acts that she used to love so much.

The idea that that had anything to do with me, has me in knots.

We're going to have plenty of time for this conversation in the future, and all the ones that will come with it. I can't imagine any outcome that could make up for the time we all lost, but once my mind gets set on something, I make it happen.

Right now, my mind is set on unraveling the gorgeous woman in my lap.

Letting my hand fall from where I'd been tracing the curve of her face, my fingers slide down her throat, feeling the quickened pulse there before slipping my hand inside the bathrobe she stole from me after showing off a day of horse hair and trail dirt.

When my fingers find a nipple, Junie arches her back and moans just from the casual brush over the hardened tip.

That sweet sound is all it takes for my semi-hard dick to thicken completely, forcing me to adjust myself behind the confines of my fly before pushing my other

Secrets on the Mountain

hand through the folds of the robe below the sash tied around her waist.

"You're so fucking wet already." I marvel at the feel of her slick folds as I slide my fingers along her seam.

June opens her legs for me, giving me better access so I can press a digit into her opening.

Her moans have changed to high pitched mewls and little gasps that have me ready to bend her over the back of the sofa right here and now.

"Let's get you into my bed before you wake Don up with all that noise you're making, baby."

Behind the closed door, I let Junie undress me, doing my damnedest not to get in her way even though all I want to do is touch her everywhere while she peels my shirt off of me, runs her soft hands down my chest and pushes me onto my back in the middle of the king-size bed.

Now it's my turn to fill the room with noise.

Junie pulls my jeans off, then takes my boxer briefs with them, freeing my cock. Her mouth is hot and wet, running over my skin, dropping kisses as she moves along my chest, my abdomen, and finally to the weeping tip of my engorged cock.

Tonight, I let her have her way; taking control of my body and making it her own in every way she asks of me.

When we're both spent and breathless, I hold Junie in a possessive grip, loving the feel of her

head resting against my chest as I slip into unconsciousness. But all too soon, I feel her slipping away from me,

"Shh, it's okay," she coos softly with her lips pressed to mine before I can panic at waking up too quickly when she slides out from under my arms. "I have to go back to the other room. I'll see you in the morning."

There's a lot left to work out, but first thing's first-- we have got to get the sleeping arrangements settled.

I need Junie in my bed for more than the calisthenics.

Chapter Nine

June

"Who's that?"

Donner eyes the photo on May-Ellen's mantle with suspicion, pointing at the baby in a very young Hurricane's arms.

"That's Raine when he was just a baby," Cane's mother patiently explains.

"How could Raine be a baby in my picture? He's a grown up already."

The four-year-old Cane in the picture really is a dead-ringer for Donner.

"That's not a picture of you, baby," I tell him. "That's Hurricane when he was same age you are now."

Donner looks between May and I with skepticism etched so deeply on his little face, I can almost see the beginnings of his father's trademark scowl setting in.

It's clear that he's trying to decide if May and I are messing with him.

It's been a week since I drove up to Moonshine

Ridge in search of the man I thought had abandoned me and our unborn son over five years ago.

A week of comparing notes and discovering the lengths some people went to to tear us apart in hopes it would convince Cane to stay in a contract so they could line their pockets, regardless of what was best for their client.

A week of making love after Donner has fallen asleep, only to have to slip out of Cane's arms and go back to the guest room before Donner wakes up.

Don gives the photo another thoughtful glare before taking off-- no doubt in search of Cane.

The past week has also cemented a bond between Cane and our son that developed unexpectedly fast. They're practically inseparable now.

Tonight, we're enjoying dinner at May-Ellen's home in the family's woodland estate after spending most of our week holding off gathering with the entire family until we were sure they understood that Donner doesn't understand that they're family yet.

It was only a matter of time till we had to give in though.

Grandmothers are a force to be reckoned with and Cane's mother and his grandmother, Mable, set the bar for insistent.

Mable eyes me through a pair of red glasses that make her eyes look comically large through the lenses.

"I need you two to get to work on the next kid *asap*," she says in a not-exactly whisper as she leans close to me, "That McAllister bitch is way ahead of me with the great grand-babies and I need to catch up."

My understanding is that she's in her eighties, but I'd have probably guessed ten years younger if I didn't know better. She can't be much taller than five feet, with a slight build that has a softly feminine figure showing under the blouse and long skirt she's wearing...with a pair of boots that look suspiciously like well-worn Doc Martens.

It's the bright pink lipstick that makes it hard not to stare when she talks.

Mable sips from a glass and waits not entirely patiently for me to respond.

I glance around nervously, hoping that April or Zephyr might rescue me the way they've been doing most of the evening whenever they see Mable managing to get me cornered.

Seeing the way my eyes keep wandering to where I can see Cane and Donner deep in conversation on a bench in the back yard, Mable smiles. Her expression goes soft as she slips her arm around me.

"You know, he never told us what really made him give up playing professionally. We all thought he came back to the Ridge to help us out when Hayle left."

There's an edge to Mable's voice that I can't quite decipher when she mentions Cane's older brother.

She takes a drink of whatever she has in her glass before continuing.

"I haven't seen him laugh like that since before we lost his father."

Through the window, we watch Cane throw his head back and laugh. He looks young again, carefree, and so much like the man I met in that parking lot carnival so long ago. It's hard to think that the Cane I fell for is the same man that his family worries so much about, the one who's been carrying the weight of so much guilt over so many things that aren't his fault.

"I'm so glad you came looking for him, June. He needs you and that boy more than you will probably ever understand."

Mable gives me a slight squeeze before dropping her arm, giving her beverage a deeply contemplative stare, and heading off without another word.

Hurricane

Donner's been telling me about the pictures in Mom's living room that look like him. He thinks it's pretty cool that I looked so much like him when I was his age-- but he's also having a hard time believing I was ever his age.

If he wasn't keeping me in tears from laughing so hard at his impression of Gran, I'd probably be feeling pretty emotional about him not understanding the family resemblance just yet.

Junie and I agreed though, we're going to try not to dump too much on him all at once. We'll answer any questions honestly and we won't keep any secrets from him-- we just figure he's got enough big changes to adjust to, we can hold off on filling in so many details at once.

"So are you going to be my dad now, Hurricane?"

Donner swings his feet back and forth nervously over the edge of the bench we're sitting on. His eyes are focused on something in the distance, possibly the soft glow of light coming from my sister's place.

Under different circumstances, I'd probably ask him how he feels about it, but being Don's father is a done deal, whether he likes it or not. Why that is, is something June and I will find a way to explain to him over time as he's ready to understand it.

"Yes, I am." I answer him honestly in the new dad voice I recently discovered I have. "You cool with that?"

I admit, the kid had me nervous for a second. When Donner looks up at me, he's nothing but one big smile.

"Yeah! That'd be awesome! Can I call you 'Dad' too?"

Behind us, the sound of Junie's gasp interrupts our man-to-man conversation.

When we turn to look her way, she's standing by the back door with her hand over her mouth and I know she's been there long enough to hear the best parts.

"Can I?" Donner looks up at me and whispers urgently, obviously eager for my answer.

He gets an enthusiastic nod. I don't trust my voice.

"Mom!" It's easy to tell why he wanted my answer so quickly. He jumps off the bench and runs to Junie, grabbing her by the hand and pulling her back to me.

I'm glad to see it doesn't take much effort.

"Hurricane's going to be my dad, is that okay?"

The sound of June's laugh makes me want to pull her into my lap and kiss her in the ticklish spot behind her ear so I can hear it again.

"I heard," she says, "and yes, it's okay. I'm glad you're happy about that."

"Are you going to get married now?"

Donner is suddenly very serious, glancing from his mother to me and back again.

"I like that idea a lot, but it's up to your mom," I answer Don, but my eyes are on June.

"Is that an official proposal?" She asks, laughter underlying the sarcasm in her voice.

"It's an official unofficial proposal." I reach for her hand and draw her closer.

I have every intention of asking her properly, with a ring to slide onto her finger when she tells me yes, but for now it seems like the right place to start.

"Then I guess my official unofficial answer is yes."

It's hard not to kiss her but even with all this talk, I'm not sure if Donner is ready to see that yet.

It's late when we get back to my place and even though I'm keeping my urge to kiss Junie under control, I haven't been able to let go of her since she said she'd marry me.

Donner lets me give him a hug before Junie puts him to bed, but only a few minutes after they disappear into the guest bedroom, I hear what sounds like an argument. Then Junie is being pushed out of the room, with what looks like her pajamas in her hands.

"No, you have to go sleep with Hurricane now," Donner is saying insistently as he shoves his mother toward my end of the house. "Mommies and daddies have to share a room, it's the rules."

Junie lets herself be pushed closer to me, hiding her face from Donner so he doesn't see the grin she's giving me.

I do my best to do the same.

"He's right, Junie-bee, the rules say mommies and daddies have to share a room." I try to make it sound as apologetic as possible.

"Will you be okay sleeping alone?" I ask Donner, who seems satisfied that we're accepting the downside of the mom and dad rules.

"Uh huh," he assures me, "I had my own room at our old house."

Donner goes back to his room and Junie looks at me and mouths the words *"our old house"* at me. Obviously, he's also expecting the new arrangement to mean that he and June will be staying.

This is going to be so much easier than I thought.

"You heard him," I say, pulling Junie through the door of our bedroom, "it's the rules."

Epilogue 1

Four Months Later
June

There's a snowman family outside the kitchen window. Cane and Donner built them last weekend, after the first trio of snowstorms for the year had blown over and the sun came out for a day.

There's clearly a daddy and a mommy and little boy, but there's also another small child in the family of oversized snow balls lined up by the plowed driveway.

Donner says it's his little sister. He tells us that now that Cane and I are married and we're a family, he's going to get a little sister and a little brother just like Hurricane has.

Of course, our son has also explained-- quite impatiently-- that we simply need to order these siblings from the internet and they will get delivered when the delivery van can make it up the mountain.

Cane and I know we'll have to explain things a little more clearly soon enough.

"You thinking up names?"

Strong arms wrap around my middle, and I feel Cane's solid frame mold to my back. His chin rests lightly on my shoulder and he asks his question in that deep purr that has me glad that Donner is up at May's place for the rest of the day.

"It's too early for names."

I stretch my neck to one side, giving my husband more room for the kisses he's trailing down the side of my throat.

"Don says he's getting a little sister first," Cane murmurs into the crook of my neck, right before he pulls my pajama top aside to start down my shoulder. "I'm thinking Sunny."

He's been like this since we found out.

Cane knew before I did, but I think he'd been paying extra close attention because he's so determined not to miss a minute of our next baby's life.

With Donner's blessing-- or more like, at his insistence-- we got married as quickly as possible, in a very small courthouse ceremony down in Slow River with a simple family dinner afterward.

My parents flew out from Illinois for the wedding, after I was sure that my dad finally understood that Cane hadn't actually kicked me out and refused to acknowledge our son for all those years. Now they're the best of buddies and my family is delighted at the way things have worked out.

We'd only been married for a week or two before

Secrets on the Mountain

we were inundated with requested from both sides of the family to start working on more grand-children. A request that both Cane and I were all too happy to oblige.

Cane brought home a shopping bag of home pregnancy tests for me the day he noticed I poured most of my morning coffee down the drain. It just hadn't tasted right and it made me feel a little sick.

He was convinced I was pregnant-- the only reasonable explanation in his mind for me eschewing coffee.

Of course, he was right.

I'm not even out of the first trimester, but this one is already different than Donner was. Or maybe I'm just getting to enjoy the experience this time around because I have a handsome, supportive, husband at my side, spoiling me rotten by catering to my every whim.

We're both trying to concentrate on enjoying getting to share this experience together, not dwelling on what we missed the first time.

Suddenly my feet lose contact with the kitchen floor as Cane sweeps me up in his arms and carries me toward the bedroom.

"You know, we could stay out here today," I remind him. "We have the house all to ourselves."

"I like the way you think, wife." Cane does a one-eighty, depositing me on the sofa and starting the fireplace. He spreads a blanket on the floor and slowly crawls between my knees.

My pajamas are unceremoniously deposited on the

floor and Cane pulls my hips roughly to the edge of the cushions so he can bury his head between my legs.

When he's left me boneless and panting, I'm sprawled on the leather sofa, glad that it's easy to clean, catching my breath while plotting to knock him down and climb on top of him.

Cane's big hand splays wide over my belly and he looks up at me with a look I can only describe as awe.

"When?" He asks, kissing up my inner thigh and then moving his hand so he can kiss my stomach too. "When will you start showing?"

"It wasn't until the end of six months with Don."

It's cute how disappointed his looks. Six months is still a long way off for this one.

"But I've heard a lot of women say they show much earlier with the second baby."

That news has him grinning.

"You are ready for the second trimester, right baby?" I pull myself to sitting and then slide onto the floor with him, pushing him back and yanking off his pajama pants.

"I'm ready for all of it, Junie," he laughs, letting me undress him and lying back to give me full access to his thick cock as I work my hand down his hardened length and run my tongue across the tip.

"You sure? Because you're going to have your work cut out for you for the next few months."

Cane's hands grip my thighs, guiding me down as I take him inside me. The feel of his girth splitting me open and filling me so completely always takes my breath away but our playful conversation is forgotten quickly when he's seated fully inside me and I begin to move.

Soon, my movements are more frantic and Cane's hands are tighter in my flesh as he keeps my rhythm until I'm coming hard and loud again.

Then I'm on my hands and knees, Cane's fist wrapped in my long hair as he enters me from behind. My knees widen, I go down on my elbows and take his powerful thrusts till this time we're falling over the edge together.

"Whatever you need, baby, just ask."

Cane's voice is hoarse, his breathing still heavy as he pulls me tight to him despite the sweat still coating both our bodies.

"Remember that when I expect you to fuck me four times a day."

"Four?" His voice cracks. He sounds a bit skeptical.

"Sometimes six," I add, twisting in his arms to look up to see his face.

"Good thing I'm tight with the boss," he says. "Sounds like I'm going to be using a lot of personal time off."

I get a kiss on the head and Cane pulls another blanket off the sofa to drape over us as I drift into a well-earned nap.

"Son of a bitch."

Cane mutters under his breath.

"What's wrong?"

"I just did the math," he kisses me near my ear, his

whispered voice light with amusement. "Now I know why I can't keep Raine on the damn camp for a full shift these days."

Epilogue 2

2 1/2 years later
Hurricane

I slip my finger under the collar of the tuxedo dress shirt, trying to loosen it around my neck.

I didn't get dressed up for my own wedding, God only knows how I got talked into this.

Looking out at the woman in the front row of folding chairs lined up in front of the stage, the bright smiles from Junie and the two-year-old baby girl in her lap remind me.

I'd do anything for the woman with the chocolate curls and the sea green eyes.

Including wearing a damn tuxedo and standing up at my brother's wedding.

The preacher says he can kiss the bride, the crowd breaks into applause, and the newlyweds get introduced to their guests. All I want to do is get back off this stage. I might be stuck in the monkey suit for the rest of the day, but at least I'll have Junie whispering in my ear about all the things she plans to do to me later because she thinks I look good in the suit.

She's been filling my head with filthy ideas since I got dressed this morning.

Sunny's almost two now and we're ready for another one. I'm planning on putting baby number three in June-bug's belly before the night is over.

By the time the happy couple has made it off the stage and through the onslaught of bubbles and birdseed that was approved for throwing, no one's paying attention to the rest of the wedding party as I follow Rapid Jones and Raine down the steps, unsnapping the infernal bow tie and loosening my shirt collar as I go.

Apparently, my girl approves. Before June's even hands the baby off, she stands on her toes to kiss the space at the base of my neck where the collar is open.

"I swear, Cane, if you roll your sleeves up, you won't be present to make your toast."

I can take a hint.

I'm also more than happy to slip the coat off.

We had a bear of a winter, but the late May weather is already bringing warm days out here on the south face of the mountains.

Dropping the cuff links into my pocket, I make a show of rolling up the sleeves on the formal dress shirt, loving the way Junie's eyes rake over my bared forearms.

"You are a bad man, Hurricane Hart," she whispers

as she takes my arm and leads me back to the big room where the reception is being held.

"Rapid's the best man, Bug, no one's going to miss me if I'm not there."

Of course-- that's not exactly true, and when it's time to raise my glass in honor of my oldest brother and his new wife, Junie and I are fully clothed again and seated in our assigned places at the reception.

Rapid's toast has everyone laughing, then he gets everyone sniffling. When he's done, he raises his glass and the hall fills with applause.

When I stand up, the big room is dead silent.

One of the caterers has topped off my champagne flute with the special batch of ginger ale that Ginger and Current Jones brewed just for the event.

The couple has made it clear that anyone who wants to take advantage of the no-host bar at the lodge is welcome to, but there's not alcohol being served at the event.

Looking around, I haven't seen any of the guests opting to go that route. Even gran and her friends appear to be sober as judges. Which can be even more dangerous than if they were passing around their flasks of whiskey from Howard's still that he thinks no one knows about.

Speaking of Howard Smalls, the man cleans up better than I'd have thought, dressed in a suit that looks like it was tailored to him, his long gray beard trimmed and groomed with his hand over gran's as they sit with Don and Vera Jones and Mom.

Their eyes follow me as I rise to my feet.

The speech I've practiced gets lodged in my throat. I clear it out a couple of times before I try to talk. My voice feels tight, like that damn bow tie was still strangling me or something.

Junie reaches up and slips her hand in mine.

If someone had told me that I'd be here today, married to the love of my life; that we'd have a couple of kids-- currently raising hell with the rest of Moonshine Ridge's next generation in a separate room somewhere in this lodge, courtesy of Terra Hawkins' daycare staff; and that I'd be getting choked up about giving a toast to my fuck-up older brother on his wedding day...I'd have punched them.

Three years ago, that would have sounded like the cruelest fucking joke anyone had ever told.

"Hayle," I cough to clear my throat again, "I can't believe I'm standing here today, in front of God and half the Ridge, admitting this but...I'm damn proud of you, brother. You've done good, and I'm glad you're back."

It's a far cry from the polished speech Junie helped me write. The one I'd practiced for two weeks. The one I thought I'd be able to get through easily, skirting the details, and avoiding the emotional shit.

But these were the only words I could remember when it was time to speak.

They're the things I really wanted to tell my brother.

Next in Series

<u>Beginnings on the Mountain</u>
Hayle Hart

January Quinn is a sunbeam in a hailstorm, bringing light and warmth to a place inside me that I thought was destined was to stay dark forever, but making her mine means coming back to the place I swore I was done with. A place that's made it all too clear it's done with me.

I swore I'd never come back to Moonshine Ridge. but my baby sister is getting married and since we lost our father when she was just a baby, I've always promised I'd be the one to walk her down the aisle.

Checking into my room at the newly renovated ski resort, owned by one of the few people left around here that's willing to welcome me back, all I'm thinking about is how soon I can get back off this mountain.

When I see the curvy ski instructor that works at the lodge, it might as well be another punch to face; because there's not a doubt in my mind that January Quinn is mine...and there's not a hope in my heart that I can have her.

This mountain community is Jan's whole life now, but the small town I grew up in is a better place without me in it.

I wish I was still the guy that could break promises as easily as I could break the seal on a new bottle, because the Ridge isn't home anymore and it doesn't want me back.

I may have managed to crawl my way out of the bottle, but January is proving to be an addiction I don't have the strength to walk away from.

Thanks for Reading

Man. I have to say-- Hurricane Hart proved to be one tough son of a bitch of a character to write. I don't think there was any way to do him justice in the short format that these books have followed.

When I set out to write Cane and June's story, I wasn't really aware of just how much trauma Cane's dealt with and he turned out to be a far more complicated character than I'll ever be able to convey.

Hopefully, it doesn't feel too much like we skimmed over important details.

Hayle finally gets his story next, as we wrap up this initial visit to Moonshine Ridge and there's a strong chance that we'll be seeing Cane make an appearance in Hayle's story-- Hayle still has a lot of work ahead of him before he can call Moonshine Ridge home again...but he's going to find something that makes it worth it.

That's how these books work.

If you're interested in hearing how the lawsuits

against Hurricane's former agent turned out, there's a short wrap up detailing that as well.

As much as Cane would have liked to have disappeared the guy over the waterfalls on the Ridge— he let the lawyers handle this one. You can get that story when you subscribe to the newsletter at rocklynwrites.net.

Love at First Sight
Mable Hart

Most days I play online poker.

The museum doesn't get much traffic, but Lord knows I need something to do with myself all day.

Till the baby comes, at least.

My hands still on the keyboard, my vision temporarily blurring at the edges.

At least I'm alone in here.

No one here to call me out for being a sentimental old woman.

Pulling a tissue from the box on the corner of my desk, I blow my nose and dab my eyes under my glasses.

Over the past few years, every one of the girls has seen a new generation born into their family trees. I was beginning to think the Hart line was going to die where it stood.

None of my grandsons seemed interested in marrying, let alone procreating.

Love at First Sight

And after what they'd been through, who could blame 'em?

At least one of the boys will be carrying on the family name.

Soon we'll be welcoming a baby into our family and I won't be the only old woman on this fucking mountain that doesn't have great grandchildren crawling all over her.

This time, my eyes tear up so bad I have to take my glasses off.

So when the door opens with the soft sound as it brushes over the industrial carpet, I'm caught off guard.

"Um...Hello?"

A woman's voice calls out.

One of these days I'll get Howard in here to move the desks around. People don't always see me behind the computer monitor when they first come in.

"Yes? May I help you?"

I dab at the corners of my eyes one more time, hoping I didn't smudge my makeup, before I put my glasses back on and stand up from my desk.

She's a pretty thing. Young, too. Can't be out of her twenties yet. She's got some meat on her bones that gives her the kind of feminine shape men adore, but she wears it like a force field. Her hair's pulled back tight so it's hard to make out if it's brown or dark blonde, not a stitch of makeup on her, and her clothes are boxy and loose like she's trying to hide in 'em.

Good luck, sweetie, I think. She's a natural beauty. Nothing she does is going to hide that.

Love at First Sight

But it's the boy beside her that makes my breath hitch.

Can't be more than four or five. He's looking around the museum at all the old photos on the walls and the display cases filled with hunting knives and bow saws, gold pans and the working model of the old sluice with inquisitive eyes that shine with the color of oak-aged whiskey.

"Do you happen to know if a Hurricane Hart still lives in town?"

The woman's voice finds me through my daze, but it's coming from far off. Like something in a dream that doesn't seem important.

"Ma'am?"

Clearing my throat, I pull myself back into the present even if I can't take my eyes off the boy.

"Cane's around," I confirm. Not sure who this woman is and torn about giving her the information she's clearly needing.

"Could...could you please tell me where I can find him?" The woman sounds terrified, like she isn't expecting to be welcomed.

I can't promise her otherwise, and I have a feeling my grandson isn't expecting her but if my gut's right, he sure as hell needs to hear whatever she has to tell him.

"He'll be up at the camp," I hear my voice in my own ears. Shaky and sounding every bit as old as my birth certificate claims I am. "Hart's Gulch Gold Camp, backtrack on the highway a quarter mile and take

Gold Gulch Way on your left. Can't miss it, it's the only turn-off."

She looks me up and down with a curious glance, like she's wondering what the hell has an old lady so tied up about a couple of strangers walking into the place, but if she's got questions, she doesn't ask.

Behind me, the back door opens. One of the girls must have decided to come in for a while.

There's a pause between us, a moment of silence hanging in the air and I know whichever one of them came in is sizing up the situation they just walked in on.

"Would your son like a sticker?" Alice's voice sounds uncharacteristically friendly. I hear her rustling through some things on my desk.

Ordinarily, I'd cut off her hand for touching my shit, but if I move, I'm afraid I'll break the spell.

"What's your name, son?"

The boy runs toward Alice, his face all smiles that have my heart in a vice as I turn to watch him.

"Don," he says proudly but when he sees Alice filling out the little visitor's card, he quickly corrects it to "Donner. It's German for thunder!"

His hands fly above his head and he makes a noise that sounds like a lion's roar. "Like Thor, but in German."

Both Alice and I grin. My heart squeezes tighter, my hand gripping the edge of the high counter top beside me for balance.

"That is a very good name, Don." Alice gives him one of her very rare smiles and hands him one of the

Love at First Sight

visitor packets for the kids that come through. "This has some information about the town, and some really neat stickers-- one is a Bigfoot even."

I watch as Alice pauses for the inevitable "cooool," from the boy.

"And this one here, has our museum address, phone number, and website on it-- in case you ever want to get in touch with us..." Alice's head tips as she looks up, eyeing the boy's mother still standing across the room..."if you ever want to know more about Moonshine Ridge," she adds, "and the people who live here."

"What do you say, Don?" His mother's eyes have gone soft, looking between Alice and me and then back. Her hand held out for her son to take so they can get on with their reason for being here.

"Thank you," the boy says almost shyly to Alice.

"It was nice meeting you ma'am." Donner stops in front of me, looking up with the sweetest smile on his little face.

"It was nice meeting you too, young man," I manage. "Hopefully you can stay longer next time."

Donner runs back to his mom, his visitor's packet clutched in one hand as he takes hers with his other.

"Thank you," the woman says softly as she leaves, taking the boy with her.

The door has barely closed behind her before the tears break free.

Alice is beside me in seconds, pulling me against her.

"Did you see?" I struggle to ask through the sobs

Love at First Sight

that are shaking the air from my lungs. "Did you see him?"

Alice's arms wrap around my shoulders, one hand stroking up and down my back as she coos softly to sooth me like I'm a frightened baby.

"I saw, honey. I know."

"He looked just like my Dusty at that age."

I keen against my old friend's shoulder, ruining her shirt with my snot and my tears and my mascara but Al doesn't flinch. She doesn't gripe. She just holds tighter and lets me cry.

"Which one do you think it is?" She asks quietly when the worst of the shock has passed and I can gather my dignity back together.

Alice pulls off the faded flannel shirt she's wearing over her plain gray tee. It's a slobbery mess, thanks to me, and I know from experience that the mascara will never come out. But she doesn't say a word about it, just tosses the shirt over the back of her desk chair while I make quick work of several more tissues.

"She was asking after Hurricane."

My voice is tight. It comes out as a croak.

Alice hands me a cup of water from the cooler.

"Thank God for that, at least," she states firmly, eyeing the door where the woman and the child left moments ago. "Heaven knows Raine and April don't need that kind of trouble showing up on their doorstep. Especially not now."

"Do you think Cane knows?"

Alice glares at me where I've fallen back into my

Love at First Sight

seat behind my desk. The look on her face tells me that what I only suspect is what she firmly believes, but she's not completely out of compassion yet.

"You know what I think of those boys."

They're cold words for harsh thoughts, but she says them kindly at least.

"Wouldn't surprise me one bit if that girl's been trying to chase him down since the rabbit died."

I pray she's wrong, and that Cane does right by that boy-- I don't think I could handle knowing that's the only time I'll see my great grandson.

Note from the author:

When I first pictured this scene for Cane and June's book, this is how I saw it-- from Mable's point of view. It does hit different, don't it? I really wanted to write it the way Mable saw it-- and I really wanted to show the friendship that lingers between her and Alice.
80 years is a long time to know a person.
It's...*complicated.*

Just in case you've never heard the term "the rabbit died:" (not a fan of Aerosmith? Or did you just never wonder about that line in Walk This Way?)
The rabbit test was a pregnancy test used from the 1930's to the 1960's where female rabbits were injected with urine from a human woman and later dissected to

examine its ovaries. In fact, all rabbits used in the tests died, but the term "the rabbit died" became a common euphemism for a positive pregnancy test.
Aren't you glad all we have to do is pee on a stick these days?

About
Hayle Hart

January Quinn is a sunbeam in a hailstorm, bringing light and warmth to a place inside me that I thought was destined was to stay dark forever, but making her mine means coming back to the place I swore I was done with. A place that's made it all too clear it's done with me.

I swore I'd never come back to Moonshine Ridge. but my baby sister is getting married and since we lost our father when she was just a baby, I've always promised I'd be the one to walk her down the aisle.

Checking into my room at the newly renovated ski resort, owned by one of the few people left around here that's willing to welcome me back, all I'm thinking about is how soon I can get back off this mountain.

When I see the curvy ski instructor that works at

the resort, it might as well be another punch to face; because there's not a doubt in my mind that January Quinn is mine...and there's not a hope in my heart that I can have her.

This mountain community is Jan's whole life now, but the small town I grew up in is a better place without me in it.

I wish I was still the guy that could break promises as easily as I could break the seal on a new bottle, because the Ridge isn't home anymore and it doesn't want me back.

I may have managed to crawl my way out of the bottle, but January is proving to be an addiction I don't have the strength to walk away from.

Hayle & January

Beginnings on the Mountain
The Hart Family of Moonshine Ridge
by
Rocklyn Ryder

Chapter One

January

"Vacation cottage is officially restocked!"

Pepper's voice rings out across the stillness of the resort's grand parlor as she and her husband, Eddy, return from their morning's outing.

"You got everything up there?" I ask, setting my book down on the table beside the chair I've been curled up in. "It's all ready for winter?"

Eddy confirms, shaking snow out of his shaggy blonde hair after pulling off his beanie, while he and Pepper strip out of their snow gear.

"Could use a few more things," he tells me, "but it'll keep ya alive if you're stuck there for a few days."

Just like that, neither of them is listening to me anymore. I stay turned in my chair, watching them over the back long enough to watch Pepper giggle as Eddy feigns stripping one too many layers off of her.

Then they're making out, showing more PDA than they usually do out here in the main area.

With a shake of my head, I turn back around, tuck my feet up under my butt and pick my book back up.

Pepper was one of the athletes on my junior competition team back when I was still coaching at that level. She was on track for a spot on the Olympic team but a nasty crash cut a promising career short.

She lost herself pretty bad for a while. I'd been worried that she wasn't going to be able to find enough pieces of what she'd expected to be to reinvent herself into what she could become after the accident.

She came to Moonshine Ridge to escape herself, met Eddy, and now-- watching my friends and new employers chasing each other through the ski resort they renovated and reopened a few years back-- I'm confident that Pepper's life is better than anything she'd imagined.

"Get a room!" I shout out without looking up from my book.

They just found out that Pepper is pregnant with their second baby and, if I thought they were sickeningly handsy with each other before, it's only gotten worse.

It doesn't help that the resort is closed currently-- despite several feet of perfect new powder gracing the runs.

Winter hit early and hard this year, dumping enough snow on the higher elevations before Halloween that we opened early to locals, but a system of storms has been hammering us this week, keeping us from being able to keep things running until the weather settles down.

Beginnings on the Mountain

Which is why it's just me, the bosses, and a handful of maintenance staff that also live on site, hanging out in an empty resort, with not much to do but read, or head out on day trips when the sun shines between the storms.

That's what Eddy and Pep just came back from; in addition to owning and operating the ski resort, they also work with the local volunteer rescue and recovery crew. This morning, they did a cross-county run up to one of the emergency shelters that dot the trails running through the mountains.

The tiny, eight foot by ten foot hut is a far cry from the "vacation cottage" we call it, but it has a wood burning stove and emergency supplies to keep lost or delayed hikers and skiers alive-- if not comfortable.

"Hey, Jan?" I look up find Pepper standing much closer to the over-stuffed chair I've claimed as my perch. It's close enough to the big fireplace to that I can enjoy the warmth, and has a clear view of the runs from the big windows running along one side.

I make a bigger show of putting my book down than necessary. It never fails: If you want it to rain-- wash your car, if you want people to talk to you-- try reading a book.

"Sorry." Pepper's eyes drop to the cover of the paperback draped over my leg apologetically. "We just got a call from the fire station in town, looks like the county is in place to close the highway if this next storm is as bad as they're predicting. Tight window left; do you need anything from the Valley?"

"You making a run?"

Pepper shakes her head. "Current's down in Slow River doing a supply run for the brewery, he's asking if anyone needs anything. If they close the road, who knows how long it'll take before it opens."

My eyes drift to the open cover of the book in my lap. It's a trashy romance I found in the free library box next to the general store last time I was in town. It's been well-loved, having no doubt passed through several hands, with the spine broken in multiple places, and all the best scenes already dog-eared. The headless torso of a shirtless man sprawls across the front cover in a high contract black and white photo that gives away the book's content in the most promising way.

"I'm good," I tell her, with a sigh that comes out more pained than I'd like. "I don't need anything."

Pepper heads back to where ever she came from, whether to ask more of the staff if they need something or to report back on what's needed, and I pick up my book and start reading again.

What I need, isn't something I can ask Pepper's brother-in-law to pick up for me at the restaurant supply store in the valley.

Hayle

Someone's in the house. Dammit.

Wrapping the towel around my waist, I make

my way from the bathroom to the front of the house not bothering to throw on clothes or grab a weapon.

The chances of an intruder breaking into my place on the family estate in the Gulch are low and none. A bear would be a lot noisier. I let gran know when I got in last night, and Zephyr's living up at the hydro plant with her fiancé.

That leaves two culprits and I'm not in the mood for either one of 'em. Especially not--

My head snaps back on my neck hard enough to make me stumble.

"What the fuck are you doing here?"

Not the greeting I was expecting, but I can't say I'm surprised it's the one I get.

My hand reflexively goes to the part of my face that's throbbing from the punch. My fingers come away bloody from a cut on my lip that wasn't there a minute ago.

"I said--"

Hurricane's voice follows me like a sonic boom as I head back down the hall, answering his question with a middle finger over my shoulder.

"It's *my* fucking house, last I checked," I grit out when I return from my bedroom, still buttoning my jeans. "What the fuck are you doing in it?"

My jaw feels off, and my lip is starting to swell but nothing's broken. It's not the worst hit I've taken, but it has been a while since I've been hit.

"Never seen that fucking truck before," my brother grunts with a jerk of his head to where my truck is in the driveway. "Thought I better check on the place."

Cane crushes his right fist in his left hand and the sound of cracking knuckles goes off like fire crackers. The ceiling lights glinting off something on his finger.

Wedding band.

Fuck.

Seeing the wide strip of metal wrapped around my brother's finger knocks me back more than the punch.

From what I hear, they're both hitched now. With our baby sister fast on their heels, with the big event planned to go down in the spring.

I wish Zeph had opted for the courthouse route, or maybe eloped on a weekend trip to Vegas. Anything that wouldn't involve bridesmaids and best men, and me having to show up to walk her down the aisle.

"Well, the place is fine." I shove past Cane, making a point to remind him I can still take him, despite the bulk he's had on me since he hit puberty. "Truck is mine. House is mine. If you want in, you can knock."

My jaw throbs, but I'll be damned if I'm going to ice it while he's glaring at me. I grab one of the amber bottles out of the six-pack in the fridge and set it on the counter while I check the drawers for an opener.

The fat-headed bastard catches me off guard--again. This time the punch lands near my eye, sending me crashing backwards against the kitchen counter before I even know he's there.

"Fucking asshole. You should have stayed gone, no one misses you back here."

Believe me, the thought crosses my mind to shove off the counter and return the sentiment, but I didn't come back up to the Ridge to fight.

Beginnings on the Mountain

Not that Cane seems willing to let me do anything else.

"Zeph'll be better off without you showing up to fuck up her wedding."

It's hard not to hold my hand to the spot where I feel my eye swelling from his last hit.

For a solid fucking minute, the two of us just stand facing off in silence. Cane's eyes burn with rage and distrust. I can tell he's confused. This is probably the first time since before Dad and Pops died that I haven't jumped at an excuse to beat the shit out of him-- out of anyone, really-- so he's probably wondering what the fuck my game plan is.

"Yeah. Okay. Got it, man. You can get the fuck out now." My voice sounds a helluva lot more pissed than I feel, but there's no way I'm going to let my asshole brother know how much harder his words hit than his fist.

"Fucking waste," Cane mutters under his breath, shaking his head in disgust as he throws the unopened bottle into the sink hard enough to shatter it before walking out.

After the walls stop ringing from the sound of the slamming door, I pull another bottle out of the pack in the fridge and hold it to my eye till my face goes numb. Then I pop the non-screw-off top from the bottle the old-fashioned way-- with a quick move against the counter top-- and guzzle half the bottle while I stare at the broken glass scattered in my sink.

That's good cream soda that my brother just destroyed. House made in small batches. I brought it out all the way from Amish country along with a pack of birch beer.

I can't even order it online.

Chapter Two

January

The storm started around three this afternoon, by four, only local traffic was allowed was allowed up to the Ridge, and now-- anyone who's on the Ridge is staying on the Ridge. Whether they like it or not.

And the snow keeps piling up.

When this system clears, it's going to leave a lot of snow behind and the resort is going to have a great season, but for now the place is starting to feel almost creepy from being so empty.

I finished my book hours ago. The internet at the resort is satellite, when the skies are clear, it's pretty good, but in a storm like this one there's no signal. So no streaming movies or doom-scrolling through social media.

I'm bored. Capital Y, A ,W, N-- *bored*.

By seven in the evening, it's pitch dark outside the windows and the storm keeps raging. I'm thinking I might take a hot bath, maybe make myself a cup of the spiced tea they carry in the cafe downstairs...maybe take my favorite waterproof *toy* to the bath with me.

I get the bath started, undress and toss on my bathrobe while I set up candles and heat water for the tea.

Naturally-- my vibrator battery is near dead. So I plug it in to charge and head back to the kitchen to make the tea.

Only to discover that I've already gone through the stash I'd liberated from the cafe.

A quick look at the clock says it's after eight already. With everything closed, I decide I'm not likely to run into anyone I don't already know, so I turn off the tap to the bath, tie the sash around my robe, slip on my sheepskin boots, and head for the cafe down stairs.

My apartment is at the back of the resort, separate from the guest rooms. I think the apartments may have originally been built as fancy suites-- there are three of them, very private, all with excellent views of the mountains, and the giant bathtub and high-end fixtures don't make me think they were meant to house staff.

But that's what they do now, and I'm more than happy to accept my one-bedroom suite as part of my staff benefits. Only problem is that, being at the back of the building, it's a bit of a trek to get up to the side of the building where the cafe is.

The cafe is really just a small coffee counter with a few table and chair sets that get set up when it's open, but they stock an impressive collection of teas and non-alcoholic drinks for anyone under age or those who just don't drink-- like me.

Reaching into the drawer, I pilfer a few bags of the decadent spiced tea I like and leave a couple dollars in their place for the barista to find when she gets back to work.

The new restaurant is across the hall. Eddy's still looking for a chef, but till he finds the right person to bring high end dining to Moonshine Ridge, they do a decent job of burgers and no-frills steak dinners.

Of course, the restaurant is closed down right now too. Dark and lifeless.

Which is probably why the man sitting at the darkened bar of the dining hall's attached lounge seems so out of place.

From here, he's little more than the shadow of a broad back and long legs bent at the knee with the heels of his boots resting on the bottom of the tall chair.

His shoulders slump forward slightly, leaning forward on elbows that are holding his weight, his left hand is working an empty shot glass like a fidget spinner while he stares straight ahead behind the bar.

Curiosity has me heading that way. I didn't think there were any guests at the resort, and if he's a traveler than got stuck on the mountain, I can't imagine why he'd come all the way up here instead of staying at the tavern hotel in town.

He doesn't even flinch as I come around the end of the counter, moving behind the bar for a better look at his face.

Even in the very dim light, I wince when I get a look at the black eye and the cut lip that mars an otherwise handsome face. His hair is dark in the low light and his beard is thick but not grown out the way the men tend to wear them on the mountain.

His eyes are trained on the back bar, and I can't tell if he's eyeing the bottles there, or the man staring back at him from the mirror behind them.

"You look like you're working really hard to find a reason to pour a drink," I whisper, wary of interrupting his thoughts. "In my experience, if you have to think that hard to find a reason, you don't need a drink."

Reaching under the bar, I pull out one of the pint glasses and fill it with cola from the wand.

I don't know what has him sitting in a closed-down bar all alone, but I've seen that look before. Whatever his story is, I know he doesn't want a drink. He wants to go back to a time when a drink would have been all it took to chase the demons away.

Judging from the bruise blackening his left eye, I'd say those demons caught up with him today.

Hayle

I saw her in the mirror, but I was afraid she might be a mirage.

Raven black hair that's mostly fallen out of the clip at the back of her head. Skin that wears the tan tone of someone who spends more time outdoors than in.

Beginnings on the Mountain

Curves that make that fluffy, yellow bathrobe look like lingerie.

I don't realize I'm holding my breath till she speaks.

She sets a glass of cola in front of me and gently stills my hand with hers, slipping the empty shot glass out of my fingers and setting it somewhere under the bar.

My hand suddenly aches for her to touch me again and then she gives me a smile that feels like renewal.

"Jan," she says, holding her hand out for me to shake it, like we're colleagues in a business meeting. Something inside of me stirs, like waking up from hibernation, and the feel of her soft hand as it disappears in my grip has that waking thing snapping to attention.

I feel it howl as a sense of longing and protectiveness crash through me and whatever the fuck is happening, the only thought left in my head is *"mine,"* echoing over and over again.

"Hayle," I introduce myself, holding her hand much longer than I ought to.

It's hard to make out the exact color of her eyes in the dark bar, but in the light from the hall filtering in, I think they're blue. A bright, clear, aquamarine hue, fringed by thick black lashes and a small mole at the lower corner of her left eye.

"So what has you sitting in a closed bar on a week night, Hayle?"

When she smiles, dimples deepen in the center of

her cheeks, making me want to keep her smiling. Especially if she's smiling at me.

Jan doesn't seem any more eager to take her hand back than I am to release it. We let them settle together on the bar top between us, my hand still wrapped around hers in an easy contact that feels natural.

"Got stuck on the mountain when they closed the highway."

I skirt around the edge of the full story, taking a sip of the soda she poured for me.

"Is the hotel in town full? How'd you end up all way up here?"

I like the way Jan's hand feels under mine too much to get into all the reasons I'm not welcome at Cedar McAllister's business. Or any other details of why I was trying to get off this goddamn mountain before the storm closed down my escape route.

"I know Eddy," I grin up at her, leaning into the best parts of the truth. "Grew up with him and his brothers, so he offered me a place to wait it out till the road opens."

I'd called Rapid from the side of the fucking road when the state troopers turned me back. Told him I needed a place to crash and hoped he wouldn't ask for details. I didn't know my own best buddy had gotten married while I was away. Has a step-son and two kids of his own already.

Made me feel like I'd been gone longer than five years.

Then he told me that his brothers are all settled

down with rings on their fingers too. Wives. Kids. Running businesses.

We made plans to catch up later, and he put in a call to his brother for me. So here I am, with a room at the old ski resort because I'm not welcome at my own damn house.

Jan's hand slips out from under mine and I'm instantly aware of the emptiness.

"That doesn't explain the staring contest with the Bourbon."

She says it lightly, with a smile curling plump lips that make it hard to remember how I got here. There's not a trace of judgment in her tone, just something that sounds like understanding.

It has me wondering what her own story is.

The yellow bath robe parts as she bends down to fill a clean bar towel with ice from the bin. I get a clear view of creamy flesh; full, lush tits that bob and sway hypnotically with her movements, but the gap isn't enough to reveal the hardened tips I can see poking through the terry cloth robe.

"Hasn't been the best of days," I grunt for an answer as she rounds the bar to press the makeshift ice pack to the side of my face.

Across the bar, I catch my reflection in the mirror again. The man in the glass looks a lot different than he did before Jan arrived. He still looks like shit, for sure, with a black eye and a busted lip. His hair's been pulled at too many times to look like it's been combed at all today, there's a trace of blood on the khaki fabric of the long-sleeved tee showing under the collar of a navy-blue plaid flannel shirt.

But now, there's a woman standing in front of him, with her feminine curves wrapped in a robe as she stands between his knees, holding the compress against his bruised face. The way his hands rest on her waist with her free hand on his shoulder-- you'd think the rough bastard in the mirror had something to live for.

"How long have you been sober, Hayle?"

Jan's whispered question drags my eyes off the lucky asshole in the mirror and back to my reality.

Realizing it's not just the guy in the mirror that has his hands on her, I pull mine back quick and put them firmly on my knees where I'm sure they're better off.

Jan holds the ice pack to my face, her eyes holding mine with an unyielding gaze, waiting for my answer.

All I can think about is how fucking close she is. Up between my thighs now, standing so close I can smell her, tending to my bruises with a touch as gentle as the tone of her voice and making me forget that we're strangers.

Making me want to be something other than strangers.

I don't remember my last drink, but I sure as fuck remember the moment I decided I was done. I'm not the guy who keeps track of the time since then in months and weeks or days and hours. I don't have a key chain full of charms or a calendar with days crossed out.

Just fuzzy memories of a man I didn't like being

Beginnings on the Mountain

and the distance between the man I am now and where I left him behind, punctuated by every fucking time he's shown up uninvited to have me staring at a bottle, wondering if I'm really any better off without him.

"Five years, give or take."

My voice is gruff. It's not really something I want to talk about. Not now. Not with Jan's sweet body close enough to make me forget those years and the ones that lead up to them.

My fingers refuse to obey my commands to stay on my knee. I've got the thick material of Jan's bathrobe between my fingers, sliding up the edge of it below the sash tied at her waist.

It'd be so easy to pull that half-knotted belt and watch the robe fall open and then I could pull her against me fully and feel her completely, naked and warm, filling my hands and my mouth.

My hands itch, my mouth waters, my dick has been hard enough to break rocks since the first touch of her hand.

She presses closer, close enough that the tips of her nipples brush my chest. The hand that's been resting on my shoulder slips down, her fingers sliding over my collar-bone before lightly falling away.

I know an invitation when I'm given one. If I drag her into my arms right now, I'd be able to have this woman in my bed all night long.

Something about that doesn't feel any more right to me than filling the shot glass would have.

A night with Jan would be a temporary fix, something that would only open a door to a thirst I'd never be able to quench. I'm sure of it.

Something about this little yellow duckling has my head full of impossible ideas. A night would never be enough, and nothing good is going to come from starting something I won't be able to stop.

"I'm proud of you, Hayle."

Jan smiles so softly, her fingers caressing the side of my face that doesn't feel like it got hit with a sledge hammer.

When she brushes my lips with the faintest ghost of a kiss, my hands have suddenly forgotten how to move at all until she places the ice pack in my empty palm and heads back to where ever she came from.

"Sun's going to back out tomorrow," she tells me from the hallway. "Maybe I'll see you around."

And then she's gone, a swaying vision of messy black hair and fuzzy yellow hips as she disappears through a side door marked *stairs*.

My balls ache from wanting to follow her, but the last thing I can afford to do is go after her. I won't be coming back to the Ridge permanently for anyone.

Touching the side of my face that's still cool from the ice, I wince at the tenderness.

The Ridge doesn't want me back.

Chapter Three

January

I have never been so glad to come home to a charged battery in my life.

There was absolutely no getting Hayle out of my head after I left him in the bar last night.

At first, he'd just been a stranger who needed to not be alone, but there was something about him that just kept drawing me in closer.

He'd had his hands on me for mere seconds, spanned around my waist in a way that made me feel...*owned*. Like I was his.

And for the first time in my life, I'd wanted nothing more than to belong to a man.

More than a little part of me had hoped he would follow me home, but when I looked back from the stairwell door, no one was behind me.

Something tells me that Hayle is still looking for what comes after his last drink, and something about the way it felt standing near enough to him that I could hear his heart beating in the silent bar last night has me wanting it to be me.

Which is absolutely not what has me hovering in the resort's lobby this morning when I could already be out enjoying the clear weather that we've been promised is going to hold till late in the evening.

"So, I met Hayle last night?"

Do I sound casual? I'm trying really hard to sound casual when I bring him up to Pepper while she's working on the computer behind the front desk.

"Oh yeah, he's...grumpy, isn't he?" Pepper searches for the right word and then laughs. "I guess he used to live on the Ridge or something. Eddy says he's friends with Rapid."

Maybe I was too casual. Pepper doesn't seem to catch on that I'm looking for more details about the man...and "grumpy" isn't exactly the word I'd use.

"Looked like he'd been in a fight, I gave him some ice for his eye." I opt out of mentioning I found him in the bar. Even if he wasn't drinking, it seems like the sort of thing that no one needs to know.

Pepper looks up from whatever she's working on and laughs like we in on the same joke.

"Yeah, I barely got a look at him when Eddy was getting him set up with a room. When I asked Eddy, he just said 'some things never change.' I guess Hayle's pretty well known around the Ridge for being trouble. He disappeared five years ago and no one's heard from him since then. Eddy didn't know why he's back but it sounded like he's anxious to get out of town as soon as the road is open."

Beginnings on the Mountain

Great. She gives me more info and it's all bad news.

"You going out while the weather is nice?" Pepper asks, eyeing my gear. "Next storm's supposed to hit just after dark. It's supposed to be another big one."

I nod, trying to put her casual remarks about Hayle being "trouble" together with the man I met last night who only looked lost and felt like home to me.

Maybe that's just it though, maybe home is exactly what he reminds me of.

The lobby door opens, just as I'm about to grab my snow shoes and head out.

In the dark of the lounge last night, Hayle was brooding and mysterious...the kind of man that gets your imagination running away with you as you fill in the murky details of the backstory he's skating around.

In the light of day, it's easy to see that the black eye isn't the only sign that he's taken at least as many punches as he's thrown, and he seems like a guy who's thrown a lot of punches.

There's a scar that cuts through the brow over his left eye, a telltale crookedness to his nose that has me guessing it's been broken at least once in his life.

As I watch him pull off his gloves, I can see white lines crossing the backs of the knuckles on his left hand, making me wonder how many times he's bloodied them and for what reasons.

In the late morning sunlight, however, his dark blonde hair shines with silver highlights, and his thick beard is more of a dark red than the brown I thought it was last night.

He looks like he probably doesn't smile much, so

when his mouth curves upward, wide and full, it makes me like I've accomplished something special.

"Morning." His voice is low and husky and the simple greeting feels too intimate for standing in front of a ski resort front desk with Pepper watching.

There's a small chip on the corner of a tooth, but otherwise, they're straight and white and I wonder how much work has been done to make them that way, or if his dental bill has somehow escaped the rough-housing that left the scars.

"I was just going out for a hike."

I ignore the raised eyebrow Pepper gives me from behind her computer monitor, as well as the butterflies that have suddenly taken flight in my stomach under the warm, caramel gaze of Hayle's eyes.

"Wanna go?"

Hayle

Eleven in the morning and it's already been a long damn day.

I woke up to bright sun, feeling lighter, with Jan's voice echoing softly in my head after a night dreaming of hearing her moans echoing in my bed.

Proud of me.

She doesn't even know me.

Something in me needs to prove to her that I deserve her words and the sentiment beneath them before I can change that.

Beginnings on the Mountain

I headed into town this morning fully aware that I might be walking into another bloody nose, but it was something that had to be done.

Can't say my meeting with Cedar and Chamomile McAllister changed much between us...but they heard me out at least. I guess that's about as good as I could have hoped for.

As I enter the resort's lobby-- *damn*. If I thought the sun was shining bright outside, it's nothing compared to the sight that greets me as soon as I walk in.

January Quinn-- I might have asked Eddy about her this morning-- standing at the front desk looking at me like she sees something worth looking at.

Her thick, black hair is pulled into twin braids that hang in front of her shoulders and brush the tops of her full breasts, pushed high and firm under a couple of shirts layered for the weather.

The bulky snow pants-- the fancy kind that snowboarders wear-- cinch in a narrow waist and flare out with those mouth-watering hips I had my hands on all too briefly last night.

A pair of high-tech snowshoes lay on the floor beside her feet with the kind of tiny backpack used for carrying water and little else.

Fuck no, I don't want to go snowshoeing.

"Yeah, what do I need to bring?"

The words are out of my mouth without thinking.

Just seeing her smile has me feeling better. I don't think I'll survive letting her out of my sight again.

Fifteen minutes later, January has me strapped into

a pair of snowshoes, while she laughs at finding out I've never done more than ride a plastic saucer down a hill in the snow.

"How did you grow up in the mountains and not learn to ski?"

"The same way people grow up at the beach and don't learn to surf," I grunt, working to keep my balance on what feels like a pair of flat clown shoes. "I was smart enough to know better."

Jan laughs again, reaching for my hand to help me balance.

"Okay, but you've never even snowshoed?"

"Had better things to do, I guess."

When we were kids, my brothers and used to spend our days making snowmen and throwing snowballs at each other like any other kids on the mountain.

Cane and I made a badass snow fort one year that managed to stay standing all the way till we got a rain in March that melted it down to about nothing.

I think I was about fifteen then-- before Dad died.

We used to go sledding, and Dad and Pops took us ice fishing on the far end of Turtle Lake, where the reservoir freezes solid enough to drive a truck out onto most years.

But no-- I never learned to ski and I sure as hell never learned to hike across the mountains with these things strapped to my damn boots.

Every damn time January shoots me one of those encouraging looks-- like she's *proud* of me-- the grip she's managed to get on me tightens.

Beginnings on the Mountain

I'm sure as hell not about to tell her I spent every winter from the time I was seventeen finding new ways to escape the chaos at home or the growing weight of my family's expectations that I was the one who could fix everything.

I like seeing the look on Jan's face that makes me feel like I'm not the fuck up that let everyone down.

So I trudge after her, kicking the deep powder with each step and wondering if these things are working right-- aren't they supposed to keep me from sinking in the snow?

Chapter Four

January

"Not really," I answer when Hayle asks if the shoes are supposed to keep him from sinking in the powder. "They help distribute your weight so you don't sink as much, but you have to compromise between a footprint sufficient to keep from post-holing and being able to walk at all."

Behind me, I hear a disgruntled snort. I'm glad I'm ahead of him, so he can't see me grinning. It's cute how much he's struggling to keep up.

In the summer, when the snow is gone, I'm sure he'd have no trouble out-pacing me on solid ground. Hayle's big, easily six, three, and the layers of winter-weather clothing I've seen him in do nothing to hide the muscular frame underneath.

"Break," I call, stopping on the trail that's only marked by the poles sticking out of the snow along the route. Most of them have snow up to the six-foot mark.

"Imagine how deep you'd be sinking without the

snowshoes," I tell him, pointing at the depth marker beside us.

Hayle drinks from a bottle of water and grunts.

"It's getting late." Hayle's hazel eyes train on the sun getting low in the sky.

The swelling has left his face, there's just a smudge of deep purple left under the outer edge of his eye today, making it easier to see how handsome he really is.

"I don't want to hold you back."

He gestures at the row of markers ahead of us, running through the unbroken snow, indicating how much of our hike lies ahead. There's weight in his words that could be interpreted as meaning more than just the trail.

"So, are you going to tell me what happened?" I gesture to his face, handing him a granola bar from my pack.

This is likely to be our turn-around point, which means we have plenty of daylight left to get back to the resort. There's time to stop, catch our breath, and get to know each other better.

His gloved hand brushes the corner of his eye and I'm surprised when he cracks a wide grin instead of just giving me a pensive glare.

"Guess I got into a fight." He laughs, shaking his head as if he's not sure that's the right answer.

"Looks like you get in a lot of them," I indicate the scar over his eye and he mirrors my gesture with his hand, then lets his finger wander down the crooked line of his nose.

"Used to, yeah." His voice has a distance in it says his memory has gone far away.

"*Used to?*" I nod toward the black eye. "Like yesterday, used to?"

"Guess my brother wasn't real happy to see me." This time his laugh is forced.

I watch Hayle munch the granola bar. He's definitely using it as a way to avoid talking, so I give him some time while I let what I know so far sink in

"Why did you come back?" It doesn't matter, of course. There's no reason for me to need to know, but suddenly I'm very aware that Hayle doesn't live in Moonshine Ridge anymore.

Eddy and Pepper said he's just waiting till the road is open. That could be tomorrow, or a few days from now. I've only been living here for a few years, but I've never known the highway to stay closed for more than a few days at a time.

This could be the last time I see him.

"My sister." His words are barely more than another of his grunts. "Getting married...Fuck! I'm gone for a minute and everybody's married. Everybody has kids now. Everybody's living happily ever fucking after and I...."

His jaw clamps shut and tightens. Shoving the wrapper from the bar in his pocket, he grabs the trekking poles and eyes the horizon.

"Weather's coming in, we should get a move on." He conveniently changes the subject, heading back the way we came with me picking up the pace after him.

"When is your sister's wedding?" I chat easily, keeping pace beside him.

He gives me a glare that makes me laugh. He's obviously not happy that he can't out pace me in the deep snow with the shoes on.

"Spring. Summer...next year sometime. She keeps talking about flowers blooming."

"Why'd you come back now then?"

Hayle shakes his head. Apparently, he's conceded to my questions.

"Don't know."

Or not.

After several steps at a quicker pace, Hayle slows again, and eyes the approaching weather.

"That doesn't look like it's going to miss us."

Not only does the storm look like it's on a collision course with us now, but it's moving faster than we can afford.

"Right turn," I tap his arm to steer him off the trail. "There's a hut just past that tree line."

Hayle

Stuck in a shack isn't how I planned to spend my day-- or my night.

Especially not with January.

Her questions have my brain whirling, her presence has my body acting like a fucking sex-crazed

Beginnings on the Mountain

teenager, and now we're stuck in a ten by eight-foot shack for God only knows how long.

The wind is already whipping up outside and, no doubt, snow's gonna be dumping on us in no time. Hopefully the storm will pass over fast.

I grew up on the far end of the Ridge. Hartsgold Gulch is a couple thousand feet lower in elevation from the higher end where we are now, and our land is more sheltered. We don't get hit with storms like this, but I remember listening to my buddies who grew up on this end talk about the severe weather and getting trapped for weeks when the mountains had a bad season.

Jan's busy opening a large storage bin in a corner of the hut, pulling out candles and blankets, so I do my best to be useful and get a fire started in the wood burning stove.

The small space doesn't take long to warm up and once I'm confident that the small stove is burning efficiently, I start to relax.

Our family hunting cabin isn't much bigger than this place and I used to sneak up there and spend days at a time hiding from the world.

What starts as a memory that brings a grin to my face turns sour. After Dad and Pops passed away, I used to hide up there for weeks. Usually with a bottle of something strong stolen from Gran's cupboard.

Standing up to stretch after crouching in front of the stove, I pull off the shell layers and my jacket, feeling the scowl that's taken grip on my features while I think of all the times Cane drove up to the cabin to kick me out of a solo bender and drag my hungover ass back home.

He was still in school at the time. I wasn't even old enough to buy my own liquor yet.

"What's wrong?"

Jan's voice catches me off guard. Not that I could forget she's here.

How the hell would I ever be able to forget she's here? This glorified shed feels like it's shrunk to the size of a shoebox. Somehow the musty wood paneling, the pine smell of the firewood stacked by the door, the smoke of the fire-- it all takes a backseat to the fresh shampoo scent that's released when Jan pulls her hair free of the braids.

She's also started peeling off layers as the air warms around us. Too damn many layers.

When I turn toward her gentle voice, yanking me from dark memories, my mouth goes dry.

She's standing too damn close to me. Not that there's any place to stand in here that wouldn't be too close. Not only is her long, black hair hanging loose in soft waves left from the braids, but she's also tossed her ski jacket and the fleece shirt she had under it onto a growing pile of our discarded layers.

Leaving her in nothing but a tank top and a sports bra that's fighting a losing battle against a set of tits that are tying like hell to escape.

My dick goes to stone without warning. The sound of blood rushing through my veins is so loud in my own ears, I'm sure she can hear it too.

My eyes fall from those gorgeous orbs and trace the

curves of her waist, down to where her board pants are undone and pulled open.

It shouldn't be lurid. It's not like she's standing there in a pair of undone jeans pushed low on those wide hips, showing a peak-a-boo lacy pair of panties or something. They're just fucking snowboarding pants, for fucks sake. She's got another layer under them. Nothing about her half-finished state of undress should have my fingers itching to push those pants down and find my way through however many layers are left till I get to her core; then start licking my way through that.

"Hayle?"

Her voice is soft with concern, reminding me she was asking about thoughts that had filled my mind before the ones currently choking out my ability act rationally.

I watch her watch me. I see the flush that rises to her face and colors her cleavage, I watch her nipples tighten and poke through the layers of fabric designed to keep them invisible.

The pulse-point in her neck beats fast and visible and if I thought this box was small before, it's suddenly tight enough that there's no way to keep space between us now that it's also permeated with desire.

Chapter Five

January

We could have made it back to the resort before the storm hit, I'm almost sure of it, but then I wouldn't be trapped overnight in a tiny emergency shelter with the first man who makes me understand what my girlfriends were talking about when we used to giggle over take-out while sharing stories about our growing experiences with boys.

I can't explain it, but I know Hayle is a good man. Whatever reputation he has around town, or however he got it, the man I met last night doesn't match up to the stories I've been hearing.

I'm safe with this man, and I want him to know he's safe with me.

It's not like there was much of a gap to close, but suddenly there's no gap between us at all.

Who moved? Me? Hayle? Or did the walls around us just close in like a photography trick from a movie?

He's standing in front of me, his broad chest radiating heat from behind the tight, black t-shirt stretched over that muscular plane.

My hands reach out, flattening against his chest. His heart is hammering under my right palm in a rhythm that lets me know it's not just me feeling this right now.

"Kiss me." The words come out so quietly, I almost think I imagine saying them, but the vibration that rumbles through Hayle's body lets me know he heard them.

I'd take matters into my own hands here, but he's so much taller than me, I'd need a ladder to get even with those lips.

Hayle crowds me, subtly guiding me backwards till I'm stopped by the wall against my back.

My pulse is racing, my hands still trapped between us while I wait to see what he does next. His eyes have gone dark, narrowed in an intense glare that's focused on my mouth, but he hasn't lowered his head.

Rust-colored whiskers frame lips that are full and sensuous even while they're twisted into the scowl aimed at me now. His jaw is tense and I see a tick near his ear from the tightness.

It's like he's lost deep in the labyrinth of some mathematical algorithm, trying to work out the possible consequences of what seems inevitable-- and coming to the conclusion that they won't be good.

Still; his hand moves to my hip, his fingers resting at the dip of my waist with only the thin fabric of my cami top between us.

How can something so warm give me the chills?

Beginnings on the Mountain

A log in the fire crackles, a gust of wind rattles the eaves of the metal roof, Hayle's other hand lands with unexpected force against the wall beside my head just as I fist both hands into his shirt and pull him toward me.

Our lips crash together.

The kiss is hard, hungry, with both of us frantic to quench a thirst we didn't work up from the hike.

Hayle's body presses against mine, and I feel the hard ridge of his manhood firm against my belly. I must not be the only one who's desperate for more, because suddenly Hayle's hands are at my hips, pushing against the thick snow pants that I never finished taking off.

I'm eager to help him get the damn things off of me, kicking myself free of them as soon as they sink around my ankles.

Now it's my turn; Hayle's still in the jeans he was wearing under the waterproof shell pants, and my fingers fumble between us to unbutton them as his mouth blazes a trail of fire down the side of my neck.

My progress is halted when my hands are forced off of him momentarily so I can lift them above my head when he suddenly pulls my tank top and bra off in one deft motion.

His eyes are glazed by lust as he fixates on my bare breasts, not looking away even as he straightens to his full height again, pulling his shirt off and letting it fall at our feet.

Now it's my turn to gape unashamedly at his chiseled torso; the broad planes of his pectorals, the flat, dark nipples pulled tight in the swirls of dusty blonde hair that runs over his chest.

The groan in the small space is all me. A primitive, guttural noise from deep in my throat that sounds wanton and needy.

From there, foreplay is an afterthought. I've completely forgotten the order of things and maybe Hayle has too.

Our mouths are competing for access to one another, his hands tugging at my base layer leggings so insistently I think he might manage to rip through the thick thermal fabric before I can wiggle free of them.

I finally manage to finish the task of getting through his jeans, even with the distraction of his hands on my breasts, his tongue teasing my nipples, and his fingers slipping low to stroke between my thighs where I'm slick and swollen and moaning every time his fingers brush against my clit.

Jeans and boxers hit the floor together, leaving Hayle naked with both of my hands filled with the most impressive cock I've ever seen.

Granted, I've seen more in pictures than in real life, but the heavy length of throbbing flesh filling my grip now even puts that one photo my team mates had passed around back in our competition days to shame.

My mouth waters as he pushes against my grasp. On impulse, I start to sink to my knees but before I can taste him, Hayle does the impossible.

Suddenly I'm off my feet, hoisted up with my back to the wall. My legs circle Hayle's waist as my thighs are pinned wide, with his large hands wrapped around my ass.

Coaching junior ski teams keeps me in damn good shape, but I lost the svelte body of an Olympic competitor pretty much as soon as I hit my twenties. I'm not a light girl and no man has ever even tried to fuck me against a wall-- let alone pinned me with such ease that I'm one thousand percent sure I'm not going anywhere unless he wants me to.

"I don't--"

Hayle's words are rushed and broken between kisses and I don't give him a chance to finish his sentences.

"I know," I gasp, cutting off his thought with another assault to his mouth.

I feel his cock between us, pressing insistently against my opening. I'm desperate for him, but he moves and slides between my folds, teasing me instead.

"I'm not--"

I cut him off again, biting his lip gently and sucking.

"I know." I nod vigorously, breathlessly assuring him without giving a damn about his second thoughts.

"I--"

"If you're not telling me how much you want to be inside me right now, Hayle, I don't want to hear it."

Time stops as we freeze in this position. My arms and legs still wrapped around him like he's wearing me, his cock firm and slick from precum, poised just seconds from where I need it most, our eyes locked on one another as if we're each looking for answers to questions neither of us are willing to ask.

"I fucking want you more than anything in the goddamn world, January."

And then he takes me.

Hayle

There are so many things I want to tell her, but Jan's right-- none of them are what I'm actually thinking about. All I can think about is her curvy little body clinging to me, the soft warmth of her bare skin, the feminine scent of her clogging my lungs till there's nothing left to do but breathe her instead of air.

Her words are fierce. The thrust of her pelvis matches her demand and I can't find the self-restraint to deny her.

Sinking into Jan's sweet pussy in one move, tears sting my eyes, my breath catches in my chest, my fingers digging into her ass as I take a motionless second to adjust within her.

"Fuck, baby, you're tight," I grit out, measuring my breath in an attempt to maintain control.

"Sorry. It's been a while." She pants out the words, breathless and sounding every bit as feral as I'm feeling.

Then she nips at my neck. The sharp, sudden bite triggers something primal inside me.

"Don't be fucking sorry," I answer, slamming back

into her willing heat with a harsh thrust that has the wall of the little building shaking from the force. "You feel amazing, baby, there's just no way I'm going to last with your hot little cunt squeezing my dick like it's begging for my cum."

January's head drops back, hitting the wall with a thud that she doesn't acknowledge through her moans.

Her hot little body manages to drag me in deeper, her ankles locked at my back, using the muscles in her thick thighs to ride me even while I've got her trapped between me and the wall.

"Keep talking like that and I will be begging for you to come." She hisses into my ear like it's a threat and just the idea of having her beg me to fill her with my seed is enough to have me thrusting harder and faster.

"Fuck, Hayle, your cock feels so good...I need--"

I know what the fuck she needs. With Jan telling me how close she is to coming, while her nails scrabble for a hold on my shoulders with both us slicked in sweat-- I need the same damn thing.

Bending my knees, I adjust my grip on her, and angle my thrusts.

I'm moving wildly, working on pure instinct now. I can't even think, I just know that together, we've found a rhythm that has both us breathing hard, desperate for the friction and each other.

It doesn't take any more than that for Jan's body go rigid. Her velvety sheath clenches down on my dick and demands me even deeper inside and it's not physically possible to resist.

My thrusts get urgent as my balls tighten and my entire body is on fire with need as January's body milks mine for more even after I've emptied myself completely inside her.

I don't let her go for a long time, just leaning into her, bracing both of us against the wall for support.

If I move too soon, my knees will collapse and we'll both be on the floor.

Jan doesn't speak and neither do I. Maybe I'm not the only one who's not ready to face reality.

"Are you going to let me go?" She asks softly after I've kept her off her feet long enough that her legs have lost their grip on my waist.

"Never," I answer, but I give her a grin that she rewards with a deep kiss that has my mind stirring back to life if not my body just yet.

"Here, let me," I offer, taking the package of wipes she's pulled out of her day pack and laying her down on the palette of sleeping bags and blankets that she laid out earlier.

I take more time cleaning her up than necessary and before we're done, my fingers are slipping between her folds while Jan makes more delicious noises for me.

"Keep that up and I'll be making a mess of you all over again, baby," I growl at her when she reaches between my legs.

"Already?"

Blue eyes look at me with a little surprise and a lot of mischief when she finds me hard for her all over again.

"With all those pretty noises you were making a second ago, how do you expect me to let you rest?"

"Who said I wanted to rest?"

Jan gives me a naughty little smile as she strokes me fully back to life, but I don't let her pull me back inside her-- not yet.

This time, I'm going to savor every inch of January's flesh, with my fingers and my tongue; find more ways to have her needy and quivering under my touch till I can't resist her begging any longer.

And when we've worn ourselves out the second time, I stoke the fire and lay down in the blankets with January nestled against my chest, letting my mind drift while she naps in my arms.

Chapter Six

January

"What are you thinking?"

The wind is still howling outside, but the sparse little cabin is feeling cozy, with the fire in the small stove keeping me almost as warm as Hayle's body.

My fingers lazily trace his chest, down the center of his sternum, along the outlines of his abs, back up along the outside of his ribs-- which makes him squirm and catch my hand away.

I move my head and watch him kiss my fingers before he places them back on his chest, just below the hollow of his throat.

"I'm not moving back to the Ridge." His eyes are fixed on the ceiling, his deep voice quiet, determined, and not exactly directed at my question.

"I know."

His hand curls over mine, nearly enveloping it completely, preventing my fingers from starting a new trail across his chest.

"I can't stay here. I can't get involved with--"

"Hayle. Shhh."

His fingers close tighter over mine and I like the soft smile on his lips as he dips his head down to kiss me.

On our hike, I told him how I ended up in Moonshine Ridge. Pepper was one of my best athletes, with a good chance of making the Olympic team before a bad landing ruined her competitive career.

I was shocked when she contacted me about moving my training program to this remote mountain community, but not as shocked as I was to hear that she and her new husband had bought a ski resort here.

Pepper had lost her passion for being on the snow in any way after her recovery, the fact that she owns a ski resort and joined the local volunteer rescue and recovery crew was a big surprise.

Of course, one I saw the resort in person and heard her proposal-- I knew this was exactly the place I wanted to be. Forever.

The ridge is home for me now, but it's not home for Hayle anymore.

It'd be easy to lose my heart to this man. I felt it the moment I first saw him and our time together so far has only made it easier to picture a life with him in it.

I'm not a starry-eyed romantic. I knew what I was getting into even before I knew we'd be spending the night in this tiny one-room hut.

This man isn't mine to hold on to, but everything in my being screams that I should hold him as long as I can.

"How did you know?"

He shifts his body under mine and we easily reposition ourselves so we're face to face, even with me still wrapped around him and his arm holding me possessively in place.

I feel my forehead wrinkle as I look into his molten caramel gaze.

"Know what?"

"Last night," he says, his fingers trace the side of my face and it takes effort to ignore the way his tender touch has my body reacting. "You asked how long I'd been sober. How'd you know?"

"My dad," I tell him softly. "I watched him struggle for a long time when he stopped drinking."

Hayle studies me silently for a moment and I can tell he's considering his next question carefully.

"You can ask," I assure him. "You can ask me anything."

"What made him quit?"

I wish I could say it was me. Or my sister. Or that he'd done it sooner, when it might have saved us from so much loss but, like so many other stories I've heard-- my father's rock bottom didn't come till things had gone truly sideways.

"My mom died," I tell him. "In a drunk driving accident."

Sympathy floods Hayle's eyes and his arms tighten around me.

"Was he..."

I shake my head.

"No. She was driving. They estimated that her

blood alcohol level was one point eight at the time of death. They'd been at a party and Dad had given her the keys because he knew he was too drunk to drive. He didn't realize she was too. He was asleep in the passenger seat when she crashed."

"Baby, I'm so sorry." Hayle pulls me in, crushing me against his bare chest and holding me tight so I the beat of his heart is against my ear.

But I'm not the one who needs comforting.

Hayle

January wraps herself around me and holds on like she knows what's going through my mind.

A series of what-could-have-beens parades through my head and I have to take a deep breath before I can speak again.

"How old were you then?"

"Nineteen...I was in Europe."

She tells me about her childhood with parents who were loving but high-functioning alcoholics. How she and her sister never thought their parents had a problem. They were just adults who hadn't outgrown partying.

Till they got older and realized that their friends' parents never got drunk at their kids' birthday parties, and other teenagers never got called to pick up their parents from Bunco nights because they were too drunk to drive home.

"I'd just qualified for the Olympic team, and we were overseas for training. When I got the news, it totally tanked my run times. I wanted to stay on the team, but I couldn't concentrate. I ended up coming home early.

"Dad stopped drinking the day after Mom's funeral. It was weird, like, he went on one last bender and then the next day Hailey and I were helping him poor every last drop of alcohol down the drain. He even poured out the mouthwash.

"I remember one time, a few years into his sobriety, we got together with Hailey and her husband and went out to dinner. Dad was really quiet all night and got up to excuse himself and never came back to the table. I found him in the bar, staring at the bottles like he was daring them to make the first move."

A sarcastic grunt is the best I can manage. I know that feeling. It's the same one that had me in the dark last night when Jan found me.

Now I know why she came in to check on me.

"After we got home, I was pretty mad at him about it," she explains, "he'd been doing so well, it'd been a few years since he'd quit and I didn't understand why he'd been so close to throwing it all away right then.

"My sister and her husband had invited us out to dinner to tell us they were pregnant. Dad said it had hit him hard, that he'd suddenly missed Mom so much and he'd just needed--"

"He just needed to be in a bar and know he was still winning," I finish for her.

I feel her nod slightly. Her hair moving over my

shoulder as her cheek rubs my chest. I can feel my heartbeat against her face and I wonder if she notices the way it quickens at the feel of her.

"What about you? What made you quit?"

I cough out a gruff laugh, my free hand mindlessly lifting to run a finger down my nose. I've been told I do it every time now, every time I think of that night and all the things I still don't remember.

"Got in a fight." I can't help but grin when I say it even though it's not the best memory I don't have.

"Sounds like a recurring theme," she teases back gently.

"I don't remember this one." My voice is low. "But apparently I got off easy."

Over the years, I've told my story dozens of times to hundreds of people. I've gotten it down to an art. It doesn't bother me to talk about it anymore-- not until now.

Not until I felt this woman, warm and naked, with her body against mine, making me feel safe and relaxed for the first time I remember since even before Dad and Pops were killed.

For the first time, I've found something that's mine and I'm worried about giving her answers that are going to make her sorry for being here.

"Tell me, Hayle. I want to hear your side."

Of course she's heard about it. This mountain is basically held together with rocks and gossip. She's heard what I did and she's here anyway.

Something breaks inside of me and I'm flooded with a feeling I'm not familiar with.

Beginnings on the Mountain

"I just remember coming to in the ER in Slow River. My nose was busted, I felt like shit, and my buddy, Rapid, was telling me I put my hands on a woman that didn't want anything to do with me."

Jan can't hide the way her body goes stiff, but she doesn't let go of me.

"That's why you're not staying at the tavern lodge," she says.

"Mmm. I still don't remember doing it. I can't imagine why I would have-- everyone knew Cami was Cedar's girl. Except Cedar-- who was being a dumbass about it. All I can think is that I must have thought I could get him to admit how he felt about her if he saw her with me.

"Apparently I was trying to get her to sit in my lap, grabbed at her but she pulled away. It left some bruises-- Cedar returned the favor."

I think about the couple I spoke with this morning. They've been married for five years, Chamomile's pregnant with their third now, and I thought Cedar was going to put me back in the hospital when I walked in asking to talk to them.

"I guess it worked, they've been together ever since."

Jan laughs, blowing warm air over my skin and making me think about all the ways that would be more fun to spend our time than dredging up the worst of my past.

"Have you talked to them yet?"

"Went this morning." I tell her. "Can't say we're on good terms now but, they heard me out at least."

"And what about your brother?"

Her question has my mind rushing back to my thoughts just before I had her against the wall and to be honest, I'd much rather roll her over and get between her thighs all over again.

This isn't part of the story I've polished and shared over the last few years, it's personal in a way I haven't spoken out loud before but it feels like something I want to tell her.

"Cane's not going to be so easy to make peace with," I explain.

Chapter Seven

January

We stay up talking late into the night. Hayle occasionally adds wood to the stove when the temperature inside drops low enough that we find ourselves reaching for more layers. Apparently, I'm not the only one who's enjoying the feel of our naked bodies pressed together.

Hayle tells me about his family, going into detail about the sibling rivalry between him and his next oldest brother-- the one that greeted him back home with a couple of punches and sent him up to the resort in search of a place to stay in peace till he can get off the mountain.

"Cane came along when I was about three and I guess I dealt with the typical shit kids go through; there was a new baby in the house and suddenly I wasn't the center of everyone's attention, but I was still pretty young and we grew up close enough, I guess.

"Then Raine was born. Cane was four, I was seven-- everything after that started going downhill. Seemed like I was always in trouble, always getting into shit, breaking shit, getting dirty, being too loud, giving my cousins shit at school.

"Cane was the golden child. He was good at everything; sports, school, sitting still, paying attention...

"When dad and pops died, Cane had his football, Raine was only eleven at that time, but he started obsessing over fixing up Dad's old truck, Mom had Zephyr, Gran had her poker nights with her friends-- her weird feud with Alice got worse--"

I want to interrupt to ask about his grandmother's feud with Alice McAllister-- the two old women are legends in Moonshine Ridge, with as much of the local gossip being *about* them as coming *from* them. But Hayle's deep in his thoughts as he talks and it's clear that I'm hearing the unedited version of his back story-- one that he doesn't tell often, if ever.

Curling up closer, I pull a blanket over us, and cuddle into the tight embrace of his arm, holding my questions for later.

"By the time I finished high school, I was already working at the Gold Camp, helping Gran out with the stuff that she couldn't handle. No one expected me to go to college-- I didn't even get the option. The family trust means none of us kids needed to worry about money, and they needed me here at home.

"Everybody had something to throw themselves into, except for me. All I had was everybody else's expectations of me.

"I started spending my days off up at our family hunting cabin. Nobody went up there after Dad passed away, so I never had to worry about getting caught.

"Mom never had alcohol in the house-- her side of the family has a history with addiction-- but Gran always had a stash. I'd jack a couple of bottles from her and head up to the cabin and drink by myself if my buddies weren't available. Didn't always sober up in time to get back to work..."

Hayle's voice trails off. He shifts position, rolling onto his side till he's face to face with me in the darkness that's only barely illuminated by the light that escapes the small stove.

"I think I know why my brother was so happy to see me," he grins in the darkness, his finger tracing the edge of his bruised eye.

"Yeah?"

His head nods against the hand beneath it.

"Cane used to have to come up to the cabin when I wouldn't show up for work. Can't tell you how many times he found me passed out up there. How many times I woke up to a bucket of cold water being dumped on my head, how many times we came to blows with him yelling that I was fucking up and letting everyone down-- *again*."

The grin slides off his face, softening his rugged features as he stares into my eyes as if he sees something there that can make these memories easier on him.

"Cane gave me hell when he got offered a football scholarship." He whispers, "Big speech about keeping my shit together and 'manning up' to 'be there' for the family while he was gone... Dumb son-of-a-bitch grew up to be a righteous control-freak bastard. He thinks he's the only one who can get shit done up here but he's the one who took off to play ball.

"He wasn't around to help Raine with Dad's truck-- never stopped to think that maybe Raine's obsession with that old Ford had more to do with finding a connection to Dad than about having wheels of his own.

"He ran off to some out of state college to play games when Gran needed him in the office at the camp-- I can't read a spreadsheet for shit, I don't know how to enter invoices, and I never gave a fuck about learning."

My hand reaches to rest against his face, and I'm surprised at the dampness on his cheek.

Hayle's hand covers mine, pressing my open palm close. He closes his eyes, but he keeps talking, his words tumbling now with a bitter edge.

"He sure as fuck wasn't around when our sister was growing up. He wasn't the one who filled in when the school had father-daughter events, he wasn't the one taking her camping, or sitting through tea parties with her-- you know, Zeph was six when I promised I'd walk her down the aisle.

"We'd been reading one of her princess fairytale books and there was the part about the wedding where the king walks the princess down the aisle to give her away to the prince--"

Hayle's eyes roll up to the ceiling, a wry grin shadowing his lips at the memory.

"She had a fucking meltdown. Right there in my lap, just tears like you've never seen. And when she calmed down enough to tell me what was wrong-- she thought she couldn't get married. Like, she could not live happily ever after like the princess in her book because she didn't have a dad to give her away at her wedding."

Hayle's hand wraps around mine and pulls my fingers to his lips. His eyes squeeze shut, with his brows drawn tight. My heart breaks for the obvious pain in this memory.

I've met his sister a few times, she's a sweetheart. I can just imagine her as a fairytale-obsessed little girl, inconsolable at the thought that she'd never be allowed to marry her prince.

More than that, my heart breaks for the young man Hayle would have been then, thrust into adulthood before he was ready, trying to juggle so many responsibilities with his own grief and the challenges of coming of age-- desperate to guarantee his baby sister wouldn't miss out on anything she deserved.

"Where the fuck was Hurricane then? Where the fuck does he get off telling me Zephyr doesn't need me here?"

I don't know who moves first, all I know is that Hayle's mouth is on mine again-- hungry and violent and seeking comfort that I'm desperate to provide.

Hayle

There's too much shit raging through my brain now and none of it is something I want to talk about.

Something about this woman though. She's got me delving into things I haven't even thought about in years. Examining wounds I didn't know were still open. Fuck! Wounds I didn't even know I had.

Anger flashes through my body, thinking about Hurricane standing in my kitchen, watching my lip bleed while he told me our sister doesn't need me-- that the whole damn town is better off without me.

Yesterday, I didn't bother fighting back because I figured he was probably right but now-- now I wish I'd knocked him on his overgrown, pious ass.

Something in Jan's eyes brings me right back here again, back to her.

The rage is gone, the hurt from the memories, the insecurities that have been plaguing me since I got back on the Ridge-- none it exists in Jan's eyes...or her lips...or the sweet, curves of her body.

When she lunges toward me, I catch her, crushing my lips to hers and giving her everything she's asking to take from me.

The fire in the little stove is dying out. There's barely enough light left to watch her when she climbs on top of me and sinks my cock deep inside her, but I'm mesmerized by the shadow of her riding me in dying glow of the fire.

Even after she cries out, flooding my cock with the slick warmth of her orgasm, she won't let me roll her onto her back.

Beginnings on the Mountain

"I want to feel you come inside me while I'm on top," she whispers low, her hands on my chest, her hips finding a rhythm that has me powerless to deny her.

This time, when I take one of the wipes from her pack to clean us both up, neither of us has energy left to start over again.

I fall asleep with January's warm body curled against me, feeling unusually at ease.

"Eddy wants to know if we want them to come pick us up with the snowmobiles?"

This morning, the sun rose in a clear sky on nearly two feet of new snow. Neither of us were eager to get out of the warm blankets, but that had less to do with the cold morning air after the fire had died in the stove, than it did with wanting to make the most of the time we have left together.

"The trail's still visible, right?" I eye the snowy landscape outside the open door as I finish packing away the emergency supplies we used.

Jan's been texting Eddy and Pepper on the satellite locator device she carried with her on our hike-- the reason no one worried about us when we didn't get back before the storm yesterday.

Jan's hair is pulled back into the twin braids that hang over her shoulders. Aquamarine eyes shine as she looks up at me with a grin.

"We're not lost, Hayle," she teases. "Are you really up for the hike back?"

"I would rather sweat my ass off trying to hike in those damn snowshoes, than have to deal with Eddy's shit if he brings a ski-mobile out here," I answer.

"Remember that when you're crying about your leg cramps."

"If I get legs cramps on the way back, it's because someone kept me up all night overworking those muscles."

We make our way back to the resort by early afternoon, talking much more easily about our pasts and how we each ended up where we are.

Jan tells me about her competitive career and how she ended up coaching, and then I answer her questions about my life since I left the Ridge.

"Vermont, mostly," I tell her. "It's where I ended up when I ran out places to go."

I tell her about the program I developed with a few people I'd met who didn't do well with the usual twelve-step programs. This is the stuff I'm used to talking about, the thing I'm proud of. The questions I have all the answers to.

"That's awesome." Jan looks at me like she's proud and it feels like something coming untied inside me. "How long do you think it'll take to go national?"

"Few more years. We're in six states back east now. Gran's been a lot of help with funding, and her friend, Howard, has helped a lot with contacts, but the program is still in development."

The resort comes into view. The lifts are running

Beginnings on the Mountain

and there are people scattered over the new snow with skis and boards.

"Looks like the road is open," January notes, her voice echoing my own disappointment.

"Guess I'll be able to get down to the valley then."

All the relief I thought I'd feel at getting off the Ridge is nowhere to be found in the flat tone of my voice as I watch the happy families milling about the resort property.

There's an unspoken agreement between us as we climb the steps to the lobby doors in silence; all the playful touches and kisses we've shared on our hike back come to a stop. We're just two friends who returning from a hike as we remove the snowshoes and push through the doors.

"Did you decide what to do about your sister's wedding?" Jan takes my borrowed gear and sets it aside, her voice sounding too formal for a woman who started the day with my cock buried inside her.

"Yeah. I'll give her call and have her and her and her fiancé come down to the valley so we can discuss their plans."

Out the corner of my eye, I can see Eddy and his wife watching us from the far end of the front desk.

January nods. I can tell she's aware we're being watched too but I can't make out what she thinks of it.

"Maybe I'll see you when you come back for the wedding then."

"Definitely." I grin, but it's forced and I know it shows.

Saying goodbye to Jan feels wrong and when she

gives me a weak smile that mirrors my own before she turns to head for her private apartment, I'm overcome by a wave of possessiveness.

Like fuck am I am going to stand here and let her walk away without letting every one of the assholes watching know she's mine.

I may not get to keep her-- but that doesn't make January any less mine.

"Jan--" I catch her by the sleeve as she takes a step and then she's in my arms, and she'd better never forget my brand on her lips.

I sure as hell won't forget her brand on my heart.

Chapter Eight

January

Neither of us made any promises, but Hayle will be back for his sister's wedding next spring.

As I watch the shiny, black truck leave me behind on the steps of the resort, there's more hope inside me than sadness.

Maybe it was that kiss right after we got back to the resort, the one I didn't think was coming. The one that threatened to trigger the sprinklers for the fire alarm. Right in the middle of the lobby, with Eddy and Pepper, the rest of the staff, and all the locals from Moonshine Ridge and the valley watching him kiss me like he owns me.

Maybe it was the kiss right before he closed the door of his truck to leave, where I did my best to make sure he knows I own him too.

"I want details." Pepper's voice comes over my shoulder, breaking me out of my daze and reminding me that Hayle's truck has been out of sight for several minutes while I've been standing out on the landing staring after it like I expect him to come back any second.

Pepper's only a few years younger than me, having already been on the team when I started coaching. We were already close when she was still competing, but after her accident, we bonded over our mutual prematurely shortened careers.

She's never seen me with anyone before. The last guy I even kinda dated was around the time she was recovering from her injuries. I can hear the curious excitement in her voice-- I can also hear the cautious warning.

"I take it you two weren't actually caught up in the storm yesterday?" She prods as I take one last look at the road that winds into the resort's parking lot before turning to walk back inside with her.

We head around the far end of the front desk, down the hall to the little cafe where Pepper grabs us each a mocha while I find us a couple of chairs.

I can't help the way my eyes wander to the bar across the hall, or the way my mind keeps wandering to the man I found sitting there just a couple of nights ago.

"Yeah, the storm really did catch us out too far," I tell Pepper as she settles into the seat beside me. "That man is shit on the snow."

Pepper's eyebrow raises. "But apparently not shit in the snow *hut*?"

I'm grateful that I didn't have my mouth full of coffee yet, I'd have sprayed it all over the both us. My

Beginnings on the Mountain

face is hot behind my grin and I know "blushing" is an understatement for what I must look like.

But I give her a small nod that has her howling loud enough to draw attention.

"You do know who he is though, right?"

Suddenly serious, Pepper sets her drink down on the little table between our chairs and leans in close.

"Eddy says--"

Setting my coffee beside hers, I straighten up in my chair and match her sober tone.

"I've been living in Moonshine Ridge long enough to know who's who around here," I say. "I've heard all the gossip and all the folklore and I've spent enough time in the back country to know where some of those legends come from."

"I know who Hayle Hart is," I say with finality. "I don't care if Eddy thinks he's bad news. No one's even talked to him in five years-- they don't know the same man I do."

Pepper eyes me stoically, her fingers tapping the arm of the leather chair.

"Eddy says Hayle's a good guy," she tells me. "Kinda fucked up, but his family's been through some shit. Eddy's brother is Hayle's best friend. Ed said Hayle seems different than before he left the Ridge. He was asking about you yesterday and then you guys went out hiking and got stuck overnight-- and then that kiss--"

Pepper rolls her eyes up to the ceiling and fans herself, back to joking around.

"Is he moving back to the Ridge?"

Picking up my coffee, I sip to see if it's cooled enough to drink yet. It gives me time to hide the pang shooting through my heart before I shake my head no.

"Too much history up here," I tell her softly, "he's coming back for Zephyr's wedding in the spring but that's it."

"So this is your last season with the resort, I take it?"

Pepper's question takes me off guard.

"Why would it be my last season here?"

She quirks an eyebrow with a tilt of her head that says she knows something I don't. Then her eyes dart across the open space to her husband, chatting amicably with guests.

Pepper gets that look on her face that she gets every time she looks at Eddy-- the happy one that shows the hearts in her eyes and always has me feeling in-the-way and kinda jealous.

"Jan-- I know you're older than me and you've had more experience in life but I also know the look I saw on your face when you watched him leave. If Hayle isn't moving back to the Ridge-- you're going to follow him back to where ever he lives now."

Hayle

The ski resort is a few miles from town and with every tick of the odometer, the feeling I forgot something gets stronger.

Beginnings on the Mountain

No matter how many times I run through the mental checklist of everything I had with me, my mind keeps coming back to January.

January in her fuzzy duckling bathrobe, slipping an empty shot glass out of my hand in a closed bar. January laughing at me sinking up to my knees in snow despite the awkward snowshoes. January soft and naked, with feminine curves yielding under my touch.

Shit.

Now I'm driving through town with a fucking hard-on.

Moonshine Ridge has changed since I was here last, but it's also so much the same.

Alice McAllister looks up from where she's sweeping snow away from the entrance of her little store to glare at my truck as I crawl by at the town's fifteen mile an hour speed limit.

The window tint is too dark for her to recognize me, but I'm sure the whole town knows I'm back by now, as well as what I'm driving.

On my right, there's a new preschool in the old community center building. It had been empty ever since they built the new center by the gas station on the far end of town.

Gran's commercial building is busy too-- Current Jones and his wife opened a brewery in one suite and I hear Current left the river rafting business to bake pizzas with his woman.

Next to that is a new coffee shop.

Must be the one that Raine's wife owns.

From the looks of things, business is good for both of 'em. The parking spaces in front of the ranch-style building are full with a few people who look like out-of-towners milling about.

My little brother is more likely to be happy to see me, but I don't see his truck anywhere.

Gran's little museum gift shop is locked up tight too.

No point in stopping.

Across the street, Cedar's tavern is busy. The windows lining the family restaurant on the street side of the building are fogged over and inside, the booths are filled with groups of friends and families laughing and talking.

Town's busy; new businesses and the ski resort reopening has brought tourist traffic and dollars to the Ridge.

Thinking about the resort has my thoughts pulling back onto January again; only this time, the scenes flashing in my head aren't the images of the last couple of days together-- I see Jan walking toward me in a white dress, and I see her stomach round and heavy with my child. She's teaching a little girl that looks just like her to ski. We're chasing grandkids, and growing old...together. Here. In Moonshine Ridge.

The tail end of the truck fishtails on the wet road from the force of the sudden U-turn I have to make to get back onto Gold Gulch Way.

Beginnings on the Mountain

When I pound on Cane's door, a kid that can't be more than five answers. He's the spitting image of my brother, including the scowl he levels at me as he stares me down from across the threshold.

"Where's your dad?"

I remember hearing about the woman from Cane's past showing up just a few months ago, thinking he wouldn't want anything to do with his own son and my grandmother's delighted account of their reconciliation.

I rifle through my memory, trying to remember the kid's name but it's nowhere to be found.

"DAD! Uncle Hayle wants you!"

Before I can ask him how he knows who I am, the boy takes off running back into the house somewhere. I hear a woman's voice somewhere inside and then heavy footsteps heading toward the door.

I'm not familiar with the floor plan of Cane's place-- he had it built when he came back after I left.

"What are you doing here?" My brother growls at me when he reaches the door. "Thought you tucked your tail between your legs and went back to whatever hole you've been hiding in."

"I'm not leaving." My voice is clear strong, making it impossible to mistake my meaning. "You gotta a problem with me being back on the Ridge, you better work it out now."

The door slams behind Cane as he steps onto the deck with me.

"I told you; you got nothing up here to come back to. Everybody's just fine without you, go back wherever you've been for the last five years and keep being somebody else's problem."

"The Ridge is my home. My family's here, my friends-- my future is on this mountain and nobody's going to get in the way of that."

"Fuck you, Hayle!" Cane's fist swings, but this time I don't let it connect. He might be bigger than me, but he's never learned to account for me being left-handed.

I block his blow and side-step the next swing.

The door opens behind him and a pretty brunette bundled up in a puffy jacket and snow boots steps outside with the boy-- *Donner*. My nephew's name comes to me in a flash.

Cane and I compose ourselves while his woman looks us each up and down, her eyes landing harshly on me before she smiles at my brother.

"We're going to go up to May's house for a visit."

There's no mistaking the edge in her voice, making it clear that she expects us to have our conversation away from young ears.

"I'll come get you when I'm done here." The softness in my brother's voice surprises me.

Cane and I stand quietly, waiting while they walk the plowed path up to Mom's house.

I'm wondering what my newest sister-in-law and nephew have heard about me. Cane watches his family with the same over-protective stance he reserves for everyone but me.

"I don't want you near them." He spits the words at me as soon as we're alone. "Raine's got a baby on the way, he doesn't need you back here dragging him into

Beginnings on the Mountain

trouble. You're not welcome at the camp, I got enough staff that actually show up for work on Monday morning, I don't give a fuck what your last name is, we're not hiring."

"I don't want to work at the damn camp." I can't help raising my voice to match his. "Zephyr wants me in her wedding and that's not up to you."

We're squaring off again and I'm ready to block his next blow when the sound of snow crunching calls our attention away from our argument.

"What the hell is so important that has you boys fighting loud enough for the whole Gulch to hear?"

The woman at the bottom of Cane's front steps scolds us as she makes her way onto the deck.

"I heard you were back," Gran coos at me, tugging on my arm till I bend down for the kiss that surely has my cheek smeared with her trademark lipstick. "Tell me you're not leaving before everyone has a chance to see you, sweetie."

"Sorry, Gran--" Cane's eyes dare me to argue with him, "he's just on his way out."

Our grandmother purses her lips and gives my brother a scowl over the rim of her glasses. Maybe the scowl is hereditary? I'll have to ask Jan if I do the same thing.

"Hurricane Hart, I heard you two shouting at each other from the house. You've got your people worrying about you over at May-Ellen's place and every one of us knows Hayle's telling you he's back to stay. Don't be tellin' tales to an old lady."

Cane and I both fight to keep straight faces. If

anyone on this mountain knows about telling tales--it's our grandmother.

"Cane says you were drinking again, Hayle. I thought you quit? How the hell are you supposed to run that program if you can't set a good example?"

Drinking? News to me.

I glare at my brother.

"Why the hell are you lying? It's like you want me stuck in the past. You worried I'm going to come back and take your big boy pants away?"

Cane steps forward, but I don't flinch. Neither does Gran, who steps between us.

"Fuck you, man," he growls at me. "You were opening the fucking bottle right in front of me. You're too far gone to even notice what you're doing."

"Is that why you smashed a good bottle of cream soda in my sink? You thought it was beer? Jesus, Hurricane! You couldn't fucking *smell* it? God knows you threw it hard enough you had to have been wearing it all the way back to your house."

All three of us stand, silently staring at each other.

"You really quit?"

I nod.

Gran moves toward the front door, subtly herding us inside with her.

"When?"

I give my brother a what-the-fuck glare, my hand involuntarily rising to my nose.

"You really gotta ask?"

Cane shakes his head like he's trying to get the

rocks out. Gran heads to the kitchen like she owns the place.

"What program is Gran talking about?"

I sit across from my brother in one of the leather chairs in his spacious living room, thinking how much better I like the house I inherited from Mom and Dad after they built the bigger place closer to the main road.

Cane's house is too modern for me. It lacks the cozy feel of an authentic cabin.

Gran brings out mugs of cocoa-- taking me back to a childhood when fights with my brother were easier to put behind us.

I tell Hurricane about the addiction program I started with some people back east when we realized it wasn't just the small group of us that benefited more from support than steps.

Gran beams with pride as she fills in details I skim over.

And for the first time in a very long time, my brother stops scowling at me.

"Now tell us what made you change your mind about leaving us again."

There's more of Gran's lipstick on the edge of her mug than left on her mouth. Her winter coat is tossed over the back of the sofa behind her, her feet clad in thick, pink socks after leaving her snow boots at the door.

Looks like Vera Jones is still knitting sweaters-- Gran's wearing one in a patchwork of grays and greens over what looks like overalls.

A glint in her eye gives away the fact that she's on to me already-- the local grapevine probably lit up like Christmas as soon as I kissed Jan in the lobby this morning.

"I'll let you fill Cane in on that, Gran--" I get up, press a dry kiss to my grandmother's cheek and give my brother a cautious glance-- sans glare, "--I need to go talk to her."

"We do dinner at your mother's house on Sundays now, Hayle. You better bring her with you!"

I'm out the door before Cane can finish asking what we're talking about.

Chapter Nine

January

My conversation with Pepper put me in a weird mood.

After spending some time cleaning gear and putting things away in the equipment closet, I make a list of things that will need to be restocked up at the hut for anyone else who needs to use it.

Then I check my schedule for the coming week.

The ski resort is a small one and, with the Ridge being so remote, we really only serve the locals and flatlanders coming up from Slow River Valley. We're not likely to stay open during the week until the holiday season starts-- despite the fresh snow.

In addition to my coaching, I help out with general lessons and occasionally lead cross country groups, but until we're open seven days a week-- I can tell my schedule won't keep me busy enough.

It's been three hours since Hayle left and I'm already a wreck.

My fingers itch to text him. He should have made it to Slow River by now.

I wonder if he's settled into a hotel room. Has he called his sister and arranged to meet up with her and her fiancé? How long will he be in the valley?

Maybe I could drive down while I still have free time during the week and spend more time with him before he heads back east. Maybe I could--

Pepper's words come back to me when I find my thoughts drifting across the country.

I own part of this resort. I've made a home in Moonshine Ridge. I've been planning on building my own house near the resort in the next year or two. This is where I planned to retire.

But now I know my future is with Hayle.

Pepper's right-- if that means moving three thousand miles away and rebuilding my career, I will.

And I can't wait till spring to make sure Hayle's on the same page.

Closing out the schedule on the resort's computer, I make my way out of the front office, grabbing my phone from my back pocket as I head across the lobby toward the stairs.

I'm texting while walking, my head down and my attention focused on making sure my message doesn't get auto-corrected to gibberish-- it's too important to get this right.

I feel the rush of cold air hit me as I cross in front of the front doors, but I don't look up.

Until I feel strong arms haul me off my feet just as I hit *send.*

"Wha--" My cell phone goes flying out of my hand and hits the lobby's slate floor with a sound that ought to make me mad as hell, but it's hard to be mad when Hayle's kissing me like it's been a year and not just a few hours.

"What are you doing here?" I'm panting when he finally lets me speak.

"Hang on, I got a text." He winks at me like he knows who it's from as he pulls his phone from his pocket and checks the screen.

His brow scrunches into a scowl and dread pools in my gut.

I hadn't expected him to read the message in front of me, of course, and now reality is setting in.

Of course, it's too soon to lay it on the line like I did. I must come off like a love-struck teenager.

Dang it! I didn't think my text was that long. It takes him forever to read it, so I nervously pick up the shattered pieces of my phone so I don't have to read into the way the corner of his mouth twists under his beard.

"I'm sor--" I start to launch into my backpedaling speech but Hayle raises a hand and cuts me off.

"Hey babe, I gotta get back to this real quick. Hold that thought, ok?"

He can plainly see me standing right in front of him, holding the six pieces of glass and plastic that used to be my phone. So there'd be no reason to text me back.

It must be someone else.

Cell signal up here is non-existent, and the resort's

internet is satellite, but it can be slow. The text probably didn't even get sent before I dropped the phone.

Relief washes through me. He smiles and gives me a wink as he types out a reply.

Also, that smile. The crooked one that promises mischief and makes my pulse race and my panties dampen. That's not the smile of a man who read what I wrote and didn't want to hear it.

Hayle's thumbs stop moving over the screen and he slips his phone back into his pocket.

"Why'd you come back?" I ask when his attention is all mine again.

"Forgot something."

"Oh." I'm glad he's happy to see me, but the hope that he came back for me crashes. "Okay, well, let me grab a key and we can go get it."

But before I can head for the desk to grab a master key, I'm upside down, looking at the floor above me in confusion.

"Got it." Hayle's voice is playful, one arm wrapped securely around the back of my legs as his free hand lands a light smack on my ass.

I return the favor-- seeing as how his ass is right in front of my face in this position and all.

"Employee housing is through that door." I hear Eddy's voice, full of laughter even more than usual, giving Hayle directions to the stairs that access the wing to my apartment.

"Eddy!" I shriek through a fit of giggles. "You're not helping!"

I lift my head to glare at my boss to find both Eddy

and Pepper grinning like maniacs as they watch Hayle carry me across the lobby to the stairwell door.

"Oh, I'm definitely helping," Eddy answers, laughing, his arm wrapped around Pepper, who gives me a wave right before I'm carried up the stairs.

Hayle

Jan has to give me directions to her place, but I don't set her down until we're behind the locked door of her suite.

"I was going to come visit you in the valley before you left," Jan tells me. Her words are breathy and rushed as she works the buttons on my flannel shirt like it's on fire.

"I couldn't wait that long," I confess, yanking her shirt off with a little too much force. The fabric protests with the sharp sound of stitches ripping.

Her cell phone is already a wreck, thanks to me. Which means she'll have to wait on any important texts that come in until I can get her a new one. We still have some time before we need to get that done-- but not much.

"Hayle, I wanted to tell you--."

"Shh, I know."

My lips keep her from finishing her sentence.

"I just need to--"

My fingers keep her from finishing her next sentence with anything intelligible.

"January, if you're not telling me how much you want me inside you right now, I don't want to hear it."

I growl the words into her ear while my fingers slide inside her. She doesn't have to tell me she wants me inside her; I can feel how wet she is already.

My mouth waters to taste her but before I get the chance, she's answering me with a noise that's something between a laugh and a moan.

"I want you more than anything in the whole world, Hayle."

Those bright blue eyes are locked on mine, her words sounding like a vow as I notch myself against her opening and take her in a swift move that has us both gasping.

"You *are* my whole world, January," I manage to get the words out before the sensation of being encased in her heat steals coherent thought from my head.

What starts off hectic and needy settles into something slower, deeper-- different than we were together in the hut last night. I want to go deeper, sink all the way inside her, and take root there.

Something instinctual has hold on me now. A need I've never felt before has me answering some primal call to breed this woman, to plant my seed deep in her belly and watch her grow my child.

The feeling slams into me, has me speeding my thrusts at the same time Jan's walls constrict around my cock, pulling me deeper and pulsing till I can't hold back any longer.

January comes hard, with my name buried in the guttural cry that rips from her throat.

It's my undoing. With one final thrust, I'm locked with January's soft body, pouring cum into her in thick ropes that feel like they're tethering us together tighter than any words I'll ever be able to say to her.

It's a long time before I say anything-- it's a long time before I *can* say anything. We stay together, catching our breath and enjoying the connection until I slip from her body. Then I pull her to me, cradling her against my chest with my chin resting on the top of her head.

"I'm not leaving the Ridge," I whisper into the softness of her hair. "I won't leave you."

I feel her lips, warm and moist, on my chest and the tickle of her smile.

"I was going to go to Vermont with you," she says softly.

"No." I kiss her again and tighten my arms around her. "This is home for both of us."

"What about your brother? Is it going to be awkward for you to be back?"

"Yup." I chuckle and lean my cheek against her hair. "But I already told him to get used to it. That's what took me so long to get back to you."

"We never talked about the future, Hayle."

"We never talked about birth control either." I can't help the grin that catches my face.

Forty damn years, and I never thought I'd be five years from my last drink with a beautiful woman lying naked in my arms and praying she turns up pregnant with my kid.

"Shot." She says it like it's supposed to reassure me.

It doesn't.

"You want kids?" I ask, steeling myself for the possibility that a woman who makes a living in sports might not want to have children.

It won't matter. Jan's my woman now. Nothing's changing that.

She's quiet for a beat longer than I'd like but then she nods.

"Yeah. I never really thought about it before--" She moves against me and tilts her head up, "--I'd like to have children with you. If that's something you want too?"

"Are you kidding right now? I'm pissed you're not already knocked up."

"I love you, Hayle."

"I love you too-- it's still early." I glance at the afternoon sun lighting her window. "We should go get you a new phone."

Chapter Ten

January

No matter how hard I try to convince him that I can wait to replace the phone, Hayle insists we should do it today.

That means pulling my boneless, post-orgasmic body away from him and then letting him drag me into the shower.

At least it means standing under the hot water with Hayle's hands on every inch of my body as he takes care to wash me thoroughly from head to toe and back up again-- and then fucks me from behind with my hands on the tile wall before washing me down all over again.

"You know, I can just order a new one online," I tell him while I dry my hair.

Driving into town is the last thing I want to do by the time we're done.

"We should at least see if Alice has something that'll get you by in the meantime." There's something in his eye that has me wondering what's so damned important about replacing my cell phone so quickly, but he gets me on board with the promise of pizza from the Brick & Porter. Even with the local pizza chef being Eddy's brother-- we don't get delivery up here.

"I just don't like the idea of you being without a phone," Hayle explains as he drives us down the mountain. "It's winter, it's the mountains-- I'd feel safer knowing you have a phone with you."

I laugh out loud at his protective papa bear routine. Although, it does feel nice to have him fussing over me-- even if we both know cell signal is iffy anywhere past Keller's Ferry at the base of the mountain.

"Are you really going into Alice McAllister's store?" I eye the tiny general store across the street suspiciously when he parks in front of the pizza place.

It's no secret that Alice is no fan of the Harts-- Hayle, in particular.

"Nope, you are." He comes around to open my door of the truck and hands me a bank card. "You pick the one you like best out of whatever she's got in stock and let her help you get it set up. I'm going to order us some pizza, and I hear Current's wife makes some good root beer.

"Meet me back here when you're done."

Hayle pockets his wallet, shuts the door of the truck, and bends down to kiss me like he's making sure everyone in town knows he's mine.

Or that I'm his.

Either way.

It's a possessive kiss designed to show off that we're together-- and I love it.

Beginnings on the Mountain

While Hayle goes in to get our pizza, I cross the street to the little general store.

The bells tied to the door jingle as I push it open and Alice McAllister greets me with a scowl that's not nearly as sexy as when Hayle does it.

"So you're with the Hart boy now?" She practically growls it out and I feel a little like I might be in danger.

Alice has a reputation for being gruff, but she's always been pleasant with me, even if not exactly friendly. Looks like I might have lost my welcome in the only store in town.

"Um. Yeah, Hayle and I are together." I hover by the door, not sure if she's about to throw something at me.

"He send you in here for something specific?"

"I need a cell phone. I dropped mine." I take a tentative step closer to the register where Alice keeps a modest selection of electronics behind the counter.

She turns to grab a few and places three models on the counter.

When I pick one that works with my carrier, I hand her Hayle's bank card and she gives it another scowl.

"At least he'll be covering the damn money I'm losing to this bet," she mutters as she runs it.

"You need help activating it?"

She doesn't really wait for me to answer that, she just rips the packing open and takes over. Fortunately, I brought everything I need from the old phone and she puts it all together like a pro, powering it up and handing it over so I can log in to my account.

"What bet? If you don't mind my asking?"

I input my password and wait for the new phone to connect.

Alice gives me some serious stink-eye and hands Hayle's card back to me.

"That bitch grandmother of his was cackling like a mad hen today, tellin' everyone that'd listen to her about how her last grandbaby was back on the Ridge to stay.

"Bet her fifty she was full of shit. Ain't no way Hayle Hart was gonna move back to this mountain...I'm real disappointed in you, Janny. You coulda done better."

It's hard to keep the smirk off my face.

"Sorry, I cost you fifty dollars, Mrs. M." I really do try not to laugh.

"Be sure you make it up by shopping local then."

And that's all I'm apparently going to get from Alice. The old lady turns on her heel and heads into the back room, making it clear she's done talking to me.

At least I'm still welcome to shop here.

Snow has started coming down and the wind is picking up when I step back onto the sidewalk.

The new phone pings with a text message. I open it up to read and then I hurry back to the pizza place as fast I can.

Beginnings on the Mountain

Hayle

By the time we get into town, it's late in the afternoon.

I'm relieved to see that Alice is still open on the other side of the street. I'm anxious for January to get a new phone, even if it's just a temporary one till we can order her a fancier model.

I stand outside and watch till she's made it inside the store. Then I wait a little longer in case Alice throws her right back out.

There's not a doubt in my mind the old lady's had her eyes glued to us since we pulled up in front of Gran's building where the pizza place is.

Snow's starting to come down again, I pull up the collar on my coat to ward off the wind as I head inside.

Warm air greets me along with the smell of wood fire and food.

I wasn't sure what to expect from the place. They did a real good job of turning a bland retail space into the kind of place you want to sit and enjoy a drink or a meal. There's an L-shaped counter running the back of the main dining area. A long row of beer taps lines the back wall underneath a chalkboard with a list of current brews available. Up front, near the windows, is a brick pizza oven that shares an exhaust chimney with a stone fireplace facing a selection of sofas and chairs arranged for gathering.

There are tables set up along the wall leading to the back of the place and that's where I head as soon as I see the people seated around the fire.

"Cedar," I nod curtly at the man watching me with cautious eyes.

"Chamomile," I offer her a small smile as she curls closer to her husband. Hoping she hears the apology still present in my voice.

Three more sets of hard McAllister eyes watch our exchange.

"Hart." Cedar acknowledges me with an edge to his voice, but he stays seated and so do his brothers.

"Hi Hayle." Cami's smile relaxes some of the tension, giving me hope that forgiveness is a possibility.

I'm not dumb enough to think we're there yet though. I make my way to the back of the place where I can see Current watching me with a lopsided grin.

"Hey man, Rapid said you were back for a few days." My old friend greets me with a half hug and reaches for the very pregnant woman behind the counter.

"Ginj, this is Hayle," he says by way of introduction.

"Ginger," she says. When I hold out my hand to shake hers, she grabs me in a hug I'm not expecting.

"Actually, I'm back for good," I correct Current while awkwardly returning Ginger's friendly embrace.

Current whistles long and low, his eyes darting to the people sitting up front and raising a skeptical eyebrow at me.

"How's that going?"

"So far, so good," I answer.

"Alice is going to be pissed." Ginger giggles at

Current's side. "She put money down on Mable being full of shit."

"Gran's already talking, I take it?"

"Oh yeah, she put it out on the webpage this afternoon that her oldest grandson is moving home...you want something to drink?"

There's a half second of awkward silence as Current shifts his weight between feet and Ginger's face reddens at the realization what she just asked me.

"Yeah, actually, I hear you brew a good root beer." It's a question I've learned to answer easily.

"Not just good root beer," Ginger beams proudly, "*damn* good root beer!"

Ginger gives me a run down of the non-alcoholic beverages that she offers-- also made in-house, along with her award-winning beers-- and Current gets started on a few pizzas, including some to take back to his brother and the rest of the staff.

Suddenly the door swings open and the hushed conversations of the intimate restaurant are hushed by January's deafening shriek as she barrels toward me.

Looks like she got my text.

"YES! OMG! YES! YES! YES! Of course I'll marry you!" She's all screams and laughter as I catch her in my arms while everyone else in the joint stares like they've never seen a man in love before.

Epilogue 1

One Week Later
Hayle

"You wanted to see me?"

I poke my head through Gran's door before walking in.

She's easy to spot, sitting at the table in the kitchen in a men's gray sweater and a pair of plaid pants tucked into her Uggs.

Mable Hart found her personal style in the racks of a German thrift store in 1968. The pink lipstick came later, sometime in the eighties, I'm told. It's her trademark, I've rarely seen her without her makeup done-- including the bubblegum pink lips.

Today's no exception.

Gran's right hand is wrapped around a mug that's likely filled with Earl Grey, her left hand tapping on the screen of her cell phone.

She's so engrossed in whatever she's doing, she doesn't notice me until I speak.

"Oh! Hayle, honey, come in."

My grandmother jumps up from her seat and wraps her arms around my middle. At eighty-six, she's lost a couple of inches she never had to spare, putting me nearly a foot and half over her. But she's remained deceptively strong and when Gran hugs you, you stand still and let it happen.

"Just let me finish this up and I'll be right with you."

That's my cue to rifle through her fridge for something I'd rather drink than tea.

A wave of nostalgia washes over me as I head into the kitchen. The last time I was here, I was still reaching for the German imports she usually has stocked on the top shelf next to the milk.

Sometimes it still surprises me how easy it is to make better choices these days. It's not so easy for others. I'm pretty damn lucky.

I pull a can of soda out and pour it in a glass.

When I take the seat opposite Gran, her cell phone has been set aside, her tea refilled, and she's smiling at me like all she sees is the grandson she's always doted on and not the years of fuck-up he threw in between that kid and the man I eventually turned out to be.

"I take it you two won't be moving in here at the house in the Gulch?"

Jan's met the family. Everyone adores her of course.

Beginnings on the Mountain

Cane's still leery about me being back. He's waiting for me to fuck up so he can say "I told you so."

Junie's a good influence on him, and Donner has declared me his new favorite uncle-- much to my brother's dismay, but Cane's slowly warming up to having me back on the Ridge and back with the family.

Still-- January's job is up there at the resort and I don't like the idea of her commuting halfway up the mountain from the Gulch during her busiest season. Especially not when the Ridge gets bad winters like we're having this year. I want my woman to stay as safe as the mountain allows.

"No, we'll be building up by the resort," I confirm. "Jan already has her eye on some property up there, so we'll probably break ground this summer."

"When are you two getting married then?"

"Didn't know we were on a deadline," I laugh at Gran's impatience. To be honest, I'd have hauled Jan down to the courthouse the day she said yes, but she wants to do the traditional thing.

"Zephyr first, Gran," I remind her. "Jan and I are probably going to wait till the house is done and then do the ceremony on our property."

"You're going to make me wait two damn years? How much longer are you going to hold out on giving me my great grandchildren? You're already way behind, Hayle."

I can't help cracking a grin. The rumor mill has it that Gran's rivalry with Alice McAllister has escalated to a great grand-child vendetta, and the Harts are losing the game.

"We're just leaving that one up to God, Gran."

She's right about one thing, I am getting a late start on the dad thing. After spending time with my nephew and Rapid's kids, I admit to being eager to start our family.

"Well anyway," Gran slips her hand into her pocket and slides something across the table between us, "I want you to give that to January."

It's not until she moves her hand to reveal that ring that I notice the pale, indention on her own left hand.

"Gran..." I let out a long, slow, breath. "That's your ring, I can't--"

I've never seen my grandmother without her wedding ring on her finger.

"You can and you will," she tells me defiantly. "You're the oldest and the last one getting married. I like Jan, I want her to have this. I can't wear it forever."

Gran's voice is steady but there's a far-off note in it. Her eyes flick to her cell phone but only for a second.

I get the feeling there's more to this decision than just passing on a family heirloom.

Honestly-- I thought we'd be burying her in this ring.

"Your grandfather bought that for me when we got to Germany." Her eyes follow the ring in my hand as I pick it up off the table. "He wanted to put a bigger diamond in it when we got home, but I didn't want to change anything about it."

"It'll look nice on Jan and the smaller center stone

shouldn't get in the way much. I'll understand if she doesn't want to wear it out there in the snow with those gloves on all winter though."

After a single knock at the door, Howard Smalls doesn't wait for an answer before he lets himself in.

"We'll just be another minute." There is no hiding the blush on my grandmother's face when she looks up at the man heading toward us.

"You know I'll wait on ya, Mable," the old man tells her as softly as a voice tempered by seventy years of whiskey and cigars gets, his hand touching her shoulder lightly as he makes his way past us into the kitchen.

"I'm looking forward to seeing that ring on Jan's hand at Sunday dinner." Gran's voice has gotten its spunk back as she begins to shoo me out of her house.

Gran reaches up and I've known her too long to wonder what she wants. I bend down so she can place her hands on the sides of my face and smear that lipstick across my cheek.

"I love you, boy. I'm so proud of you. Now, don't forget to stop by and see your mother before you leave the Gulch."

I get one more kiss and then I'm standing on Gran's front porch in the snow with the closed door making it pretty clear that Howard Smalls isn't just my grandmother's friend anymore.

Epilogue 2

One Year Later
January

Not only can my husband-- *shhh*, that's a secret! Our wedding isn't till next spring, but we fast-forwarded the legalities when the stick turned blue four months ago-- out-pace me on dry land, he can also paddle a raft over white-water as well as any one of the Jones brothers.

Fortunately, the river isn't too rough and I'm not too pregnant yet to ride in the raft instead of driving down to meet everyone at camp like Meadow and Ozzie Lancaster did with their precious new baby girl, while their son got to ride in the rafts with River Jones who took the littlest kids on the easy route.

So far, pregnancy has been easy. I made it through the first trimester without any of the morning sickness that my friends had prepared me for-- the exhaustion is real though; it seems like I'm napping more than I'm awake and I still have five months to go.

The thing Pepper and the girls warned me about that *is* holding true is that this second trimester shit is no joke. I need sex as often as I need a nap.

After our morning run down the river with everyone, the younger kids weren't the only ones that disappeared into tents for an early afternoon siesta after lunch, but from the sounds of the camp outside, I might have slept longer than anyone else.

Poking my head out of our tent, I look around in search of my husband.

It's later in the afternoon, the fire has been started but it's got a while before it burns down to the coals that they'll need for cooking.

Families are scattered about, wrangling little ones, and keeping watchful eyes on older ones. Current and Ginger are missing, but their kids are with their grandparents-- meaning it's likely that I'm not the only one with ideas in my head of getting some private, adult time in before dinner.

Hayle's across the big group camp site, on the other side of the center fire ring where River and Cinnamon are singing together.

For a few minutes, I just watch the scene and enjoy the fact that this is the life I'm living.

Hayle grabs a couple of bottles out of a cooler, hands a beer to his friend, Rapid, and opens the root beer he grabbed for himself.

I watch him talking with his buddy, both of them taking turns pointing in various directions over what-

Beginnings on the Mountain

ever they discussing, a broad smile on Hayle's handsome face that I see more often than his old scowl these days.

When his eyes roam over this side of camp, I crook my finger and beckon him my way.

There's a glint in his eye as he jumps to his feet and heads toward me that says he knows what I want and he's ready to give it to me.

"Shhh." He laughs against my ear when I squeal as he pushes inside me as soon as we're able to get the relevant parts exposed and the tent door zipped shut.

"Shhh." I hush him back with a stifled giggle, slapping my hand over his mouth. "I'm not the one who can't be quiet."

Truthfully-- neither of us are good at being quiet and this camping trip is the first time we've had to try.

This is just a quickie to tide us over till later, when we might just have to sneak off from the rest of the group.

Hayle catches my mouth with his-- I'm not sure if I was getting too loud or if he was worried he was-- his thrusts rough and deep to hit the angle that I crave.

We don't waste time; we just race for the finish and collapse when we get there together.

"I can't wait to fuck you properly in our own house," Hayle whispers, raising my hand to his lips. "Where it won't matter how loud I make you scream."

Our house is still under construction, but we've been assured it'll be move-in ready before the end of the month.

We bought a piece of land near the resort and

opted for a house with a traditional cabin feel, but for now, we're still living in my private suite at the resort and spending occasional weekends at his house on his family's land while I have more time off through the summer months.

"If I get any worse, you're going to have to figure out how to run the program from the Ridge. There's no way I'm going to be able to handle you being over an hour away from me when I need you twenty times a day."

He steeples our fingers against each other and then weaves them together.

"I think the chapter has enough established members now that someone can cover for me."

Hayle started a chapter of his new recovery program in Keller's Ferry early this year. A few of his partners from back east moved out to help and it's been really successful. They hope to expand throughout the west over the next few years.

"Twenty times a day though," he says, running his hand under my shirt and finding my nipples hard in anticipation, "I'm going to have to build up to that level of stamina...where do you think I could find an athletics coach that I could train with?"

"I might know someone."

And then I have to cover my mouth because his is very, very busy.

Thank you for Reading

I waited a long time to see Hayle Hart get his happily ever after and, I admit that when I first introduced him-- I didn't think he was going to deserve one.

As the series expanded and I got to know each character and each family better, I got more curious about Hayle's internal story and more eager to see things work out for him.

By now, there have been plenty of glimpses into the future of Moonshine Ridge and its founding families that we know that feuds will be set aside, and wounds will mend.

I'm sure Hurricane Hart is still a bit of a grumpy control freak well into his future, but his relationship with his older brother is solid.

Cedar McAllister even lets Hayle back into the tavern at some point, although they are probably never going to be friends.

Eddy and Pepper Jones find a chef to run the high-end restaurant at the ski resort, April Hart finds a baker to rent out the kitchen at the coffee shop, Finch Diaz may, or may not, get her own personal Bigfoot sighting, and Alfred the goat lives an extraordinarily long life to play match-maker to a second generation of McAllisters.

There are so many stories left in Moonshine Ridge, we'll be back soon! But there are also a lot of ranchers down in Slow River Valley that can't stay single much longer, and there's a very tiny mountain town at the end of the Devil's Driveway called Paradise Point-- where the mountain men are more reclusive, and rougher around the edges.

Did I leave something out? Did I fail to tie up a loose end? Are you dying to know something about Moonshine Ridge or one of its residents?

Feel free to reach out to me and ask. If I don't know the answer, I'll make something up. It's kinda what I do.

Stalk me in the usual author spaces and visit RocklynWrites.net to join the mailing list so you don't miss out on what's coming next!

Start the Series

Are you new to Moonshine Ridge? Start at the beginning with the McAllister brothers:

Welcome to Moonshine Ridge and the rugged wilderness surrounding the remote mountain community where the history is long, the local lore is deep, and the men are as wild as the mountains they come from.

Protective, possessive, totally obsessed; the men of Moonshine Ridge will do anything necessary to claim the women they love and give her the happily ever after she deserves.

The Moonshine Ridge books contain a lot of insta love, some swearing, some steamy scenes, zero cheating, and a lot of swoon-worthy happy endings.

More From Rocklyn Ryder

The World of Moonshine Ridge continues in the Slow River Valley Ranches.
Start the new series with Gunner O'Leary in the Cowboy's Close Quarters Claim

Oh...my...darling:

Rocklyn Ryder

With everyone else on the ranch busy, it's up to me and our new herdsman to head into the hills to round up the strays that have wandered out of bounds before they get rustled by the unsavory neighbors on the other side of the property line.

Except, my brother didn't bother to tell me that "Clem" was short for "Clementine" when he mentioned the new hire.

Now I'm stuck in close quarters with a woman that hates my guts; a curvy goddess with a sassy mouth and an attitude that has my body aching to show her who's in charge out here.

Clementine warns me that she can't be claimed, but I'm going to prove that I'm the man who's up to the challenge.

Welcome to Slow River Valley and the historic ranches that made men rich when their search for gold in the nearby mountains didn't.

You'll find the men here are as rugged as the land their cattle graze in, with loyalties-- and rivalries-- that run as deep as the river that defines this valley.

Protective, possessive, totally obsessed, the men of Slow River Valley know what they want when they see it and won't be swayed from claiming what's theirs. A woman who wins the heart of one of these cowboys can count on getting her ride into the sunset with a happily ever after that stands the test of time.

Beginnings on the Mountain

Set in the same world as Moonshine Ridge; The Slow River Valley Ranches books contain a lot of insta-love, some swearing, some steamy scenes, zero cheating, and a lot of swoon-worthy happy endings. They're interconnected with recurring characters but can be read as stand-alones in any order.

About the Author

Rocklyn prefers her romance reads to be short, cute, and dirty; low drama and a little over-the-top: extra points for growly, alpha heroes with beards.
Originally from the farms and ranches of Central California, Rocklyn grew up in the lap of the Sierra Nevada mountains. Those small towns will always be home, but Rocklyn was born to roam.
These days she spends her days exploring America's back roads in her camper trailer, writing steamy happily-ever-afters while looking for internet.
Keep in touch when you join her (mostly) weekly newsletter and never miss updates on what she has in the works-- and what's working and not in a life full of adventure and shenanigans.
Sign up here or by visiting Rocklyn online at https://www.rocklynwrites.net

Printed in Dunstable, United Kingdom